"... a page turner. I found I could not put it down until I had reached the end. It makes you think about how you are handling your life and if you are stagnating because you are too afraid to take a chance. I enjoyed reading this book from the first page to the last and found the ending the best, due to the fact that I had started rooting early for the main characters."
—*Readers' Favorite*, 5-star review

"Overall, the book creates a suspenseful journey for characters—and readers— trying to navigate life's big questions. A reflective, witty, and fun story that elegantly crosses genres and addresses intriguing themes."
—KIRKUS REVIEWS

"A heartfelt journey of two lost souls finding grace . . . and each other. *Waterbury Winter* is a must-read for anyone who believes in second chances and the power of kindness—or who wants to believe in them. This is one of those books that, when you have to put it down, you can't wait to pick it up again."
—DONNA CAMERON, Nautilus Award–winning author of *A Year of Living Kindly: Choices that Will Change Your Life and the World Around You*

"*Waterbury Winter* is a heart-warming story of loss and love, challenge and resistance, and the power of creative expression. Henley's masterful descriptions of character and place make these pages the perfect spot to hang out. Readers will make themselves at home, cheer for the protagonist, Barnaby, and be totally charmed by his opinionated parrot, Popsicle."
—ROMALYN TILGHMAN, award-winning author of *To the Stars Through Difficulties*

"A *tour de force* reminiscent of *A Man Called Ove*. Barnaby Brown's interactions and experiences unfold in such a way as to endear him to the reader. He's not perfect, but his imperfections are what reveal his gentle and generous spirit, and we root for him at every upturn and downturn. *Waterbury Winter* is a memorable masterpiece."
—SARALYN RICHARD, award-winning author of the Detective Parrott mystery series and *A Murder of Principal*

"Linda Henley manages to combine drama, romance, humor, and even an art theft mystery in the highly entertaining *Waterbury Winter*. The novel introduces us to Barnaby Brown, an artist who is so down on his luck there's no farther to slide. Through fast-paced writing and a series of remarkable plot twists, Henley constantly surprises the reader as Barnaby (accompanied by his faithful parrot, Popsicle) stumbles mightily in his efforts to redeem himself and become the man he wants to be. A many-layered novel, *Waterbury Winter* is, above all, a moving tribute to the healing power of art."
—LAUREL DAVIS HUBER, award-winning author of *The Velveteen Daughter*

# WATERBURY
# WINTER

# WATERBURY WINTER

A NOVEL

## LINDA STEWART HENLEY

SHE WRITES PRESS

Published 2022
Printed in the United States of America
Print ISBN: 978-1-64742-341-4
E-ISBN: 978-1-64742-342-1
Library of Congress Control Number: 2021920007

For information, address:
She Writes Press
1569 Solano Ave #546
Berkeley, CA 94707

Interior design by Tabitha Lahr

She Writes Press is a division of SparkPoint Studio, LLC.

To all creative spirits

# CHAPTER 1

Barnaby Brown winces as his shovel hits concrete. He scrapes jagged ice from the driveway, then hurls it into a pile of snow. The shards scatter, pock-marking the white surface. A slate-gray morning sky bristles with the sensation that more storms are on the way. Barnaby pulls his shabby coat tighter around his lanky frame and looks up. Snowflakes pinprick his face, chilly reminders of his so far failed plan to change everything. He tugs his wool cap over his ears as he lifts the garage door. It's Christmas Eve, and he vows again that this will be his last Christmas in the house, in this God-forsaken climate, in a dead-end job.

"Merry Christmas to you, Barnaby," a neighbor shouts as he passes by on the sidewalk.

Barnaby raises his hand in reply. He never looks forward to the holiday. He'll spend it alone, as usual. Well, not quite alone. Popsicle, his green Amazon parrot, is excellent company. He waves at the bird as he catches a glimpse of her iridescent feathers through the front window and almost laughs in spite of himself. "Be a good parrot," she tells him when he leaves the house. God knows, he tries.

The old station wagon needs to warm up before he can take it to work. He turns the key in the ignition and waits. After several minutes, he backs out of the garage, stops long enough to pull down the door, and steers the car into the street. The exhaust spits grime onto the freshly fallen snow.

Carano Hardware, where he has worked for seventeen years, is situated two miles away on Main Street in Waterbury, Connecticut. Like other former industrial cities in New England, Waterbury's commercial center has seen better days and its disintegrating roads beg for attention. Barnaby rattles along the first mile before he notices the car faltering. When he approaches the traffic light at the top of the hill, the accelerator fails, and the vehicle grinds slowly to a halt. The light turns green, cars behind honk, and he mutters obscenities under his breath. He allows the vehicle to roll downhill, aiming for a side street where he can investigate the problem. The car slides and swerves on the icy road, and he clutches the steering wheel in his attempt to control the vehicle as it fishtails its way down. The motion throws him from side to side with giddying force. His stomach somersaults. The tires squeal as they scratch the frozen surface. The thought flashes through his mind that his life is over. He lets go of the wheel, shuts his eyes, and braces himself for the impact. Seconds later, the car crashes into a snowbank. His heart thumps wildly as he wipes his forehead. *Well, if I've survived this crisis, perhaps the old car will, too.* He checks the dashboard. The odometer shows over 150,000 miles, and the gas tank is almost full. He turns the ignition off and on, but the engine just grates without engaging.

A passer-by taps on the glass.

"Are you okay?" he mouths.

Barnaby winds down the window. "Seems I am. Car's not, though."

"Looks all right to me. You were lucky. I saw it all. Spinning out of control. Are you sure you don't need help? Shall I call a tow truck?"

"Thanks all the same, but there's no time. I need to get to work. She's okay where she is for now."

"Good luck, then," the man says and takes off down the road.

Barnaby is not a mechanic, but he figures the transmission has died. He got the vehicle from his parents when they died fifteen years ago, and it wasn't new then. It must be eighteen years old, at least. He drops his head onto the steering wheel and waits until his heartbeat returns to normal.

The snow falls in heavier flakes, covering the windows, and he supposes once more that he'd best leave the car where it is and walk to work. He can't miss again. He's already come in late twice that week, losing pay, and his boss Salvatore—Sal for short—is counting on him to be there today, the last day for Christmas sales. Besides, now he'll have the expense of the repair, and he's stretched to the limit already. It'll put a dent in his already forestalled plan to drive out West and start a new life. As he examines the car for further damage, he sees that the fender has crumpled in the spinout. *More dents, damage, and debt.* His mood darkens as he locks the door, feels for gloves in his pockets, and trudges to work. He draws the collar of his coat up and huddles his shoulders against the raw wind. Half an hour later, his feet numb and one sock wet from what must be a hole in the sole of his boot, he arrives at the store.

"And about time, too," Sal greets him. Observing Barnaby's snow-encrusted hat and beard, his face softens. "Whatever happened to ya?"

"Car broke down. Sorry I'm late."

"Well, take off those wet things and get yerself a cup o' coffee. What are ya gonna to do about the car?"

"Nothing for now. I know you need me today."

"I appreciate that. Yer a good man, Barnaby," Sal says.

Barnaby hangs up his coat and changes his shoes. He keeps an extra pair at the store and gratefully rids himself of heavy boots and the one wet sock. He examines the display of new socks hanging on the wall.

"Mind if I take a pair of these?" he asks. "You can take the cost from my pay."

"Sure, but let's call 'em a Christmas gift," Sal says.

Barnaby nods his thanks.

The store has large windows, old wooden plank floors, and tall shelves neatly piled with cleaning materials, cans of paint, brushes, tools, nails, and buckets. The windows reflect lights from a small Christmas tree mounted on a wooden crate near the cash register bringing a magical glow to the workaday space. Customers are already browsing in the aisles as Barnaby puts on the new socks and his blue apron with BARNABY embroidered in yellow letters on the front. He takes a sip of hot black coffee. At least he's getting warm. He forces thoughts of the stalled car out of his mind. *One day at a time*, he tells himself. That had been good advice from Alcoholics Anonymous. It got him off the booze years ago. How many years? At least fifteen, before his parents passed away. But since then, he's fallen off the wagon. Perhaps the old wagon is sending him a warning: both it and his sobriety are up for renewal. He dismisses the uncomfortable thought.

Behind him, a young woman's sharp question startles him. "So you only have coffee filters in these sizes?"

"Yes, ma'am. They seem to fit most coffee makers. What kind do you have?"

"A drip coffee kind with a cone filter. I'm staying at my mom's. Not sure what size."

"Well, how about if you get a plastic holder that fits these filters? Then the size won't matter," he says, handing one to her.

"Thanks," she says, grinning.

Another customer approaches him.

"Where do I go to file a complaint?" he asks, holding a pot of paint.

"Well, you can start with me, I guess. What's the problem?"

"This paint's the problem. Don't cover the wall. Put three coats on and still no good."

Barnaby takes the can and reads the label. "This is white paint, top of the line. What's the color of the wall you're trying to cover?"

"Red. Blood red. Makes me puke. Now it's pink with red streaks. Looks like a side o' meat."

"Okay. You'll need to prime the wall first. Here's the stuff you need. But I'm telling you, red's not an easy color to hide. You may need two coats of primer before you try the white again."

"Don't I get my money back? No one here told me about primer. What's the matter with you folks? Ever heard of customer service?"

"Well, of course. Service is our business," Barnaby retorts. Then, attempting to tone down his voice, he adds, "If you want your money back, you'll have to talk to the owner, Mr. Carano. He's over there."

The man jerks around and storms to the front of the store. Barnaby shakes his head. Difficult customers—that's what he hates most about the job. He likes helping people, but when they complain and act rude, he feels like quitting. And, he reminds himself, he would have done so years ago, except for the drinking that robs him of all ambition. He hears the door bang and guesses that Sal's goodwill didn't extend to solving this man's problem. Pink walls, indeed. He sniffs. Serves him right.

The day wears on. Outside, the snow continues to fall, smothering everything.

"We're getting a white Christmas," Sal says, moving away from the window. "We'll close early. Folks won't get out much in this kinda weather. Come to think of it, how're ya getting home without a car? Guess I'll give ya a ride."

"I appreciate that," Barnaby says. It's the first good news he's had all day except for the new socks, and despite himself, his face breaks into a grin. He knows his smile is infectious, and Sal returns his smile and slaps him on the back.

"And a merry Christmas to ya, too," he says. "*Buon natale.*"

The store door opens, allowing a blast of arctic air inside. A large man of about Barnaby's age, dressed for the weather in a thick overcoat and ski cap, approaches the front desk.

"Got any Christmas lights left?" he asks.

"Sure. Over there, aisle two," Barnaby replies.

The man, clean-shaven and smelling of expensive after-shave, wanders to the aisle. "My wife wants them. She likes the white ones," he says over his shoulder. He takes several boxes down from the shelf and deposits them next to the cash register.

Barnaby rings up the sale. "That'll be twenty dollars and fifty cents."

The man reaches into his pocket for his wallet and hands over the cash. He stares at Barnaby's apron, then blinks and peers at his face.

"Wait a minute, I know you . . . aren't you Barnaby Brown?"

Barnaby meets his gaze. "Oh my God!" he says, "Sylvester Goldstone . . . Sly! What on earth brings you to these parts?"

"Well, I'll be damned." Sylvester bangs a fist on the counter and grins broadly. "My wife's parents live here. We came for the holiday. We're putting up the tree tonight, you see. That's why we need the lights."

"I never knew that Melanie—that's her name, isn't it?— came from Waterbury."

"She didn't. This is wife number two. Her folks live in the Hillside district. I forgot that you're from here," Sylvester says. "Almost didn't recognize you. You're different. Changed."

"Guess I am. But you're exactly the same. Are you still working at St. Mary's in Providence?"

"Nope. Got into the business of selling art. I have a gallery. So how about you? Are you still painting? You were doing well, and selling, when we were teaching art at St. Mary's."

Barnaby tilts his head. "Not painting much these days, but you can see a mural I did a few years ago out there," he says, pointing.

Sylvester squints through the window at the wall of the neighboring building covered with giant figures dancing in a circle on the beach, palm trees towering above them. "Wow, not bad! Are you a muralist now, then?"

"Not really. The building owner paid me to paint it. He was from Hawaii. I used a discontinued brand of paint from the store here to complete it. Took a lot of paint, too."

"Did you get much recognition for it?"

"Not really," Barnaby says again.

"Well, you know those Philistines, people with no appreciation of art. Your mural is sort of Matisse-like. Reminds me of us in the old days, down at the beach in Rhode Island. Yep, those were the days," Sylvester says, with a crooked smile that widens his square jaw. "Do you have anything else I can see, something smaller?"

"I do, but not here. I have some things at home."

"Well, look here. How about if I give you a call? We're staying until the twenty-seventh. I'd love to see what you've been doing."

Barnaby scribbles his phone number on a slip of paper and passes it to Sly.

"I'll be damned," he says again. "Never thought I'd see you working in a place like this. You sure have changed. Got to run. I'll be in touch."

Barnaby collapses onto a stool by the counter. He feels hollow inside. It's surprising Sylvester recognized him at all. They had last seen each other in 1990, eighteen years ago, after Barnaby lost his teaching job at the school in Providence. It was also the year his beautiful wife died. The date stayed emblazoned in his memory. He'd been fit and healthy then at twenty-seven, not stooped and frail, as he now appears at forty-five. And it's true that he painted regularly then and earned part of his living as an artist.

His passions, painting and Anna, both died that year.

He stares outside. The late afternoon gray sky has taken on a sickening yellow glow at the horizon.

"Time to get outta here," Sal says. "We got company tonight—if they can get there, that is. Gina's making lasagna."

The two men douse the lights, close up the store, and hang a MERRY CHRISTMAS! SEE YOU DECEMBER 27TH sign on the door. Barnaby pulls on the still damp boots and coat and climbs into the passenger side of Sal's truck.

By five o'clock he's standing on his front doorstep. Too early for dinner. He has only one bottle of scotch, and he's saving that for Christmas. He steps down onto the driveway. Heavy flakes have already covered the tracks of the truck's wheels. He turns toward O'Malley's, his local hangout. The encounter with his old friend and colleague Sylvester Goldstone had embarrassed him. Was Sly serious about wanting to see some paintings? Probably not. How Barnaby wishes he were still young with a bright future as an artist ahead of him.

One drink for Christmas wouldn't hurt. It might dull the ache in his gut.

# CHAPTER 2

Barnaby wakes up slowly. His head pounds woozily as he opens his eyes and focuses on the wallpaper opposite the bed. The rose pattern seems out of order, fading in and out. He turns over and glances at the clock. Past ten. He sits up in a panic. He must have forgotten to set the alarm, and he's late for work! With a shock, he remembers it's Christmas, and a holiday. *What a relief.* He swings his legs over the side of the bed, stands up unsteadily and heads for the bathroom. It's cold in the house—it's always cold—he doesn't want the expense of heating all the rooms. Hands shaking, he runs the tap until the water warms, then splashes it on his face. So much for his idea that he should stay off the booze. But what was he supposed to do with all those old memories stirred up? Damn Sylvester and his obvious shock at finding his former teaching colleague selling lights at a hardware store. Barnaby feels like Scrooge being visited by the ghost of Christmas past.

His mind wanders back. He and Sly had spent Christmas Eve together in Vermont one year. They rented a lodge, planning to ski on Christmas Day, when the slopes would be empty, but they lapsed into talking by the fire and drinking eggnog until well after midnight. They woke with headaches, never made it to the lifts, and went snowshoeing instead. It didn't matter. Barnaby privately preferred the sparse beauty of a silent hike through snowy woods, anyway.

Shaking his head to clear the memory, he throws on his frayed robe and shuffles to the kitchen. Popsicle must be hungry. Strange that she hasn't yet woken him up with her usual cries of "hello, good morning, hello, top o' the morning." They had a custom of calling to each other. He had heard parrots did that in the wild as well to maintain connections. Popsicle would call and he'd answer, the parrot would call again, and so it went, sometimes for a full five minutes or more.

But this morning, Popsicle is silent.

The large metal cage by the kitchen window is empty, and the door gapes open.

His heart skips a beat.

"Popsicle?" he calls. "Hello! Good morning! Where are you?"

An icy breeze draws his attention to the sash window, also gaping wide. Stomach clenching, he rushes to it, and leans outside.

"POPSICLE," he yells.

His voice, swept away by the wind, sounds weak and forlorn. He senses at once that it's useless. She's probably dead already. How could she, a tropical bird, survive in the frigid temperatures outside? Barnaby shuts the window and sits down at the kitchen table. On second thought, he opens it again, thinking there's a chance the parrot will fly back in. Resting his head in his hands, he lets tears run through his fingers onto the wooden table top as he gives way to his grief, and sobs. He remembers opening the window the evening before to leave breadcrumbs for the birds outside. He must have forgotten to close it, and Popsicle's cage as well. He had been drinking. A cold, dead feeling fills his chest, and he sits there with it for a long time, shivering in the drafty room, knowing his luck has finally run out, not that he ever had much of it in the first place. But this time, it's his fault, and he hates himself. Reaching for the bottle of scotch on the counter, he pours a glass. He has never felt worse in his life. Perhaps life isn't worth living.

After his fifth glass, his mind swimming in circles, he staggers to the threadbare couch in the living room. He plops down, allows his head to crash against the cushions, and soon falls into an uneasy slumber.

He wakes in darkness. Five o'clock. He has slept the day away.

Remembering his parrot has disappeared, he stumbles into the kitchen to see if by some miracle she's back. But the cage remains empty, and fresh snow on the windowsill blocks the three-inch gap between the window sill and sash. *Popsicle is dead, and I murdered her.* Screaming with shame, he slams the window shut.

He wonders if O'Malley's is open. At least he can have a drink, get something to eat, and talk to the bartender. He stops at the bathroom on his way out, gets dressed, then reaches for his coat, ties a scarf round the collar, crams a hat on his head, and bends to pull on the damp boots. The right one leaks, he recalls, and finds a plastic bag to stuff in it. It's freezing outside, but the snow has stopped falling. Few cars pass as he sets out to walk the several blocks to the bar, and he meets no one along the way. Bright lights sparkle from trees in neighbors' windows. He ignores them, not wanting to think too much about the holiday he isn't celebrating. Head bowed, he plods slowly along the slippery sidewalk.

As he nears O'Malley's, the flashing red neon signs of Budweiser beer beckon. An orange glow glimmers through the windowpanes. *Thank God they're open,* he thinks. He picks up his pace as he senses gnawing hunger pains. As an afterthought, he reaches for his wallet. He hopes he has enough cash for a few drinks and dinner.

O'Malley's has been his home away from home for years. It's dark inside, but the bottles filled with multi-colored liquids on the shelf behind the bar shine, lending a warm ambiance to the place. The long counter, made of heavily varnished mahogany, is edged with brass. This metal strip, polished by decades of unwitting patrons, reflects the yellow lights above. An old army jacket hangs in a frame on the wall facing the customers. Two pool tables take up space in the middle of the room, their green linings lit by low-slung lights. Wooden booths and tables occupy the sides under small slitted windows with blinking signs. Barnaby takes his usual place on a stool near the cash register at the bar.

"Santa been good to you this year then, Barnaby?" Sean asks.

Sean, the bartender, is a few years older. He has a shock of dark hair, and his sharp blue eyes peer directly into Barnaby's.

Barnaby drops his head. "Not this year, Sean. Lost my parrot."

"*You lost Popsicle*? Now that's too bad. Fly away, did she? Forget to feed 'er, did you?"

Barnaby meets the bartender's gaze with cold eyes.

"Nah, just kiddin'," Sean continues. "I know you take good care o' that bird. She used to like comin' here when you brought her in, sittin' on your shoulder. Got people laughin' when she started talkin'. 'One for the road,' she'd say. 'One for the road.'" He smiles. "I'm real sorry. What'll you have?"

"The usual, scotch on the rocks. And a burger and fries."

"Burger and fries on Christmas? Don't you want the special? In honor of the occasion, we have a turkey sandwich with dressin' and cranberry sauce. Five bucks."

"Thanks, but I'll just have the burger. Not in the habit of celebrating. Haven't done so since my wife died. Anyway, who are you to talk? Working tonight, I mean. Surprised you're open."

"Yeah, well, things don't go so well sometimes at home, and there's always folks like yourself, needin' a place to go," Sean says.

"How's your mother?" Barnaby asks.

"Not so good. We had a late Christmas breakfast. She didn't want a big meal for dinner. Doesn't eat much anymore. Think she's been depressed since my dad passed away."

Barnaby nods. "How long has she lived with you now? Must be going on two years."

"Yep. Two years this Christmas. It's always a hard time for her."

Only two customers sit at the counter and Barnaby doesn't know either of them. The tables are empty.

Sean puts a glass of scotch in front of him. "So tell me what's goin' on, Barnaby," he says. "I can see from that glint in your eye that somethin's wrong. Out with it."

"You never miss a thing, my friend. Of course, the big thing is Popsicle, but my car bit the dust as well."

"That old clunker? No surprise there. Why don't you talk to Phil over at the auto-body shop? He's got cars, cheap ones."

"I need a good one. That guy sells lemons. I plan to go out West next year."

"I know, but you don't seriously think you'd get there with that old wagon o' yours, do you?"

"Sean, I don't know. Just need to get away for a while. Start again."

"You mean, leave off the drink. Well, you don't hafta leave town to do that."

"What are you saying? You want to lose me? I'm a good, regular customer."

"You are that, but I know what's good for folks, and the drink ain't doin' you any favors."

"Okay. Like I said, I want to start over."

"Fine. As your friend, I wanna help. Have one drink tonight and go home."

"We'll see."

New customers arrive and take seats at the far end of the bar. None are regulars. Sean goes over to take their orders. Barnaby downs his drink.

"Hit me again," he says to the bartender.

Sean sighs, but refills the glass.

The food arrives and Barnaby digs in. He feels better. The world does, too, as the familiar warmth of alcohol spreads through his body. Unaware of time passing, he sits at the bar, comfortable with the low lights and quiet conversation around him. He orders several more drinks.

"Another," he says as he again shoves his glass across the wooden bar top.

"I think you've had enough, Barnaby lad."

"Tis my business, and it's Christmas," Barnaby says, slurring his words.

"Go home, Barnaby. I'll see you later."

Sean places the glass in the dishwasher and wipes the counter. Barnaby stares at him for a moment, slides off his stool and plants his feet on the floor. The bartender hands him his hat and coat.

"I'll be back," he says, and shuffles unsteadily out the door.

# CHAPTER 3

December twenty-sixth. *What's special about this day?* Barnaby asks himself as he rolls over in bed. Nothing. It's the day after Christmas, the day he doesn't celebrate, and he has a hangover. Well, so what else is new? Then he remembers. This might be the day that Sly will call about the paintings. Barnaby climbs out of bed. Yes, that's what he said. He wanted to see them before he left town on the twenty-seventh. Barnaby surveys the surrounding scene. God, what a disaster. He has allowed the place to fall into disrepair and messiness. The only part of the house that's even halfway presentable is his studio. He could do a little cleaning to improve things for the visitor.

His head hurts. Too much scotch the night before. He takes two aspirin and stumbles into the shower, allowing the water to stream over him. There's still a little shampoo left in the bottle, and he suds his hair, stinging his eyes as he rinses. Amazing what hot water will do. He's almost human again. Stepping onto the bath mat, he envelopes himself in a towel. He really should do laundry to keep the towels from smelling sour. Scrutinizing his reflection in the mirror, he decides he probably could use a shave. He soaps his chin and runs a razor through the uneven strings of his beard. After washing off and reapplying the soap several times, he succeeds in removing all remnants of it. The raw skin flushes red, and he nicks his skin, but he's clean-shaven for the first time in years.

Sylvester calls later that morning. "Hey there, Barnaby. Wanted to let you know I can't make it this time to check out your stuff. But I'm interested. How about if you send me some images so I can get a sense of what you're doing? My email address is Sylvester@cuttingimage.com."

Barnaby gulps, clearing his throat before answering slowly, "Sure, Sly. It may take me a few days to get them to you, what with the holidays and all."

"That's cool. Shoot me the info. By the way, I go by Sylvester now. Great seeing you."

Damn him. He's always been Sly. *Shaved for no good purpose.* And Barnaby is not accustomed to having his work photographed and sending it anywhere, especially not online. He doesn't own a computer or know how to use one. Where's he going to get the money and time for all that? He's got a car to repair. *Lower your expectations, Barnaby boy*, he tells himself. This is a pie in the sky, like his plan of moving to California.

Stomach growling, he opens the cupboard. A few packets of crackers and two tins of tomato soup. Those will do for lunch. And breakfast? He opens the fridge. Three eggs and half a carton of milk. A chicken. That would have been his Christmas dinner, with the drumstick for Popsicle. Chicken was the parrot's favorite—she would hold a drumstick in one claw, biting it as she sat, perching on one foot and tearing at the meat with her large hooked beak. "Good stuff," she would say.

Good stuff, indeed. Barnaby shuts the refrigerator door. *No chicken for the parrot this year*, he thinks sadly, and none for him either. He couldn't stomach it, eating by himself, without Popsicle. His eyes mist as he glances out the window.

He had shut it the night before, when he came home, drunk and hopeless.

He fries the eggs, makes coffee, sits down at the table, and wolfs down his breakfast. Then he puts the dishes in the sink, adding to the pile that's already there. For a minute he considers washing them, but quickly dismisses the thought. He has too many other problems to deal with and needs to make good use of the day. He needs to get organized. First things first. He finds a pencil and makes a list.

Hang up signs about Popsicle.

Fix car.

Drive west.

He takes some large sheets of paper and scrawls the words: *Missing. Green Amazon parrot. Answers to name of Popsicle. Please call if found 203-555-7875 or contact owner at 55 Russell Road.* Then he puts on his hat and coat and goes outside.

As he tapes the first sign to a lamppost, a woman taps him on the shoulder. "I know that parrot. Are you the owner?"

"Yes. Have you seen her?" he replies, his face brightening.

"No, but I've heard her. Amazing vocabulary. I heard her counting."

"Yes, she liked numbers," he says dully. "She knew how many tubes of paint I had. If I put them out on the table, she could count every one of them."

"Did she like the colors as well?"

"Not sure about that. She liked people more. Sat on my shoulder and talked to strangers. Better than me at socializing, I'd say."

"So you've lost her?"

"Guess so. I left the window open."

"Are you sure about that? I saw someone go into your house on Christmas Eve."

"*You did?* My God. You're kidding me. Excuse me, but who are you, anyway?"

"I'm Lisa. I live two doors down, at number 57."

Barnaby scans her face. Almost as tall as he is, she is younger, her long chestnut hair gathered in a tail. She levels her gaze, her hazel-flecked eyes solemn.

"I wouldn't lie to you," she says.

"All right. Can you give me more details about the person who went into my house? I never leave the door unlocked, so how could anyone get in?"

"She seemed to have a key. I didn't see her face. She wore a long coat and boots. I keep myself to myself and don't like to pry, but I pass by your house regularly and I hardly ever see anyone going in the front door. Except for yourself, of course. That's what caught my attention."

"I'll be darned. An intruder! How dare she . . . maybe she took Popsicle. If so, she'll have hell to pay." He shakes his head and stomps from one foot to the other. "Did you see her come out?"

"No. It was snowing, and I didn't want to stick around. None of my business, anyway."

"Well, thanks for telling me, Miss Lisa. I'm Barnaby. Surprised we've never met, but then I'm kind of a loner."

Heading back to his house he ponders, so someone may have stolen Popsicle. *Who on earth could that be?* No one ever expressed interest in having the bird. And who has keys to his house beside himself? The contractors who did the work on his studio, but that was years ago. His parents, but they're dead. He hasn't changed the locks, and they could have given someone a key. Perhaps he should call the police. No point. Chances are they wouldn't be able to help.

He'll try to find clues about the woman's identity himself.

He goes back inside, taking in every detail of the house as though seeing it for the first time. As he notes the torn wallpaper, the dusty floors, the pictures askew, and the shabby furniture, he feels ashamed. He's done nothing to improve the place since his parents left it to him except build his studio. That had been a foolish project, too. It cost him all his savings, the small inheritance from his parents, as well as the equity loan he took out to pay for it. He still has loan payments to make each month, and he could definitely use another source of income. That, or he should sell the house and move out West, as planned. In any case, he needs to clean the studio. He climbs the stairs with a bucket and brush.

The doorbell rings and he clatters downstairs to open the door, holding the scrub brush dripping on the floor. Lisa stands outside.

"Sorry to bother you again, but I remembered more information about the woman who entered your house," she says.

"Kind of you. Please come in, out of the weather."

"It'll only take a minute," she says as she steps into the hallway.

"Let's go to the kitchen where it's warmer. I have the oven on. Please excuse the disorder. I'm cleaning up today." He throws the brush into the sink, splashing water onto the wall, and pulls out a chair for her. "Coffee?" he asks.

"Thank you. Black."

He pours her a cup. She takes a sip and sheds her coat.

"The woman came in a car. It stopped on the curb, and the driver, a man, waited while she slipped in. As I told you, I didn't see her come out, but I have a description of the car if that would help when you talk to the police."

"Thanks, but I haven't called them."

"You haven't?"

"Not yet, anyway. I only want my parrot back. Not sure the police would care about a missing bird. I expect they have more urgent matters to attend to."

"Yes, I guess so, but someone came into your house without your permission. That's trespassing. And she may have stolen something besides the parrot."

"Good point. I hadn't thought about that. I've been distracted. You see, there's Popsicle, and then my car broke down on Christmas Eve. I need to get it fixed."

"Oh," she says, standing up. "Well, I wanted to let you know about the car I saw. A dark green Mercedes."

"Really? That's curious. Someone with money. I might give the police a call, but I should probably find out if anything else is missing first, though there's not much to steal around here. Actually, I was about to go up to my studio."

"You have a studio?" she asks.

Barnaby watches her eyes light up.

"Do you have some paintings there? Mind if I see them? I love art. I majored in art history in college."

"Sure."

He leads the way up the staircase.

The studio has high ceilings and windows facing north. Paint of all colors splatters the floor and a rack with partitions holding canvases of different sizes extends along one side of the room. Brushes, tubes of paint, and piles of rags are scattered around. In the center a large oil painting rests on an easel. Lisa ambles over to it.

"Wow! I like this!" she says, turning toward Barnaby.

He shrugs. "Yeah, it's not finished, but it's the last piece I worked on before . . . well, before I lost interest."

"Lost interest? In this subject? How could you? It's so full of life and color. I love the figures fighting their way against the storm. Expressionist style. Fantastic."

Barnaby's face brightens. Then he takes a deep breath, as though readying himself to plunge into the high wave in the painting. "Thanks," he says, exhaling. "I did a series of weather paintings, usually with figures, often at the beach. I didn't really lose interest." His eyes meet hers. "It was the drink. After I started drinking again everything went downhill."

She grimaces. "I've got relatives with that problem. I

understand how it is. But you've got something here, if this painting is any example."

Barnaby blinks, then squints as a beam of sunlight streams through the window, illuminating the wall behind him.

"Do you have another to show me?" Lisa asks.

He strides to the rack of paintings and inspects them, pulling out each one. "It's here somewhere, the best I did in that series."

She examines some pictures propped against the easel while he continues to search. "I take it these aren't yours—different style," she says at last.

"Right. Those are by artists whose work I like. Damn it all, where could it be? I always kept the weather paintings in the order painted, and the one I'm trying to find must have been one of the last. Oh God. Maybe it was stolen. Maybe that woman, whoever she was, took it."

He gazes at Lisa. Her mouth has dropped open. "Well, now you have another reason to call the police."

"Guess so. First, I want to find out if any others are missing. Damned nuisance."

"Okay, I'd better leave you to it. Sounds like you'll be busy for a while."

"I'd like to keep looking for that painting. I don't want to report it missing unless I'm certain."

"Sure. I'll come back another day and see more of your work, if you'll let me. Let me know if I can be of any help to you."

"You've already done a lot. Thank you," he says.

"Anything to help a struggling artist. You said your car broke down. I'd be happy to give you a ride to wherever it is. Here's my phone number." She hands him a business card, pauses for a minute, then retraces her steps downstairs.

Barnaby watches her go, but her words resonate in his mind. *Struggling artist.* Well, he's certainly struggling, but no one has called him an artist in a long time. He reads her card. *Lisa Nettler, Social Work, New Haven County.* Straightening his shoulders, he leans over the stairwell banister and calls down. "Lisa, actually I'd appreciate a ride to the car, if you have time."

"Sure. How about this afternoon? The snow's stopping and the streets will be clearer by then."

"Okay. I'll knock on your door. Thanks."

After she leaves, he continues to sort through the rack of paintings. His best painting is definitely missing. He remembers how happily he completed it at the beach—how happy he'd been in those days. Thrilled by the way he'd rendered the viridian waves swirling around squealing children filling buckets, he'd attempted other, more challenging water scenes, stretching his skills as an artist. And those summer afternoons . . . how he misses those times sitting with friends at the water's edge, watching sanderlings chase then withdraw with the tide, and the warm nights sipping margaritas on the shore.

He slouches in the studio's frayed armchair, his mind floating like flotsam bobbing up and down as the old memories wash over him. His head drops to his chest. After a while he can't decide if any other paintings have disappeared because it has been so long since he worked on them and he can't remember them all. It was a good and productive time for him after he got sober. His parents allowed him to move home on the condition that he quit drinking, but after they died, he slipped. He should now quit drinking and find inspiration to paint once again. It feels good to have someone appreciate his work, even someone who cares enough to steal it. Who would do that? Can the same person have taken Popsicle as well? It made no sense at all.

At two o'clock Barnaby bundles up for the weather and trundles along the sidewalk to Lisa's house. The temperature has risen to above freezing and all around he hears melting snow dripping from skeleton trees, poking dark holes in the slush. A truck roars past, throwing a tide of black sludge onto the sidewalk, narrowly missing him. He curses under his breath.

Her modest two-story house has wooden siding and sash windows like his and others in the mostly Irish East End neighborhood. But she has kept hers in good condition, with fresh white paint. A fence surrounds the property. She spies him through a window, waves, and steps outside. Her car sits in the driveway.

"Hop in," she says. "Where to?"

"Jackson Street. I'll have to get it towed."

"Okay. Let's find it and go to a repair shop on Broadway. I know a first-rate mechanic there."

After a while they turn onto the side street where Barnaby left the car.

"I parked right here," he mutters. "Goddamit."

"Are you sure this is the place?"

"Definitely. It ended up in a snowbank. They've plowed the street. Must've towed the car already."

"Bummer. You sure seem to have had a run of bad luck lately. There's a place nearby where they keep towed cars. Let's go there."

They stop at a parking lot surrounded by a chain fence. The gate is locked, but he spots his car inside the lot. There's a sign with a phone number to call to retrieve vehicles. She hands him a pencil and scrap of paper, and he writes it down.

"Guess there's not much more we can do today, a Sunday. Looks as if no one's around," he says. "You've been a great help, Lisa. Can I buy you a drink or something?"

"Thanks, but not today. I'll take you home."

Back home in his kitchen, he considers having a drink but thinks the better of it and puts a kettle on the stove to make tea. Lisa is a kind woman, and attractive. He wishes he had met her under different circumstances, when he wasn't in such dire straits and when he had more to offer. Possibly she can become a friend. He needs one now, especially since Popsicle has disappeared from his life.

He feels hopeful until he contemplates all the things he has to do and the expenses to come. It will cost money to get the car to the shop and more money to repair it. He should call a locksmith to change the locks, and he supposes he should call to report the thefts as well. That can wait—he doesn't want the hassle of dealing with the police. He stares at the parrot's empty cage. There's no way he can drive out West without Popsicle. She has been the one genuine pleasure in his life for the past several years, a loyal friend who doesn't judge him, and something to care for. In fact, he takes better care of his parrot than he does of himself . . . and she's gone. Perhaps he needs a drink after all. For comfort.

He turns off the stove and reaches for the bottle of scotch.

# CHAPTER 4

His alarm goes off at six. Barnaby crawls out of bed as he remembers he has to take the bus to work. He checks himself in the mirror. No bloodshot eyes. He must have stopped drinking early last night, he thinks with relief. There's no doubt that he appears better—younger—without the beard. He takes a quick shower, dresses, and leaves the house. The bus takes him downtown, to a stop close to the hardware store. He picks up a donut at a coffee shop on the way.

"Morning, Barnaby," Sal says when he arrives. "How was Christmas?"

"Don't ask. Lost my parrot, and I think someone broke into my place. I'm afraid I'll have to make some phone calls on my break."

"I understand. Did they take anything?"

"Don't know if the same person took the bird, but one of my painting's missing."

"Bad luck."

"I'll say. So how did yours go?"

"Great. Family came over, brought presents. Got a new sweater," he says, pointing to his chest. "Hey, see you got rid of that beard. Looks good."

"It'll grow back. Don't know if I want to make a habit of shaving."

The first customer arrives, and soon both men get busy. There's a lot of demand for shovels and sand. At ten, Barnaby goes to the office in the back of the store and pulls out the scrap of paper with the towing service number.

"Barnaby Brown here. You've got my car in your lot, and I need to get it out. Can you tow it to the shop on Broadway?"

"You have to come by and pay first."

"How much will that be?"

"Depends on how long it's been here."

"I think you towed it yesterday or the day before."

"It's one hundred dollars, then twenty for each day."

"So how late are you open?"

"Close at five."

Barnaby groans, hopes sinking to his boots. That means a hundred and twenty dollars already, and the clock is ticking. He must retrieve the car today. He picks up the phone again and calls the repair shop. If he can get the car there, they might work on it tomorrow.

"Sal, I need to leave early today to deal with the car," he says.

"Okay with me, but yer'll have a short check this week. Ya missed a lot of days before the holiday, and we agreed no work, no pay. Sorry to do this to ya, Barnaby, but business is business."

Barnaby nods dully. He needs the car. He also needs the job. He takes the bus to the tow lot and enters the office.

"I'm here to pick up my car," he tells the attendant.

"Which car is that? Do you have proof of ownership?"

"Somewhere, but not on me."

"We need a document."

"I think I put a copy of the registration in the glove compartment. If you let me go to my car, I can check," Barnaby says.

"Okay. Need to see your driver's license first."

Barnaby takes his wallet from his pocket and pulls out the license.

"All right. You can go check."

Barnaby goes through the door into the back lot and rushes to his car. He unlocks the passenger door and slides into the seat to search the glove compartment. There's nothing there except a flashlight.

"Goddammit," he says out loud and returns to the office.

"Let's see what you've got," the attendant says.

"I have the papers somewhere. They must be at home. I took off work to come here. Will you let me pay now so you won't charge me for an extra day? I can come back tomorrow with the documents."

"Sorry. Got to follow the rules," the man says, pointing to a sign on the wall.

Barnaby grunts with annoyance as he leaves. As he passes Horace's Joint, a bar he would normally avoid, he thinks a drink might be the thing to soothe his nerves. He's about to enter the saloon when the door bursts open and three men emerge, two dressed in black leather, their necks collared by a beefy man with a red face. A smell of vomit emanates from inside.

"Get outta here, you bastards, and don't show your scrawny asses here again," he roars.

The men rev their motorbikes and screech out of sight.

"Freakin' yahoos," the man growls. He catches sight of Barnaby. "You comin' in?"

Barnaby wavers.

"Barnaby!"

He turns to see Lisa's car by the curb.

"Saw you as I passed by," she calls through the lowered window. "Did you get your car back?"

"No. Forgot the registration."

"Oh. Need a ride?"

He throws a glance at the saloon. Could be a bad idea to go in that place. He's not that desperate, and he'd prefer to drink at O'Malley's anyway. He shakes his head at the man waiting by the door.

"Sure," he says to Lisa. "If you've got time."

He climbs into the car, and they head to Russell Road.

"Have you figured out who your intruder was?" she asks.

"No."

"Did you call the police? Get the locks changed?"

"No."

Out of the corner of his eye he sees her glance furtively in his direction. Squeezed next to the door, slumped in the seat, he stares at his hands. They drive to Barnaby's house without talking. He opens the car door and steps out.

"Thanks again," he says.

He knows he ought to be grateful to her, but feels vaguely irritated. He's embarrassed that she has helped him yet again, and he'd rather have had a drink. He turns toward O'Malley's, then stops in his tracks. He wants the car back and needs to find the registration.

He lets himself into the house and makes for the living room, opens the desk drawer stuffed with bills, receipts, and envelopes, pulls everything onto the floor, then kneels to sort through the jumble. He sees a notice with PAYMENT OVER-DUE printed in red letters. It's his loan invoice for November. He must have forgotten to pay. Now he'll have a penalty on top of the usual bill. He can hardly stand to search any further. It's time to fix the car and drive away from his miserable life in Waterbury.

But he can't leave without Popsicle. Somehow, he believes he'll find her. She's been his companion for years, and he can't conceive of life without her. It's only been two days, and his life already feels bottomless. She has given him roots, a grounding of sorts, and a continuing connection to Anna. He has to find her. He'll hang up more signs. Surely someone noticed a person coming out of his house with the big green bird, a sight hard to ignore, or saw her flying away somewhere. He's half crazed worrying about it all and resolves that if he gets Popsicle back, he'll muster the strength to change everything.

He stuffs the papers back into the drawer. As he does so, a piece falls out of his hand. His car registration. *Thank God!* He picks it up, folds it carefully, and puts it in his pocket. If he hurries, he might still make it to the towed car lot before they close.

⁂

Three hours later, the car is at the repair shop and Barnaby's back home. Having successfully accomplished one project, he wants chicken for dinner. Even though he'll eat alone without Popsicle to share it, a meal will help his state of mind. Perhaps he'll have a drink to go along with it. Only one drink. There's not much left in the bottle, anyway. He considers inviting Lisa to share dinner, but he has nothing to go with the chicken except some stale crackers, and that's hardly a meal. Perhaps he can invite her another time, after he's had a chance to go grocery shopping and clean the house.

He turns on the oven. He'll roast the chicken and open a can of tomato soup for an appetizer. If he puts the cracker pieces in the soup, he won't notice they're stale. He pours himself a drink and sits at the table while he waits for the oven to warm up. Life already seems brighter. After a while he puts the chicken in the oven.

The doorbell rings, and he rises to answer it. A young woman stands on the doorstep.

"Hi," she says. "I read your sign, and I think I have your bird."

"What? You do? You're an angel!"

His mouth breaks into a wide smile, and he has a strong urge to fling his arms around her. She does look like an angel, and pretty too, with shiny blond hair and cobalt eyes. She smiles back.

"The bird flew into my window. I live next door but I only saw your sign this morning. I came earlier to tell you, but you weren't home. Problem is, I don't know how to pick her up. She has those claws, you know?"

"No problem there. I can come and get her."

"Please do. I don't know anything about parrots. I called the pet store to ask what to feed her. They said give her peanuts. So that's what I did. She made a big heap, spitting out the shells and dropping them on the floor."

"Yes, she does that. She likes chicken, too. I'll give her some tonight. Well, let's go."

They walk to the house next door. On the way she tells him her name is Mary, and that she moved into the neighborhood a few weeks ago. She opens the front door cautiously.

"I don't want the bird to fly out," she says. "I've kept her in the kitchen, but this morning she got out and flew into the living room. She's perching on the curtain rail."

Barnaby follows her into the room.

"Popsicle!" he calls.

The parrot squawks loudly and flies down from the curtains, landing on Barnaby's shoulder.

"Hello, hello, good parrot," Popsicle says. "Hello. Good parrot!"

"Yes, good parrot!" Barnaby says.

The bird rubs her beak against his ear, and he strokes her back.

He beams at Mary. "I can't thank you enough. I'll think of a present to give you. This bird means the world to me."

"I can see that," she says. "I didn't know what to do with her. If it hadn't been Christmas, I probably would've given her to the pet store."

"Glad you didn't. I'm so happy she's back."

"How old is she, and how long have you had her?" Mary asks.

"She's twenty-three. I've had her for eighteen years. My wife Anna gave her to me before she died. She had cancer." He blinks, sniffs, and lowers his gaze, then glances sideways as Popsicle climbs down his arm and pecks at his sleeve. "I know, you're hungry, old girl. We need to go. I've got a chicken in the oven."

"Now I can understand why you're so attached to her," Mary says. "Thanks for telling me."

"Good-bye, and thank you again," Barnaby says.

He leaves with the parrot on his shoulder. The aroma of roast chicken greets them at the door. He sets Popsicle on her perch, pulls the chicken out of the oven, and gives her a drumstick. Between them they eat the whole bird, and Popsicle says, "Good stuff." Barnaby grins, musing not for the first time that the parrot's favorite food is another bird. It's almost cannibalistic. After the meal, he washes the dishes and cleans the cage. It takes him a long time to complete the overdue chores. It's late when he's done—too late to go to O'Malley's. His problems are far from over, but at least he has his bird back. Thank goodness for that—she is a lifesaver. His other troubles pale compared to losing her.

A full moon glows in the window. Exhausted by his labors, he sinks into the nearest kitchen chair. He half closes his eyes, trancelike, and stares at the moon's silvery face. When he opens them again, the unusual sight of moonlight reflecting off clean dishes turns his thoughts to Anna. She always kept the house sparkling. Dull days with her simply didn't exist—until the end, when the light in her eyes faded, rendering them almost transparent. He aches at the recollection.

It was during one of their last weekends, before she became bedridden, that she'd insisted on going to the local veterinarian's office. She wouldn't tell him why, only that it was important. He had resisted, knowing her weakened state made even small excursions taxing, but he couldn't dissuade her and he wanted to please her, so they went. The parrot was perched in a large cage in the waiting room. She eyed them as they entered, then clawed down the side wires to meet them.

"Good looking bird," Barnaby said. "Is that why we're here? You wanted to show me the parrot?"

"I want you to *have* the parrot. She's for sale."

"What? I—we—don't need a pet."

"You might, later. For company."

"But I have *you* . . ."

She held her finger to his lips, silencing him. Her pale eyes had taken on a faraway expression, as if she was already leaving. He'd gazed at her, full of love, his heart breaking.

❄❄❄❄❄❄❄❄❄❄

That night, grateful for Popsicle in his life again to fill the aching hole, he sleeps soundly for the first time in days. Next morning when he wakes, he hears the familiar sound of the bird calling from the kitchen in her almost-human voice.

"Hello!"

"Good morning, Popsicle," he replies.

"Top of the morning!" she says, ending with a loud squawk.

*Top of the morning, indeed*, Barnaby thinks. It's a good day. He goes into the kitchen, and opens the cage door. Popsicle sidles out, climbs down the bars and flies the short distance to the table. Barnaby sets some peanuts down, and she picks up each one with her gray beak, then holds them with a claw while she pecks. She eats the nuts and spits out the shells.

"What a mess," she says.

"You're telling me," he agrees, smiling.

She's a messy bird, but he doesn't mind. Noting the piles on the floor, he remembers his project of cleaning up. No time now because he has to get to work, but he vows he will do something to improve his living conditions. That includes having the locks changed. Obviously, since the bird wasn't stolen, the thief wanted his painting. But why? No one had shown any serious interest in his art for years—*except for Sly, of course.* But he is a friend, and trying to help him out. Barnaby tells himself he should call the police and get the locks changed right away. He can't afford to lose any more paintings—it's possible they're even valuable.

He picks up the phone to call the police and gives the officer details about the burglary.

"What's the value of the stolen property?" the officer asks.

Barnaby frowns. "No idea."

"Okay. So I guess you're not worried about the loss. How did the perpetrator enter the house?"

"Actually, the person didn't break in. Had a key."

"Well then, that's not burglary. It's robbery. Trespassing, if the person entered without permission. Where does the person of interest live?" the dispatcher asks.

"Possibly right here in Waterbury, since she has a key. A neighbor saw her."

"Now we're getting somewhere. Do you have a description?"

"She wore a long coat and hat."

"Oh, did she now? It's winter, so that's normal. Anything more to identify the individual? Physical characteristics? Height? Age?"

"I'm afraid I don't know. I could ask my neighbor. She arrived in a green Mercedes."

"Okay. License number?"

"Don't know that."

"All right. You let me know if you have more details and we'll include them in the report."

Barnaby sighs, feeling slightly foolish. As he'd thought all along, to find the culprit he'll have to do some investigating himself. Meanwhile, he has to go to work. He can talk to a locksmith there about changing the locks. He knows several good ones who regularly buy supplies at the store.

Barnaby strokes Popsicle's head before shutting her in the cage for the day.

"Bye-bye. Be a good parrot," Popsicle says. She always knows he's leaving when he puts on his coat.

"I'll be a good parrot," he replies, chuckling. "You, too. See you soon."

The bus comes quickly, and he arrives at work on time.

"We need to take inventory before the new year," Sal says. "Can ya get up the ladder and check the paint on the top shelves? Hard for me to get up there with my big gut hanging out. Might fall. Too much good home cooking," he says, patting his stomach.

Barnaby carries a ladder to the shelves, puts a pencil over his ear, and picks up a notepad. He climbs up and whistles as he checks the cans and expiration dates.

"Yer in a good mood today. Something good happen?" Sal calls to him.

"Yeah. Got my bird back. She flew into a neighbor's house."

"That's great. Happy for ya."

An hour later the store is full of customers and Barnaby descends the ladder. Billy, a locksmith, is there buying tools.

"Hey Billy, got a job for you," Barnaby says. "Can you go by my place and change the locks today?"

"Sure. Where do you live?"

"On Russell Road, number 55."

"I can go by right away. What kind of lock?"

"You can switch out the cylinder. Yale lock. I'll need a couple of keys. Front and back doors. Let me know how much I owe you."

"Oh, that's okay. You've always served me well here, ordering parts and so on. Happy New Year to you."

"You're all right. Thanks, Billy." Barnaby says. Can you drop off the new keys here when you're done?"

"Will do," the locksmith replies as he goes out the door.

Despite the broken car and mystery of the stolen painting, things are looking up. Barnaby's amazed how much happier he is now that Popsicle is back. That's really the most important thing. People have been kind and helpful. Now he only needs to get the car running, and he can turn things around. He didn't even have a drink last night.

Maybe 2009 will be the year he'll finally move out West.

# CHAPTER 5

Monday is Barnaby's day off. He has new locks on the doors and a day ahead of him to take some control over his recent luckless life. He'll call the repair shop to find out when the car will be back in service and he'll buy some groceries. Payday isn't until Friday, but he has enough money for food and a new pair of boots. Outside, the weak sun flings blue shadows on residual snowdrifts, but the temperature has risen. It's a good day to take Popsicle out, something he'll have time to do after he runs errands. He takes his coat from the hall closet and bundles up.

"Bye-bye, see you later," Popsicle calls.

He splashes along watery streets to the nearest grocery shop. As he passes Lisa's house, he again wonders if he should invite her to dinner. He'll buy some extra vegetables just in case. Women like vegetables. In the market he fills his sack with as much food as he can carry and heads back. There's a SALE TODAY sign in a discount shoe store, and he goes in. He buys a pair of boots and wears them on the way home. They're stiff, but comfortable, with non-slip soles, and his toes feel warm and dry. At home he takes the boots off, fills the fridge with food, props up his feet, and calls the car repair shop.

"Barnaby Brown here. Could you tell me when my car will be ready?" he asks.

"Yours is the 1980 Ford Pinto station wagon, right? Probably in a few weeks. We'll have to locate the parts first."

"Okay. How much are we talking about?"

"I'd guess somewhere between one to two thousand bucks. If we can find the parts, that is. We'll need your authorization to go ahead."

Barnaby moans. "Let me think about this. I'll get back to you."

He already missed two equity loan payments. Another will come due for January, and his next paycheck will be short because he missed some hours of work. Also, he splurged on cognac for his birthday last month. A thousand dollars is more than his pay. He needs another source of income. He might get in touch with Sly about selling some paintings. Under the circumstances, even if Sly is involved in the theft, Barnaby would gladly forgive him if he bought some. After all, he's an old friend, and friends forgive each other, don't they? And besides, he has no proof that Sly is guilty. He ponders who else could have taken his painting, and why.

"What do you think, Popsicle?" he says, handing her a banana. "Shall I sell a painting? Get money to pay bills and buy you peanuts?"

"Heavens to Murgatroyd!" she says, peering down at him from the top of her cage.

Popsicle always amuses him. He and Anna used to repeat those words from the old Yogi Bear cartoons, often giggling at the corniness of it all. "Silly bird," he says, and Popsicle obliges by bowing. Sometimes he's sure she understands him, or at least his feelings. He has debts that will be difficult to pay off. But he has Popsicle, and that's cause for a celebration: a drink at O'Malley's.

He dons a scarf, buttons his coat almost to the top, then invites her onto his arm and tucks her inside, leaving her head out. He knows she likes traveling with him this way, heart to heart. On sunny winter days he takes her out as often as he can. The vet had told him she needs fifteen minutes of direct sun a week, and she's safe outside, as long as she's protected and the temperature is above freezing. They head out to O'Malley's.

"Well, look who's back!" Sean welcomes him as he observes the parrot. "How did you find her?"

"Neighbor had her," Barnaby smiles, removing his coat and allowing Popsicle to climb onto his shoulder.

⁂

Three hours later he's still at the bar. He wasn't planning to have more than a couple of drinks, but Ben, a former employee at the hardware store, talks to him, and the drinks keep coming. Professor Logan Miller sidles up to the counter.

"How's it going, Professor?" Barnaby asks.

"So-so. Can't complain."

The history professor, recently retired from the University of Connecticut, sports a neat gray beard, thick glasses, and a worn tweed jacket over brown flannel trousers. He uses musky aftershave. It doesn't mix well with the beery bar air, and Barnaby leans away from him. He hopes the professor won't begin lecturing about some of his favorite subjects like the history of the Industrial Revolution and the demise of the Waterbury brass business, but then he remembers that the older man usually only waxes eloquent after his third drink. He must miss his students.

"Sean, give me a shot of Jack Daniels and a splash of soda," the professor calls.

The bartender pours the drink and sets it down.

"Thanks. Brooke been in today?" the professor asks.

"Not today. Haven't seen her in more than a week."

"Good looking woman, that one," the professor says.

"I'll say," Sean replies.

Barnaby stifles a smile. Brooke Taylor is way out of Professor Miller's league and probably Sean's as well.

Popsicle is happy on Barnaby's shoulder. Every so often she flies to the pool table, walking pigeon-toed and pushing the balls around with her beak. The players shoo her away, laughing.

"Behind the eight ball," she says.

"Would you get the damned bird off the table, Barnaby," Charley Carson calls at last.

Barnaby wanders over to the table. "You should let her play. She'd add interest to your game," he says with a lopsided grin.

Charley, a chunky man wearing a baseball cap and a tattoo of a dragon on his right arm, points his cue at Barnaby and glares at him. "You don't play, so what do you know? I've got money at stake, and she's in the way."

"Okay. Come on, Popsicle." He holds out his wrist and the bird climbs on.

"Popsicle pickle eater!" she says, squawking.

"I know. You're hungry." Barnaby says.

Back at the bar, he asks Sean for a pickle. He has no idea why a parrot would have a taste for pickles, but there's a lot he doesn't understand these days. Sean offers one, and the bird reaches for it with her beak.

"So when are you going out West?" Sean asks.

"Not till I get my car fixed. Had a lot of expenses lately. Someone broke into my place and stole one of my paintings."

"Really? Any idea who?"

"I have a hunch. Need to follow up on it, but I don't have a computer."

"Why is that a problem?"

"I only have the suspect's email address so how can I contact him, if I don't have a computer?"

"That's easy. You could go to the library to use one. Or what the heck, I can send a note for you. What's the address?"

"I don't have it with me. If you're willing, it would be a big help."

"Sure. Bring me the info."

Barnaby finishes his drink and shakes his head when the bartender offers a refill.

"Haven't done much paintin' these days, have you?" Sean says. "I remember you were always bringin' stuff in back when your parents were alive. I liked it. Think you should pick it up again. You could probably sell some, too."

Barnaby yawns. "It's not so simple, Sean, my friend. The muse has to speak."

"The muse? Well, if you wanna paint a masterpiece, maybe so. But you can paint ordinary pictures that people would like. Paint us, here at the bar. Hell, I'd buy one. Put it right here on the wall."

"Perhaps I will," Barnaby says.

He orders a grilled cheese sandwich and gives Popsicle the pickle. He's warm inside and glad for the company in the bar. The hum of conversation around him and the *thwack* of balls on the pool table and occasional cheers from the players relax him. His troubles seem to vanish when he's there. The professor has found a willing listener, bending some poor guy's ear about the terrible Waterbury floods in the 1950s. Time to go.

Back home with Popsicle, Barnaby ponders Sean's suggestion of painting the regulars at the bar. Not a bad idea. There are some colorful characters, all there for reasons known only to themselves. He'll bring a sketchbook next time and make a preliminary drawing.

✦✦✦✦✦✦✦✦✦✦

On Tuesday Barnaby takes the bus to work again. The sun's out. It's almost time for the February thaw, the balmy interlude before the last savage snowfalls of winter. He buys a donut and eats it as he strolls to the hardware store. He's right on time, but the building is dark. Sal hasn't arrived early to open, as he usually does. Barnaby peeks through the window. Eight o'clock, and no one is there. Something's amiss. He reaches in his pocket for the key, unlocks the door, and turns on the lights.

"Glad you guys are here," a woman says as she wanders in. "I desperately need some light bulbs. Don't know why, but all my lamps went out at once and I can't live in the dark, can I?"

"No, ma'am. What's the wattage?"

"Wattage? I don't know. Regular, I guess. My husband died. He always took care of things like this."

"What do you use the lamps for? Bright ones for reading or low lights for atmosphere?"

"For atmosphere, I guess. I don't read much. Don't want them too bright."

"All right. Sixty watts will probably work. If these are too dim, bring them back with your receipt, and we'll be happy to exchange them." Barnaby goes to the aisle stacked with light bulbs and brings a few packages to the counter. "They come in packs of two. How many do you need?"

"Well, there are six lamps, so three, I guess, plus one extra. That makes four."

Barnaby rings up the sale. It bothers him to think of the woman sitting by herself in the dark. Perhaps she'll be back for brighter lights. What could have happened to Sal? In all his seventeen years of working there, his boss had never missed a day without telling him ahead of time. He picks up the phone to call Sal's home. As he does so, Billy, the locksmith, comes in.

"Hey, Billy, thanks for changing my locks," Barnaby says.

"No problem, happy to help out. I wanted to tell you. Strange, but when I went into your house, I remembered I'd been there before. Must've been when your folks still lived there. They wanted the locks changed and asked me to make an extra key for the house cleaner. That's not too common, for home owners to tell me the reason for extra keys. Stuck in my mind."

"Interesting. Thanks for letting me know," Barnaby says.

He frowns. So maybe that's the person who broke into the house. Sly may have had nothing to do with the robbery. But why would the housekeeper want one of his paintings? His parents died fifteen years ago, he didn't keep the housekeeper on afterward, and he doesn't remember that she'd paid any attention to his art. Very puzzling. In any case, now he can follow up on Sly's interest in seeing the work without suspecting him of stealing it. Or so he imagines. He prefers to think Sly had nothing to do with the theft and that he'll become a promoter of Barnaby's work in the future.

The phone rings.

"Barnaby? Gina Carano here. Sal's had a heart attack. He's okay, it's mild, but he's still in the hospital for tests and needs to take it easy for a few days."

"Oh my God. Terrible news. Sal's a regular bull of health, uh, I mean, he's always had a clean bill of health, hasn't he?"

"Until now, he has. Can you manage to keep things going while he's away? Today's the thirtieth, and the store's not open on New Year's Day, so you'll only have to cover today and tomorrow."

"Of course I can manage. What a shock! Poor Sal. Please send him my best wishes and tell him not to worry."

"You're a brick. Thanks, Barnaby."

Sal had a heart attack? He's only a few years older than Barnaby, though he eats rich food and has the bulging waistline to prove it. Barnaby's sorry for Sal, but now he, Barnaby, can't take time off to manage his own problems. But that's okay. He's tired of dealing with them, anyway, and he's glad to help his boss. He'll manage the store, even work overtime. It would be good to have the extra pay.

The day passes quickly. He counts the cash, deposits it in the safe, locks up, and takes the bus home. On his door mat he finds the mail in a pile, mostly bills, but there's a handwritten envelope as well, a woman's hand, curvy and neat. He takes the card out. It's an invitation to a New Year's Eve party at Lisa's house. He sets it on the mantelpiece next to the framed photograph of his wife. No one has invited him to a party for years, and he usually celebrates the new year at the bar. It might be good to have a change. He picks up the phone and leaves voice mail for Lisa telling her he's pleased to accept her invitation.

He goes to bed at eleven. From a deep sleep, the shrill sound of the telephone startles him awake. He throws the covers off, leaps to his feet, and fumbles in the dark for the handset. A woman's voice screams into the line.

"You thief! You lying bastard! I only took what's mine to take. You're a life wrecker, Barnaby Brown."

And the phone goes dead.

He drops the receiver. *Who on earth can she be? Who did I hurt, and whose life did I wreck, apart from my own?* Whoever it is must be deranged. She said she only took what was hers to take. Could that be the painting? *Of course.* His parents' house cleaner who had a key has taken his painting. He still doesn't remember her name. He'll investigate tomorrow. Grateful he has re-keyed the locks, he goes back to bed imagining shadowy figures peering at him from behind the curtains of his bedroom, his parents' old room. Those ghosts again. How can he ever escape them, living in their house, with their former maid stealing precious pieces of his earlier life? He falls into an uneasy sleep.

In the morning he wonders if the phone call was just a figment of his guilty imagination.

# CHAPTER 6

On New Year's Eve, Barnaby manages the store alone again. He doesn't expect many customers, and more storms are forecast. Icy winds buffet the few brave pedestrians, hunched over and scurrying along the sidewalk. *God-awful weather*, he thinks. He brews a pot of coffee to drink with his morning donut. At lunch time, he debates braving the cold and running out for a sandwich. Hunger pangs win out, and he posts a BACK IN 15 MINUTES sign on the door.

He spends most of the day after lunch taking inventory. He knows this will please Sal, and having it done will spare him some stress—bad for a person with heart problems. Wanting to know how his boss is doing, he picks up the phone. A woman's voice answers.

"Gina? Barnaby here, calling to see how Sal's getting along."

"Well, thanks. He's okay. Wants to get back to work. They're discharging him this afternoon. I'm guessing he'll be in on Friday. Wants to pay you."

"Tell him there's no hurry, though I'd appreciate the check. I could stop by and pick it up, if that would be easier."

"Let's wait until Friday and see how things go. How's everything at the store?"

"Fine. Taking inventory. Tell him not to worry, and happy New Year to both of you."

He hangs up, turning his thoughts to the party that evening, thinking he should have done some laundry last night. What does he have to wear that's halfway decent? He might still have a good shirt and some dark pants. Time to shave again to get rid of the stubble from several days' growth. Conjecturing why that matters, he recognizes it's because he'd like to make a good impression on Lisa. A new sensation—he can't even remember the last time a woman caught his attention.

Barnaby closes the store early, as he knows Sal would do on New Year's Eve, and goes home. Popsicle squawks hello when he opens the front door. He returns the greeting, then cuts up an apple for her. She takes it, eyeing him with appreciation. The party starts at nine, and he has plenty of time to find suitable clothes. Why is he so nervous, acting like a teenager? He hasn't concerned himself much about his appearance for years, but now he regards himself critically in the full-length mirror in the bedroom. Unable to see through it, he fetches some window cleaner and wipes the glass. He's a little taken aback at the face that emerges. His stringy hair is in need of a good cut and his hollow cheeks give him an emaciated expression, as though he hasn't eaten well in years. Well, there's some truth to that. He hasn't paid much attention to the food pyramid advised by the government for healthy eating, and he knows he's had more than his quota of alcoholic beverages. That reminds him: he must be sure not to drink too much tonight.

It's too late to go to the barber, but he can shave, take a shower, and trim the worst of the shaggy hair around his face. His smile is his best feature. He practices smiling in front of the mirror. He finds a blue shirt that compliments his eyes and a pair of corduroy pants. They're a bit large in the waist, but he tightens his belt and figures they're all right. At least he has a brand- new pair of boots to wear.

"Well, bless my buttons," Popsicle says, extending a wing and preening the feathers.

Has she noticed he's wearing different clothes? And that his trouser button needs to be tighter? Surely not. She's not prescient. Or is she?

"See you soon," he says, slipping a smile.

As he approaches Lisa's house, he hears music and laughter. He stops. Does he really want to go in? Socializing was never his strong point, and it has been a long time since he attended a party—he'll go home and tell Lisa he's sick. As he vacillates, rocking from one foot to the other by the front door, a couple passes by.

"Guess you're going to Lisa's. I'm Harry, and this is Olivia," the man says.

"I'm Barnaby."

"Well, come on in," Harry says, holding the door open.

Barnaby squares his shoulders and steps inside. Lisa takes his coat.

"So glad you came," she says. "Don't you look nice. How's it going?" Dressed in a silvery blouse and black pants and her hair swept up, she appears stylish.

"Got the parrot back," he says.

"Well, that's good news."

At that moment, two women wearing fur coats and heavy perfume arrive. They hug Lisa and talk to her, gesticulating wildly.

Lisa gives Barnaby a wink. "Talk to you later."

He'd prefer to continue the conversation with her, but obviously she has other guests to attend to. He surveys the scene. The floor plan is similar to his, but renovations have changed the appearance entirely. It's much better. Her kitchen, a separate room in his house, opens to a sitting area with a fireplace. On the table there are piles of sandwiches, bowls of fruit, oatmeal cookies, various cuts of meat, and a platter of cheese, olives, and sliced baguettes. In the middle of the spread, like a monument, stands an enormous chocolate cake on a platform. He saunters over and stares. It's at least three layers high, with "Happy 2009" on top in pink icing.

He turns to the woman standing next to him and tries to think of something to say. "Better than a donut," he says.

She turns to face him. "What's better than a donut?"

"That cake. I bet it's better than the donut I eat each morning."

"Well, I guess so," she says, giving him an uneasy stare and moving away.

Barnaby considers going home. He's no good at small talk, and the crowd of strangers talking with such animation intimidates him. Then he hears a woman's soft voice behind him.

"Is that Barnaby Brown? What are *you* doing here?"

He spins around. A younger woman smiles up at him. A sparkling barrette accents her long dark hair cascading over her red dress, holding back a curl, artfully arranged above one ear.

"Julia!" he says. "Haven't seen you in a donkey's age—sorry, don't mean to use that old expression—it's been years. How are you? What brings you here?"

"I'm a friend of Lisa's. We work together. Why don't you get a drink and we can sit down and catch up?"

"All right. Can I get you something as well? What will it be?"

"A Diet Coke, thanks. Don't drink alcohol much anymore."

He makes his way to the kitchen counter, finds a can of Diet Coke, and pours himself a glass of scotch over ice. He hands her the can, and she goes back to fetch a glass. Flinching—he's forgotten his manners—he starts to apologize. She smiles and holds her hand up to silence him, and they sit together on the couch.

"So Barnaby, tell me what you've been up to. I last saw you in Providence, twenty years ago or so. You taught art at that girls' school. Are you still teaching?"

"Sadly, no. You may not have known that Anna died. Cancer. I left after that. Haven't kept up my teaching career."

"Oh, I'm sorry to hear that, and about Anna. What a lovely girl, and you both had so much talent."

Barnaby looks down at his hands. "There has never been anyone like Anna."

Julia touches his shoulder. After a minute Barnaby clears his throat and says, "What about you? You were still in college when we knew each other. I remember you dated my old friend Sly."

She smirks. "Yeah . . . along with everyone else, I guess. Still, we had fun in those days, didn't we?"

"We did. Strange, seeing you here. I ran into Sly right before Christmas, here in town."

"You did? Is he still teaching?"

"No. He said he's in the art business, buying and selling art. He has a gallery. Seems to be on his second wife."

She nods. "Sounds like him, always a bit of a salesman. I'm sorry—he was our friend. I don't mean to speak badly of him."

"It's okay. He and I haven't kept up our friendship. Anyway, what are you doing now?"

"As I said, I work with Lisa. Social work. Not always easy, but necessary."

"I should think so. Helping people is important."

"So is painting. We all need artists. I remember your fascination with the weather in Rhode Island. You'd go out on the rocks to watch approaching storms so you could paint the gathering clouds. Very dramatic!"

Barnaby's face flushes. "Well, that was then," he says, swallowing the last of his drink.

"Do you remember the time we all went night sailing? You, Anna, Sly and me? Now, that was wild."

"Stupid, more like. We couldn't see a thing."

They both laugh.

"You have that same irresistible smile," she says. "Dimples and all!"

He covers his mouth with his hand, and his flush deepens. "Think I'll help myself to another drink," he says, getting up. "Can I get you something?"

"No, thanks. It's great to see you again, but I don't want to stop you from visiting with everyone else."

He sits back down. Maybe he doesn't need another drink yet. "I'd rather talk to you. You're the only person I know besides Lisa, and I've only newly met her."

"I don't know anyone else, either. Lisa thinks I need to get out more, so she invited me. I have to admit, I tend to stay home a lot."

"Me, too." Barnaby glances at her left hand. No wedding ring.

"I'd love to know about your art," she says. "What are you working on these days?"

Barnaby waits before answering. He doesn't want to tell her he's not painting anymore and that he works at a hardware store. He's already humiliated enough by running into Sly, and he likes Julia and wants her to think well of him. "Actually, I've started a new series of paintings of people in ordinary walks of life," he lies. "Working, you know? Sly may even want to buy some."

"That's terrific. Do you have a studio? And do you live here, in Waterbury?"

"Yes, to both questions. What part of town do you live in?"

"North End. I have a condominium there."

"Ah yes. I remember you were into acting. Are you still performing?"

"Occasionally, with a local group. It's not as much fun as theater in college, though." Her eyes light up. "Do you remember when we all had parts in *South Pacific*? You were Emile, and I was Bloody Mary. Anna played Nellie. She had a beautiful voice. It was loads of fun." She searches his face. "You were perfect for the part, with your sun-bleached hair and deep tan."

Barnaby shrinks at the notion of himself now, so much older. He runs his hands through his limp tawny hair as he struggles to think of a fitting response. After a few moments, he says, "It *was* fun. It's where I got to know Anna. You know she taught English at the same school where I taught art, but I never knew her well at work. Then when she tried out for the play, I saw a different side of her."

"I remember. We all envied you two, especially when you sang, 'Some Enchanted Evening.' It was obvious you were singing it to her."

He smiles. "She did well with the song about washing that man right out of her hair, too."

"Which she apparently couldn't do with you," Julia says, nudging him with her elbow.

He laughs. "It's good to talk about those times," he says. "Makes me young again."

"Me, too," she says.

He sees a shadow pass across her face. "Do you have a family? Any kids?"

"No."

Noting her sad expression, he figures it's best not to pry. That would allow her to inquire more about his life, too, and he's not prepared with answers.

The disc jockey in the adjoining room announces that he will accept requests for songs from the guests.

"Let's have him play something from *South Pacific*," Julia says.

Before he has a chance to respond she jumps up and marches to the DJ. In a few minutes he hears the strains of "Bali Ha'i." Julia grabs his hand.

"Want to dance?"

He hesitates. He's not sure he knows how to dance anymore.

"Come on, it's New Year's Eve," she says.

He sets down his empty glass and eases himself off the couch. She leads him to the living room, and they join the dancers. Grasping her right hand, he winds an arm around her waist. She feels light and agile in his embrace. He catches the rhythm of the slow song and dances perfectly in step with her. A faint fragrance of coconut wafts from her hair. When the music stops, he's suddenly aware of his heartbeat. As he steals a glimpse at her face, he notices her eyes are moist.

"Thank you, I enjoyed that," she says.

"First time I've been dancing in a donkey's age. There's that old saying again. What's a donkey's age, anyway?"

She smiles. "How long do donkeys live?"

He returns her smile. "No idea, but I have a sudden yearning for a piece of that chocolate cake. Care to join me?"

"Only if it's already cut. Lisa may be saving it for midnight. She likes ceremonies."

Barnaby peers over her head at the table. The cake sits untouched. "Too bad. Guess that means we'll have to wait until midnight. I had only planned to put in an appearance here, but thanks to you I'd like to stay longer. Would you like to dance again?"

She nods, and they step back into the throng. The music's tempo picks up. They jump and sway and move their feet.

Lisa appears at Barnaby's side and whispers into his ear. "Didn't want to ignore you. Can you spare a minute for a chat?" She glances at Julia. "If you have time, I mean. Don't mean to interrupt," she says loudly.

Barnaby stops moving and looks apologetically at Julia.

"Go ahead and talk to Lisa. She's the host." Julia says. "I need to sit down, anyway. Dancing's hard work. I'll see you later." She gives Barnaby a brief wave and leaves them together.

"Come into the kitchen, away from the mob," Lisa says.

Barnaby follows her to the sink. Bottles of wine and liquor are assembled on the counter nearby. "Think I'll help myself to a drink, if that's okay." He drops some ice cubes and pours scotch into a glass.

"So tell me. I'm dying to know. How did you get the parrot back?"

"She flew through my neighbor's window."

"Oh. Then I guess the woman I saw going into your house didn't take her. How about the missing painting? Did you find that?"

"No, and I've no idea what happened to it. Maybe the woman you saw stole it, but maybe not. I called the police, but I didn't have enough useful information."

"That's too bad, but I'd still like to see more of your paintings," Lisa says. "May I come over sometime soon?"

"Sure. Name the day."

"How about this weekend? Saturday?"

"Evening's okay after seven. I work during the day."

"Fine. I want to thank you for coming tonight. Hope you're enjoying yourself. I have this party every year. We have cake and champagne at midnight, and we make all kinds of silly toasts. It's a good way to begin the new year. Are you making any resolutions?"

"Sure. I want to solve all my problems. You know about some of those. And I plan to move out West."

"I'll be darned. Where, and why?"

"Oh, I don't know. Tired of the snow. Santa Barbara or San Diego. Anywhere warm."

"Well, you'll have to get the car fixed first, right?"

"Of course." He stares at his feet. He's doesn't want to be reminded of his problems after enjoying himself talking and dancing with Julia. "Lisa, it's a very nice party. Thank you for inviting me," he says, taking a sip of his drink.

"You're welcome. Don't overdo the booze."

He pushes through the guests, wanting to find Julia. She's dancing with a tall man, an accomplished dancer, and doesn't see him. He sits in a corner with his drink. Julia was always popular. Why would she be interested in him, other than as an old friend?

He had enjoyed holding her in his arms, though, and the music from *South Pacific* had brought back happy memories of his wife. The exotic setting of the musical had inspired them both to think about moving to California, a place where palm trees grow by the sea and the sun shines all year, a place of endless opportunity. The old dream has now become more urgent as an escape from a life that he doesn't know how to fix. He checks his watch—only eleven, an hour to go until midnight. What's he going to do to kill the time? He could have another drink or two, but then he remembers: he promised himself he wouldn't drink too much. In fact, he probably should give up drinking altogether. He'll stay long enough to ask Julia for her phone number.

The jostling crowd becomes rowdier as the midnight hour approaches. Barnaby has had enough to drink to feel slightly tipsy, and he sits with his eyes half shut, opening them every once in a while to search for Julia. He doesn't see her. Perhaps she has met someone else. A man hands him a glass flute.

"What's this for?" Barnaby asks.

"Champagne," the man replies, "and there's cake. You'll have to stand up. The toasts are about to begin."

The music stops, and the dancing couples separate from one another. Barnaby stands, and someone fills his glass. Lisa climbs onto a chair in the middle of the room.

"Listen up, everyone. We'll have speeches now. Anyone who has anything to say, please stand in line. Then at midnight it's time for cake and 'Auld Lang Syne.' Thanks for coming."

The first person takes his place on the chair and raises his glass. "This is for parties like this one. Here's to our host. To Lisa."

"To Lisa," the crowd roars, and applauds.

A second man stands up. "To the people of Waterbury, who are all about to get older."

"Whoa, speak for yourself," a young man yells. He sways as he attempts to stand on the chair, and several hands reach out to steady him.

"I think he's had a few too many beers," Julia says, suddenly appearing at Barnaby's side.

His face lights up as he sees her. He takes her arm, guiding her to the side of the room. "I've been looking for you. Would you be willing to give me your phone number? I'd like to stay in touch."

"Sure," she says, digging in her purse for a pencil and paper.

"You know, that guy has a point," Barnaby says. "Why should we act older each year? Why not try to find our way back to ourselves when we were younger? To our best selves, I mean."

"I agree. When we talked this evening about our younger days, I felt transported back. I'd love to recover the sense of optimism that I knew then. Is that what you're thinking?"

"Exactly," Barnaby says. "I've resolved to make a fresh start this year."

"Good for you."

He wrinkles his forehead and takes a breath.

"Uh, just wanted to ask. Would you like to go out for coffee sometime?"

"I'd love to. Or dinner. Call me."

His face relaxes as he exhales.

The guests count down to midnight: "Five, four, three, two, one, *Happy New Year!*" and begin singing, "Should auld acquaintance be forgot . . ."

Julia gives Barnaby a hug. "Happy New Year. I'm glad we met again."

"Me, too," he says and kisses her lightly on the cheek.

Barnaby walks the few steps home elated. Seeing Julia so radiant and friendly gives him hope. He resolves to make a real effort to turn things around this year. As he opens his front door, Popsicle greets him from the kitchen.

"Hello, hello, top of the morning."

"Top of a very good morning," he says. "And a happy New Year to you, too."

"One for the road," the parrot says.

"Not today," he says, throwing a handful of peanuts into her food dish and covering her cage for the night. "Not tomorrow, either."

# CHAPTER 7

Julia Morgan keeps a close eye on her rearview mirror as she drives home. Sparse traffic in the first hour of the new year allows for easy viewing of the few speeding drunk drivers. *Inconsiderate folk, endangering the lives of others*, she thinks. Her thoughts turn to the party.

Lisa's considerable accomplishments include lavish entertaining, and this evening's event proved no exception. She's a superb baker—the chocolate cake tasted luscious. Julia sighs. Compared to her friend and co-worker, Julia lives a dull life: she works too much, and doesn't pursue hobbies in her free time. She hasn't had a role in a theater production for over three years now. When younger, she'd fancied playing a character on stage added spark and intrigue to her everyday presence. Now she wants to make the most of the next phase of her life, her middle years. She needs a change. Her efforts to dress up tonight had paid off, though. She'd caught the attention of Barnaby Brown. Now, *that* made attending the party worthwhile. She hopes he'll call soon.

She locks the car in the garage and enters the condominium. Her cat, Molière, curled up in a chair in the living room, opens a lazy eye when she comes in but doesn't stir.

"I know. You're annoyed with me for not celebrating the new year with you," Julia says. "I'll give you a special treat."

She goes into the kitchen, opens a can of his favorite cat food, and spoons it into a dish. Molière springs from the chair and struts into the room, tail high. Julia ponders if Barnaby has a pet he talks to. If not, he might find her strange for having conversations with an animal. The cat joins her on the bed in due course, a warm presence at her feet.

The next morning, the phone awakens her.

"Hey Julia, happy New Year! Nancy here. The sun's out! Want to go for a walk?"

"What time is it?" Julia answers sleepily.

"After ten. Did you celebrate last night?"

"Yes, sort of. I went to a party. I *would* like to walk. Give me an hour and I'll be ready."

Nancy Hamilton and Julia would both turn forty this year and had already promised to celebrate together on their birthdays. *Celebrate, or commiserate?* Julia asks herself. Nancy and she had met years ago at the gym where they had agreed to follow an exercise program to stay in shape as they progress into their forties.

Julia pulls on blue jeans and a thick sweatshirt and downs a glass of orange juice with a slice of toast before jogging the three blocks to her friend's house. Nancy appears, dressed in a rainbow-colored wool hat, a purple coat, and red running shoes. Her intense brown eyes twinkle in the winter sunlight.

"It's a new year," Nancy says. "Let's make it happy."

"All right. Where are we going? Our usual trail?"

"Let's go to the Green, run downhill to the river, and then climb back to get a cardio workout."

Nancy sets a fast pace, and Julia increases her stride.

"If you keep this up, I won't have any breath left for talking," Julia says.

Nancy slows down. "All right. You want to talk. So talk."

"Don't you want to know where I went last night? Lisa invited me to her New Year's Eve party. First time. Pretty nice, more than I expected."

"Not like you to go to a party. What persuaded you?"

"I think I agree with Lisa that I need to get out more. Anyway, I met a man. Actually, I re-met someone I knew more than twenty years ago."

"Really? What's he like?"

"He's different from when I knew him back then. Older, of course, and somehow sadder. He told me his wife died. That obviously affected him."

They stop at a spot by the Naugatuck River and watch the water swirl past. Two mallards hug the edge, dipping and muttering softly to each other. The male's green neck shimmers opalescent in the sunshine.

"I've always admired ducks," Julia says. "The way they don't let things get to them."

"Uh huh. Good to have a thick skin, sometimes. It sounds as though this new man has a softer side, though."

*Just like me*, Julia thinks.

"He does," she replies. "But when he was in his twenties, he was a hunk! All the girls adored him."

"Was he a boyfriend?"

"No. He and I never dated, partly because I went out with Sly, his friend. We spent entire days at the beach swimming, playing volleyball, and sailing. Sly had a sailboat."

"I didn't know you sailed." Nancy rubs her hands together. "It's getting chilly, standing still. Let's move on."

They sprint along the Main Street, dodging families with dogs and children. A scarlet cardinal darts from a tree, reminding Julia of the party and the special red dress she had worn. After a while, they slow to a walking pace.

"The best thing about Barnaby is that he's an artist," Julia says. "A good one."

"Cool," Nancy says. "I hope he's a decent guy. You, my friend, have a genuine talent for falling for losers."

"True." Julia growls. "The last one was a disaster. But I think this one is okay. I've known him for a long time."

"Sure, but what do you actually know about him now, with all those years in between? He could be an axe murderer."

"Silly girl. If you saw him, that's the last thing you'd think."

"So tell me more," Nancy says. "Why are you interested?"

Julia takes a breath. "I'm not sure. He's sort of tired. But he has the same warm smile. And he has a romantic streak."

"How do you know that?"

"We danced together. I could tell."

"Aha. Has he asked you out already?"

"No, but he wanted my number and said he'd like to go out for coffee. I think he's actually rather shy. He used to act more confident, like our friend Sly."

"You've never talked about Sly. Another mistake?"

"Yep. Good looking. A womanizer, I learned later. I fell into his trap. But I was still in college, and he was five years older. At least I have an excuse for that one."

Nancy rolls her eyes. "Okay. Good luck. Keep me posted."

They reach the downtown area. No one is around, and some of the industrial brick buildings they pass gape hollow, with broken windows.

"It's too bad about this crumbling old town," Nancy says. "Did you know that last year *Forbes* magazine rated it one of the worst places for businesses and careers in America? Hard to conceive that for nearly a century Waterbury was the brass capital of the world! Still, I wouldn't mind moving to one of the older neighborhoods, the ones where the houses have brass doorknobs, but they're way out of my price range."

"I've no idea where else I'd go if I left." *Certainly not back to Boston, not as long as my father's still there*, she thinks. Pushing the uncomfortable thought away, she turns to Nancy and says, "Anyway, where else would you want to go?"

"California, a place full of opportunity, Problem is, I'd need to find a job first. I'd have to pass the bar exam there, too. That's not easy. Most people fail the first time."

"You've built a good practice here. Why would you want to give that up?"

"I wouldn't. It's only a pipe dream."

"Right. You have to have a dream, otherwise how can it come true? Remember the song from *South Pacific*?"

"Sure. Saw the musical in New Haven a few years back. Robert Goulet sang the main role. Loudly."

"Well, they played the song last night at the party. Brought back memories. Barnaby and I both took part in a production of that play in Providence."

"Oh, so he's an actor as well as an artist. Sounds fascinating."

"That's what I think."

"Let's stretch and speed uphill. Kick off the new year," Nancy says.

"You and your health nut routine. Drives me *nuts*."

Nancy laughs. "Come back to my place and I'll make us coffee and you can talk to me about Barnaby."

She takes off. Julia follows more slowly, flashing on the image of her friend soaring in her career, while she, despite considerable skills in social work, flies closer to the ground. Casting her mind back, she reflects that she has never been able to help those closest to her. Her former husband, for one. She had known they were headed for trouble the first time he raised his voice, saying green didn't suit her and she should never wear green. He had practically ripped the bright emerald blouse from her body. At the time, she attributed his behavior to his color blindness and forgave him. But she should have recognized then that he was blind in more ways than one.

Maybe a new relationship would add some fresh color to her life.

# CHAPTER 8

Barnaby starts New Year's Day with a song in his head. After greeting Popsicle and removing the cover from her cage, he shaves, then makes for the shower. Then he determines, in keeping with his new resolutions, to do laundry. He collects towels, various items of clothing, and Popsicle's cover, and throws them all in the washing machine. After he sets it going, he strips the sheets from his bed. He can't remember the last time he changed them, so they're surely overdue for a wash. He whistles as he works. It's a few minutes before he realizes the tune is the enchanted evening song from *South Pacific*. His thoughts turn to Julia. His heart skips a beat. He'll pluck up courage to call her soon. This evening.

While he's waiting for the washer to finish its cycle, he decides it would be a good idea to pay some bills. He receives his paycheck the next day so he can write checks before he spends too much of his money on booze or at the pub. Then he remembers: he's giving up drinking. Damn. He'll miss it. But it has caused so many problems in his life, it's the new year, and he wants a different life in California. He opens the drawer containing the paperwork. Right on top sit two bills from the bank with red PAYMENT OVERDUE stamps on the envelopes. He slits the envelopes. The first bill is for $150 plus a late fee of $15. The second is for $150 plus a late fee of $50. Goddammit, that's already $365. His two-week paycheck nets less than $700. So much for paying for the car repair. They cancelled his credit card years ago, and he has no other source of income—*except for the sale of his paintings.* He can go to O'Malley's and ask Sean to send an email to Sly, as his friend offered to do.

He pushes his arms into his old coat, responds to Popsicle's "bye-bye" salutation, and heads for the bar.

Barnaby's eyes adjust slowly to the relative darkness inside O'Malley's. Sean stands in his usual place behind the counter. The place reeks of stale beer.

"Well, hello there, stranger," Sean says. "Missed you last night."

"Went to a party. Nice change, but not my style."

Sean places a glass on the counter and reaches for the scotch.

"Not today, thanks. I'll have a cup of coffee instead."

Barnaby perches on a stool and faces the bartender who regards him with raised eyebrows.

"Overdo it last night?" Sean asks, pouring coffee.

Barnaby shakes his head. "No. I'm giving the stuff up. New year resolution."

"Well, I'll be damned. Good luck to you with that."

"Reason I came in, besides seeing you, is to take you up on your offer to send my friend an email. I need to contact him about selling my paintings."

"Sure thing. What's his address?"

Barnaby pulls it from his pocket and hands it over. Sean puts a laptop on the counter and takes a seat beside him.

Barnaby casts his eyes around the room. No one else is there. He'll miss drinking with his companions—and the booze, for that matter. This isn't going to be easy. He's tempted to ask for a drink.

"Okay," Sean says. "What do you want to say?"

"How about, 'Hello Sly. I'd like to talk to you about the paintings you said you'd like to see. Give me a call or send me your phone number. Thanks, Barnaby.'"

Sean types the note and presses the send key.

"Guess I'm going to have to get myself a computer some-day," Barnaby says.

"Yeah, hard to get by without one. So what else is new?"

"I met an old friend at the party last night. A woman." He fingers his coffee cup, raises it to his mouth, then sets it down. "Might ask her out."

"Yeah? Well, I guess you're already havin' a happy new year. Goin' off the drink and gettin' a girlfriend. Good for you, fella. We'll miss you."

"I'll still come around. I might even do a painting of the place, as you suggested."

"That'd be nice." Sean wipes the counter, takes glasses out of the dishwasher and sets them on the shelf. He turns to face Barnaby again. "What's her name?"

"Julia."

"Julia. I knew a woman with that name. Used to come in with a guy who caused trouble. Forget his name. He'd drink too much and start fights. Had to throw him out more than once."

"That doesn't sound like someone this woman would know. Can you describe her?"

"Pleasant smile, dark hair. Sometimes wore somethin' sparkly in her hair."

"Hmm. Could be Julia. Has she come here recently?"

"Nah. A few years back, I guess."

Barnaby is relieved. Julia had not given him the impression that she was in a relationship, but then she might only con-sider him an old friend, not a potential romantic partner. Or perhaps she likes that guy she danced with. It doesn't hurt to try, though. He'll call her soon. "How are things with you?" he asks Sean.

"Oh, not too bad. Goin' to hire a guy to work the bar when the weather improves so I can go fishin'."

"That's good. You work too much."

"I do, but I like the job, talkin' to people, you know?"

"You're lucky to have work you enjoy. Got to go. Thanks again for your help."

"No problem. Come back in a day or so when the guy's had a chance to reply."

"I'll do that. See you later."

He retraces his steps homeward, hears the phone ring as he opens the door, and rushes to pick it up.

"Got your email. Sylvester here. Happy New Year! No time like the present. When are you going to get those images to me? I expected them already."

"That's what I want to talk to you about. I don't have a computer and can't send you anything electronically. But if you have time to come over, I can show you some original work. That's better, anyway."

"All right. I can get away this weekend. I live in Manhattan now, not far from my business, Goldstone Gallery in Greenwich Village. What's your address?"

"55 Russell Road. How about Sunday?"

Barnaby hangs up the phone and sits down. Then he remembers he forgot to ask for the guy's phone number. Damn. Now he really needs to clean up. How can he bring his wealthy friend into this dump? It would further humiliate him, and Sly would soon see that he's no longer painting. Feeling panicky, he climbs to the studio. He can create something new that very day and find the paintings in the weather series, ones that might attract buyers. A small blank primed canvas sits on the floor, and he lifts it onto the easel, replacing the painting that's there. Then he pulls more paintings out of the racks. It's been several years since he examined them, and he's surprised how good they are. Sunlit scenes burst with color and life—figures on beaches lying on striped towels with umbrellas, children splashing in the waves, white spray obscuring their faces. Other paintings are mysterious, with rocks and lighthouses barely discernible through the mist. He lines the canvases up against the wall. Twenty altogether. Too bad the one he considers his best isn't among them, and he debates contacting the police with additional information about the cleaning woman who has a key . . . but he doesn't have time now. He needs to paint—and clean.

He opens the drawer where he keeps his oil paints and chooses colors, then opens the tubes and squeezes the contents onto a palette. Thank goodness the paints are still usable. After pouring turpentine into a jar and picking up a thick brush to dip into the liquid, he coats the canvas with an underpainting of burnt sienna, a good choice for a bar painting. He'll go to O'Malley's to complete sketches of the figures and background. As the familiar smells of turpentine and linseed oil fill the room, a warm wave courses through his body. He has missed painting. It's what he was born to do. *How have I let so many years go by without following this lifelong passion?* He needs to make up for lost time. Soon he has covered the canvas with a thin layer of the coppery-colored paint. He pours fresh turpentine into a tin and stashes the brush. That will keep the bristles soft until he can return to work on the scene.

He plans to spend the rest of the day cleaning and then go to the bar to sketch. He can have dinner there as well.

At four o'clock, he stands and stretches. Scrubbing the kitchen floor for hours makes his back hurt. Years of accumulated grime and dirt have disappeared and the tiles are dark red again. The parrot watches from her bird's-eye view at the top of the cage.

"Helluva job," she keeps saying, turning her head from side to side.

"You're right, Popsicle. It *is* a hell of a job. Now don't you go throwing food on the clean floor. No peanut shells, either."

"Peanut," the parrot says, opening and shutting her beak.

"All right," he says, fetching a bag of nuts and putting a handful into a dish in the cage.

Popsicle claws her way down to reach them. Soon she pecks the shells off, drops them on the bottom of the cage, and eats the insides. A few shells drop onto the floor.

Barnaby shakes his head. Cleaning is a thankless task. He's hungry. Grabbing a sketchbook and pencil, he heads for the door. Popsicle is too busy eating to tell him goodbye.

# CHAPTER 9

After she returns home from her walk with Nancy, Julia calls Lisa.

"I had a great time last night," she says. "Hope there wasn't a pile of clutter to deal with afterward."

"Glad you could come," Lisa says. "I didn't touch anything until this morning. Some guests stayed until three. Had to kick them out, finally."

"Guess that's the problem with New Year's Eve. People drink too much."

"Right. By the way, I noticed you got along well with Barnaby Brown."

"Yes. I knew him years ago in Rhode Island."

"Did you? Be careful. He has a lot of problems, you know."

"Really? I wasn't aware of any."

"He sure does. Alcoholic. Lives in a pigsty. Could be one of our classic cases."

"Oh. I didn't know that. You've been to his house?"

"Yes. He's a neighbor."

"Well, he seems to be a decent guy. He's an artist, too. A good one."

"I doubt he's painting much these days," Lisa says. "He works at Carano Hardware."

"He didn't mention that. I've got to run. See you at work. I only wanted to thank you for the party."

∗∗∗∗∗∗∗∗∗∗

Julia slams the phone down. Good grief, she's done it again: made a connection with a loser. She had high hopes this time. Oh well, best to find out sooner than later. There's a pile of laundry. She'll wash it along with Barnaby out of her hair, but can't help feeling disappointed. The memories of the *South Pacific* musical that they performed in together evoked nostalgic recollections. How sad that Barnaby slid downhill. That explains his changed appearance. But he told her he is working on a new painting. It's possible Lisa is mistaken. In fact, why has she gone to such pains to tell her those unflattering details about the man?

Julia takes the rest of the day to run errands. There's no point waiting for Barnaby's call, especially since she's no longer sure she wants to see him. She doesn't need an alcoholic in her life. She shoves a pile of wet clothes into the dryer.

The phone rings several times before she answers.

"Hi, Julia? Barnaby here. I enjoyed seeing you at the party yesterday. Would you like to go for coffee and continue our conversation?"

"Uh, I'm pretty busy these days."

"Okay, how about you call me when you have some free time. I'm busy during the day, but I have evenings and Sundays free." He tells her his phone number and she jots it down.

"All right. I'll call you. Thanks."

She slowly replaces the phone. She needs space to think. It wouldn't hurt to meet for coffee. That's hardly a date, and he has given her the option of calling to set it up. Anyway, possibly he only wants friendship. Coffee is safe. She'll think again about calling.

# CHAPTER 10

On Friday Barnaby takes the bus to work. Sal is already there making coffee.

"Hey, how are you feeling?" Barnaby asks.

"Not bad at all. Still need to watch myself. I'm supposed to cut down on work hours for a while, so I'm only staying until lunch. Can ya handle things for the rest of the day?"

"No problem. Are you taking any meds?"

"Yeah, and I have a checkup at the hospital next week. Have to change my diet, too," Sal says, groaning. "They told me this is a wake-up call."

Barnaby nods. "Don't worry about things at the store."

"That's a comfort, thanks. Saw ya did the inventory."

"Most of it. I'll finish this morning while you're here to deal with the customers."

"Great. Listen, don't let anyone go in the basement. I've locked the door. Don't want people poking around when I'm not there. Thanks again, and here's yer paycheck."

Barnaby pockets the check and sets up the ladder so he can access the higher shelves and continue taking inventory. His thoughts turn to Julia. He's disappointed she didn't agree to meet him for coffee when she'd seemed so agreeable the night before. Did something change? Did she learn more about his present conditions, which he took pains to hide? As uncomfortable as the thought makes him, he still wants to get together. He's taking steps to improve his life and wants her to see him at his best. He'll sell some paintings, fix his car, paint the kitchen. As he counts the bottles of Pine-Sol and cans of Comet, he's reminded that he needs more cleaning supplies. Sal always gives him a discount. He'll take some home.

He breaks early for lunch and calls the car repair shop. "Barnaby here. Want to ask if I can pay you in installments for the repair."

"We don't usually do that. You pay when the job's done."

"Well, in this case I hoped you could make an exception. I need my car."

"How many payments are you talking about?"

"Two. I get paid every two weeks."

"Tell you what. We'll order the parts. You can pay for those. Then when you're ready to pay again, we'll start the work."

"That sounds good. Please go ahead and place the order."

He's satisfied with the arrangement. He'll have enough money left for at least one of the equity loan payments and can talk to the bank about those as well. Anyway, he plans to work every day now. If he doesn't hit the bottle, he shouldn't need to miss.

After work, Barnaby stops by the bank's ATM to deposit his paycheck. If he sells the paintings and works regular hours, he'll pay his equity loan off faster. In fact, he had planned to apply for a refinance so that the monthly payments would be lower. He can do that soon.

At home, he gathers the pile of mail on the doormat. He tosses it on the desk in the living room. An envelope from the bank catches his eye with the words LOAN PAST DUE stamped across the front. He tears the envelope open.

*Dear Mr. Brown,*

*We regret to inform you that since you have missed three payments on your home equity loan, the bank has initiated proceedings to reclaim your property. Your house will revert to the bank's ownership unless you make your payments immediately. If you fail to make them in a timely manner and wish to stay in the property, you will be charged rent. Otherwise, you will be expected to vacate the premises.*

*If you have questions, you may call or talk to your local bank.*

*Sincerely,*
*Bank of Boston*

Barnaby drops to the floor. He reads the letter again. Surely they wouldn't take away his home. His chest tightens. How could things have gotten to this point, right when he's getting his life in order? He plans to talk to the bank the next morning and tell them his circumstances have changed, and he now has additional sources of income. He'll ask for a reprieve. Surely they'll understand.

*Damn it all. Damn everything.* He heads to O'Malley's for the TGIF special.

The packed bar forces him to push through the crowd to his usual seat at the counter near the cash register. Professor Miller is already uncertainly perched on a stool, one foot reaching toward the floor as if to steady himself.

"Hello there, Barnaby," he says. "TGIF, right?"

"I guess so." Barnaby would prefer a different companion on this day, but the professor is already in his cups and ready for conversation. A monologue, anyway.

"Did I ever tell you about my button collection?" the professor asks.

Barnaby yawns. "I expect so. I don't always remember barroom conversations."

"No." Professor Miller nudges him. "I'll bring mine in one of these days. It's valuable. The designs are unusual, and you being an artist, they might interest you."

"Whoever told you I'm an artist?"

"Your friend Sean here. He's a fan of yours. Didn't you know?"

Barnaby shrugs. He waves at Sean. "The usual, please."

Sean places a tumbler of scotch in front of Barnaby. "Thought you were layin' off . . ."

Barnaby holds up his hand. "It's Friday. Thank God."

Sean tightens his lips and moves along to serve another customer.

"As I was saying," the professor continues, leaning closer. "I'm a member of the National Button Society. You're aware that brass buttons were the first products made by the industry right here in Waterbury. They were actually the first buttons made anywhere in the country. They produced them for military uniforms. Envision that—in 1822 the Chase Company made twenty gross of buttons per day! The ones on that uniform Sean has hanging on the wall were undoubtedly made here."

"You don't say," Barnaby says. He has finished his first drink while listening to the professor's lecture and needs another. As he peruses the crowd, he identifies others he'd rather talk to, but he doesn't want to give up his seat at the counter. It might be a night when he needs several drinks. The professor's story has left him strangely depressed. He calls for a refill.

"One of these days I'll make a deal with Sean for those buttons," the professor says.

"He'll never sell them. The jacket belonged to a relative who fought for the Union in the Civil War."

"Is that so? I'd no idea Sean's roots went back so far."

"He's of Irish descent, and his relatives came here early and worked in, of all places, the brass industry."

"Interesting. I'll have to talk to Sean about that. Did you know that brass is made of copper and zinc?"

"No, I didn't."

The professor opens his mouth to say something else, then turns his head and leaves his mouth hanging, speechless. Barnaby follows the man's gaze. Brooke Taylor stands by the door wearing a form-hugging purple coat with shiny brass buttons. She doesn't have to push through the mostly male patrons, who move aside to let her pass. There's a noticeable hush in the room.

Sean immediately comes to take her order.

"Could you make me one of your specials tonight, a gin gimlet?" she purrs.

"Coming right up," Sean says, smiling.

The buzz of conversation resumes, and the professor slips off his perch.

"Would you like a seat?" he offers.

"Thank you," she says, as she takes it. Her perfect white smile dazzles.

Barnaby gulps two mouthfuls of scotch. What's he going to say to this beauty, the heart throb of O'Malley's, who's sitting right next to him? Her scent teases his nostrils, reminding him of gardenias. He wishes the professor had stayed put.

Brooke holds the cocktail glass in a slender hand and sips the green drink.

"That drink reminds me of my parrot," he says at last.

She turns toward him. "You have a parrot?"

"Yes, Popsicle. She's a yellow-naped Amazon. Has green feathers."

Her silvery laugh sounds like bells. "Does Popsicle talk?" she asks.

"Oh, yes. Keeps me company."

"I had a parrot once. He died."

"Oh, sorry. Do you miss him?"

"I was a child, and I did miss him."

Professor Miller stands beside Brooke sitting in his old seat. He'd left his drink on the counter and, unable to attract her attention, reaches around her to grasp it.

"Excuse me!" Brooke says, shrinking from him. "Please keep your hands to yourself, mister."

Barnaby watches the professor's face contort with horror.

"I'm sorry, didn't mean anything . . ." he stammers. "Just wanted to get my drink."

She hands him the glass. "Please thank Sean and do me a favor and give him this book." She lays a slim volume on the counter. The white lettering of *Shakespeare's Sonnets* gleams in the dusky room. She leaves cash for her drink by the till and gets up to leave. Once again, the crowd stands aside to let her pass. A whiff of perfume hovers in her wake.

Barnaby pats the stool beside him. "Sit back down, Professor. I know you didn't mean to harass the lady." He feels sorry for the old man. "Tell me more about the brass business."

Professor Miller hauls himself up. "You know, people come here for different reasons," he says, "but what brings a woman like that into a bar, alone? I've never seen her come in with anyone, and she never goes out with anyone, either." He hands the book to Sean.

"What happened? Did you scare her off, Barnaby?" Sean asks, winking.

"Nah. But maybe you know the answer to the professor's question. Why does a woman like her come here, apart from enjoying your superb gin gimlets, of course?"

"She doesn't usually come on Fridays, when the place is crowded," Sean says. "Her favorite time is early Sunday afternoon, when no one else is here. She only has one drink. I like to think she's here to see me, but more's the pity, I don't think that's so. I'm thinkin' she wants peace. She makes an impression wherever she goes, and she must get tired of bein' stared at. 'And I shall have some peace there, for peace comes dripping slow.'"

"My heavens, do you know what you're saying, man? That's Yeats, from 'The Lake Isle of Innisfree,'" the professor says, his eyes brightening.

"My father used to quote those lines. He came from Ireland, you know."

"Are you a poet, by any chance?" the professor asks, staring at the book of sonnets.

"Are you kiddin'?" Sean laughs. Barnaby looks from one to the other in surprise. There are always surprises. That's one of the reasons he frequents this bar. And that the people amuse him, and he feels accepted. He doesn't really want to give up drinking. What else would he do with his time, and where else would he find such good free entertainment?

"Hit me," Barnaby says, pushing his glass toward Sean. "Double."

# CHAPTER 11

Barnaby wakes up on Saturday with the familiar headache and foggy mind. He overdid it last night. Sean understood, as always. His drinking buddies expected no less from him than the usual too many glasses of scotch. Charley, a regular customer on Fridays, had treated everyone to a round, he remembers, or maybe two. He grunts. He has to go to work. *It's late, but better late than not at all*, he tells himself. He skips the shave and shower, dresses in overalls, his usual work clothes, and catches the bus downtown.

"Sorry I'm late," he tells Sal.

"Looks like ya fell off the wagon, Barnaby my boy," Sal says. "Thought ya were giving up."

"I am, I am. Got some bad news last night, is all."

"Shouldn't let that stop ya. Perhaps ya need some help. Ever gone to an AA meeting?"

"Not for a while. I need a cup of coffee."

Barnaby pours a cup and sits in a chair by the cash register. He's already miserable, but the thought of losing his house makes things worse. What on earth can he do? If he misses work again he'll lose pay, but he must talk to the bank. The thought crosses his mind that he can hardly afford his life anymore.

"Sal, I've got some important business to attend to. Do you mind if I take a longer lunch hour today?"

"How long? I'm leaving at noon. Doctor's orders."

"I'll leave at eleven. Should be back by twelve thirty. Can we leave the store for thirty minutes?"

"Barnaby, I've been depending on ya. Can't keep closing the place. How about ya leave at ten forty-five? Be back by noon."

"All right. Thanks," Barnaby says.

He leaves promptly at ten forty-five and runs to the bank ten blocks away. Breathless, and sweating despite the bitter January wind, he opens the glass door to the building and makes for the teller line. "I need to talk to someone about my loan," Barnaby says, pulling the envelope out of his pocket.

"You'll need to see a banker. Take a seat."

He waits awkwardly in an armchair in the lobby, drumming his fingers. Finally, a man with graying hair wearing a gray suit approaches him.

"Mr. Brown? I'm Lloyd Purser." The hand he extends, soft and slippery like a fish, does nothing to ease Barnaby's discomfort.

They enter the banker's cubicle. Barnaby places the envelope on the desk and sits across from the man, painfully aware of his own day's growth of stubble and overalls. At least they're clean. Lloyd opens the envelope and reads the terse letter.

"This looks pretty clear to me," he says. "Pay the past amounts due plus the late fees or the bank will start foreclosure proceedings on your house."

"I understand, but I'd like to ask for a reprieve."

The banker meets Barnaby's anxious gaze and averts his eyes.

"Not for me to say. You'll have to talk to the manager, Mr. Olivetti. I'm afraid he's out today, but he'll be back on Monday."

Barnaby clenches his hands and grasps the arms of the chair. His heart is beating so fast he wonders if he might develop a heart attack like Sal. "Are you sure no one else can help me? I'd like to resolve this as soon as possible."

"I understand, but you must wait for the manager. Cursing, Barnaby hastens back to the store. He's annoyed with himself. His life is a jumble, and each time he takes steps to make things better, he fails. He shouldn't have gone out drinking last night. He'll renew his resolution.

He's on the bus after work before he remembers Lisa is coming over that evening. Damn, he really doesn't want to see her. He has too many other problems to deal with at the moment, and she has the effect of making him feel worse about his life. She knows too much. She's sympathetic, but he wants women to respect, even to admire him. Accustomed to hiding behind his drinking for so long, he values his recent attempts to come across as a different person, and Lisa is someone who won't let him forget his troubled past. Outside, everything has turned colorless. Showers of sleet bash against the window panes. He shivers and tugs his hat over his ears before getting off the bus.

At seven o'clock he hears a firm knock at the door. Lisa is right on time. She stands smiling on the doorstep.

"Come on in," he says.

She takes off her hat and coat and places them on the staircase rail. She's wearing a low-cut frilly blouse and black pants. Her perfume clashes with the Pine-Sol smell of the freshly scrubbed kitchen. He wrinkles his nose in disgust.

"Smells like you've been doing some cleaning," she says.

"Trying. Guess I've let things go a little. I'll have things clean by spring, anyway. Spring cleaning, you know?"

"Sure, though spring's far away when the weather's this ugly."

He clears his throat. "Uh, would you like something to drink?"

"Tea or coffee would be great. You don't still have liquor in the house, do you?"

"I do. I should give it to you to avoid temptation. Come on back to the kitchen."

She follows him, stepping gingerly on the clean floor. "You *have* been busy," she says. Approvingly, he thinks.

At that moment Popsicle flaps her wings. "Heavens to Murgatroyd! Helluva job! Helluva woman!" she says.

Lisa jumps.

"Don't mind her. She gets rowdy sometimes, especially when new people come around."

"But she insulted me. *Hell of a woman*. What does that mean?"

"Nothing. Don't take offense. She sees that you're a woman, that's all. Probably feminine rivalry. I'm her man, you know."

"Okay, but who'd want to compete with a parrot?"

Barnaby takes the whistling kettle off the stove. "Tea or coffee?" he asks again.

"Do you have drip coffee?"

"Somewhere I do. Usually I make instant."

"Well, tea then."

He places a tea bag in a cup and pours water over it. "Sugar or milk?"

"Black is fine." She takes the cup and sits at the table. "So how are things going?"

"Could be better, could be worse," he says. "Why don't we talk about you? How's work?"

"Work is work. It's not much fun. Sometimes it gets you down, seeing people in difficult circumstances. The worst part is that you do all you can to help, and still people struggle. Worse still for people in my profession, we don't always know the results. We can only follow cases so far, and it gets discouraging when you spend a lot of effort only to find out that the person has moved or is no longer in contact."

"But there must be cases where you feel you've been helpful, with a good outcome."

"Sure. Problem is, many people who find themselves in a deep hole can't dig themselves out. That's especially true of people with substance abuse problems." She stops, and casts a quizzical glance at Barnaby.

He flinches, but ignores her comment, turns his back to her, and takes her empty cup to the sink. "You came to view the paintings," he says stiffly. "Let's go upstairs to the studio."

They climb the stairs, and Barnaby turns on lights. Lisa walks over to paintings lined up against the wall and examines each one.

"They're very good. Full of life. Even those that are sub-dued show mystery and intrigue. How much are you selling them for?"

"Don't know yet. Are you interested in buying one?"

"I might be. Depends on how much they cost."

"I haven't priced them yet. I'd like to wait until a friend in the art business comes by to appraise them, and I can let you know then. Are there any that appeal to you?"

"There are several. Hard to choose. I like them, Barnaby. I see you've got a new one, too, on the easel."

"Yes. I plan to start a new series. Getting back into painting again."

"You should. These show a whole new side of you."

"One that most people don't know any more," he replies drily. "Of course, Julia does. I'm glad she came to the party."

"Yes. Julia. I want to warn you. She's had her share of problems, too."

"So have we all, except for yourself, of course. You spend your life helping other people solve theirs. Must be nice."

"I don't think of it that way," Lisa says, then meets his eyes as she continues. "Let's talk more about this. Have you had dinner yet?"

He shakes his head.

"Well then, why don't you come over to my place? If you don't mind leftovers, I have a tuna casserole."

"Thanks, but not tonight," Barnaby says. "May I have a rain check?"

"Sure. Thanks for the tea, and for showing me your work. I'd like to help you, you know that. Call me."

"I will. See you later," Barnaby says.

After she leaves, he speculates about her abrupt departure. Perhaps he has offended her. She means well—doesn't she?—but she makes him uncomfortable.

Besides, Popsicle doesn't like her, and that's a bad sign.

# CHAPTER 12

On Sunday morning the sleet turns to rain. The streets glisten shiny and wet, like water on a whale's back. Why does he think of whales?

It takes a minute, but then it comes back to Barnaby. Of course! He and Anna had gone whale watching. Anna leaned on the boat's rail, never taking her eyes off the horizon. When they at last spotted a whale, she grabbed his arm.

"Look! It's spouting, like a fountain. Pure joy, don't you think?"

That's one of the things he had loved about Anna. Her unbridled enthusiasm.

✤✤✤✤✤✤✤✤✤✤

Since Sly is due in a few hours to see his paintings, it's time to stop dreaming and get to work, Barnaby tells himself. He shaves carefully. He looks healthier without red eyes, and this morning his eyes shine, a clear blue. Smiling at his reflection in the mirror, he hopes this will be his lucky day. It would be wonderful if all his problems would vanish into the sky like kites on a lost string. But he hasn't held a kite since those long-lost days in

Providence. The kites appeared in his paintings, firmly clutched by small children with no problems to lose. Sighing, he tells himself to stop pinning his hopes on a proverbial cloudless sky.

After coffee and whole wheat toast—healthier than a donut, he thinks—he collects cleaning materials and a bucket. This time he mops the stairway leading to his studio. He can shut the doors to the bedrooms and living room. If he has time, he'll wash the kitchen windows. Thanks to Popsicle, no spiders have taken up residence there.

Since they didn't arrange a time, he doesn't know when to expect his friend, and when he discovers he doesn't have much to offer him to eat, he reckons he doesn't have time to buy anything. If Sly is driving from New York, he may be on the road already. By noon he judges the house mostly presentable and smelling fresh in all the public places.

Sylvester arrives in the early afternoon.

"How was the drive, Sly?" Barnaby greets him.

"Not bad. No accidents on the freeway. Please remember, I go by Sylvester now." He hands Barnaby a business card. "Is this a shoeless house?"

"What do you mean?"

Sylvester chortles. "I mean, do you want me to take my shoes off so I don't make your house dirty?"

Barnaby laughs feebly. "Oh. No, that's okay. The floors don't mind a bit of dirt." He's tempted to add "a lot of dirt," but restrains himself. "I can offer you tea or coffee, or would you like something stronger?"

"A beer would go down well."

"Sorry, no beer. Scotch or bourbon?"

"How about scotch on the rocks? Will you join me?"

Barnaby hesitates. "Trying not to drink before dinner these days." He pours a drink and hands it to his friend. It smells good, and he wishes he could have a glass.

"Where can I leave my coat? It's wet," Sylvester says.

"Let me take it. It'll dry here in the kitchen. Warmest room in the house."

"Yeah, kitchens are the heart of a home. I've always liked them. Don't do much cooking these days, though. My wife Carol is an excellent cook. Have to watch my weight," he says.

"What happened to Melanie, your first wife?"

"Oh, that's a long story. We had two kids, a boy and a girl, and then things went wrong. Don't know why, exactly. Her decision. She didn't like it when I quit my job at St. Mary's. I wanted to make more money. You know there's no money in teaching."

"Yeah, I remember. But there are other rewards."

"Sure, if you're happy with the lifestyle. My older brother Gregory—you remember him?—did well and bought a second house in the Hamptons. I'm not there yet, but I'm working on it. As I told you, I got into the business of buying and selling art, which is why I'm here. Besides seeing you, and getting caught up with my old and talented friend," he says, smiling broadly.

"Don't know about talented. I'm not selling much these days."

"Why not? You have your day job at the hardware store. Pays the bills and leaves you time for painting, right?"

"Not really, but this year I'm turning over a new leaf. I've a new series of paintings in mind."

"That's good. And you live here, by yourself? Never remarried?"

"No."

"Too bad. I remember Anna. Quite a looker, and nice, too. I see you have a companion, though," Sylvester says, ogling the parrot.

Barnaby's insides churn at Sly's simplistic assessment of his wife, but remembering his friend's womanizing nature and not wanting to confront him, he lets the comment pass.

"Popsicle's good company," he says. "Today she's on best behavior. She can be pretty noisy at times."

The parrot eyes Sly sideways as though sizing him up, but says nothing.

"Your new wife Carol, what's she like? Her parents live here in town, I understand."

"Right. In the Hillside district. Nice historic house. Her parents are quite active socially, and the night I saw you—Christmas Eve, wasn't it?—they threw a big party."

"Where are you living in New York?"

"Upper East Side."

"Business going well?

"I'd say so. Wish I could get away more, especially in summer. You remember how much I like sailing. This year I'm going to rent a place by the water on Fire Island so we can take a boat out. Maybe you'd like to come along sometime."

"Maybe I would," Barnaby says. "If you're finished with your drink, do you want to take a look at the paintings?"

"Sure do. Lead the way."

They mount the stairs to the studio. Sylvester immediately crosses the room to the canvases stacked against the wall.

"Yup. That's how I remember them. Spectacular." He checks them all once, then rechecks some. "I'll take them. How do you want to do this? Want to sell 'em all to me outright, or give 'em to me for consignment sales?"

"I haven't thought much about it. How much are we talking about?"

Sly scratches his head. "I'll give you $15,000 for the lot. That's $1,000 apiece for the big ones and $500 for the smaller pieces. I'd give you more, but they need framing."

"How would that compare with the price if you take them on consignment?"

"Hard to say. You're not a known artist, so it might take a while for them to sell. Commission is fifty percent. If I pay upfront, you'll have the cash today. I can write you a check."

Barnaby takes a breath. The idea of suddenly having a check for $15,000 is hard to resist, but something tells him not to sell all those paintings at once.

"Tell you what," he says. "You can take half of them. I'll keep the rest for now. If sales go well, I might sell you the others."

"Okie dokie. Sounds like a deal. They're nice. Are you painting more like these?"

"Not on this theme. You probably remember from your painting days that artists paint what interests them at the time. Those scenes, mostly seascapes, don't represent my life anymore."

"True enough, though I don't understand why you haven't painted more during the intervening years. I see some others in the racks. Are you going to show me those?"

"They're no good. I went through a lean phase. No inspiration. Sort of like writers' block."

"Well, find a muse," Sylvester says. "Talent doesn't disappear, and you do have that, I must say."

"I'll let you know when I've done some new ones that I think are any good. Do you want to take the paintings now?"

"May as well." Sylvester picks out the ones he wants and stacks them near the door, then takes out a checkbook and writes a check for $7,500.

"I can't give you a proper receipt. Okay if I write you a note?" Barnaby asks.

"That'll do for now, but follow it up with an email, if you would. I need proper documentation."

Barnaby scribbles a note and wraps the canvases in newspaper. Soon all are ready to go.

"Car's outside, in the driveway," Sylvester says.

They carry the paintings downstairs. Sly retrieves his coat from the kitchen. It's still pouring rain.

"Let's make a dash for it. I'll open the trunk. We can put some in the back seat as well."

Barnaby helps his friend load the car. Sylvester slams the trunk and goes round to the driver's side. He holds his hand up in a farewell gesture. "Thanks a lot," he says as he turns the ignition.

As Sly backs out of the driveway, Barnaby gasps. The car is a dark green Mercedes. Wasn't that the description Lisa had given of the one driven by the woman who entered his house? *Was Sly involved in the theft?* He puckers his brow. Strange, but not worth pursuing yet. He's solved one of his biggest problems.

He has some money.

# CHAPTER 13

It's Monday again. Wanting to be sure the previous day hadn't been a dream, he rushes to the studio to find the check, picks it up, and examines it. The check is indeed made out to him for $7,500. It's like a miracle. Now he can go to the bank, settle his debts, and decide what to do about the car. He might consider buying a newer used one instead of paying to fix the old clunker. He whistles as he fixes breakfast. Popsicle dances on the top of her cage, keeping pace with his excitement.

"Good parrot, heavens, good parrot," she says, finishing with a squawk.

"We're both good parrots today," Barnaby says. "Rich ones."

Sometime he imagines he's a bird, parroting his way through life, calling like Popsicle in her cage, waiting for a comforting echo. But lately that's not the case. He's not simply repeating his routine—he's on the verge of making some real changes. He hasn't felt so optimistic in a long time. After he finishes his coffee, he washes the cup and goes to the hall closet for his coat. His threadbare coat. He might treat himself to a new one with his newfound wealth.

He takes the bus to the bank and asks to see Mr. Olivetti.

"I'll check if he's free," the teller says. "Have a seat."

Barnaby scans the room. He has always hated banks, the sterility of them, and the way the employees look at him suspiciously when he comes in clothed in overalls. Today he's wearing street clothes, but it's possible the old coat sends the same poor impression as the overalls. He'll enjoy wearing a new one. Finally, the teller informs him that Mr. Olivetti will see him.

The manager sits behind a shiny desk perusing a file. A plush green carpet compliments several similarly colored paintings on the walls. Barnaby wants to examine them but thinks this might not be the time to do so. He sits down in an upholstered chair facing Mr. Olivetti and stares at the perfect part in the man's hair.

"Ahem," the manager says. "I understand you're having some trouble meeting the terms of your home equity loan. What seems to be the problem?"

"I've had the loan for ten years. It's almost all paid off. I fell behind in my payments because I got sick."

"Sick? In the hospital, you mean? Incapacitated?"

"Yes, incapacitated. But not in a hospital."

"Can you provide proof, a doctor's note, for example?"

"Uh, no. But now I'm recovering and I'm back at work full-time. I'd like you to stop the foreclosure process on my house."

"I can only do that if you make up the two payments you've missed. And you have another one due this month."

"I can do that. I have a check here," Barnaby says.

"Let's see." The manager examines the documents on his desk. "You work at Carano Hardware, right?" He nods slowly. "I know it. Sal's a relative of mine. He's a good man."

"Did you know he had a heart attack?" Barnaby asks.

"I didn't. Poor guy. I'll have to give him a call . . . look here, I'd like to help you out. I'll have Lloyd Purser make the payment adjustments to your loan and give you a revised statement."

"Much obliged to you," Barnaby says, as he stands up to leave. For perhaps the first time, he understands the value of his long employment in a business where the forgiving owner is a respected member of the community. Unlike other alcoholics of his acquaintance, even during his darkest days, he had never quit his job.

Half an hour later he has deposited Sly's check and made the three payments on his loan. His next stop is the car repair shop.

"Morning, Mr. Brown," the man at the front desk says. "The parts arrived on Saturday. Do you want us to start the work?"

"Not yet. Could I have a word with the mechanic?" Barnaby asks.

"All right. Wait here."

The man goes into the garage. Barnaby examines the pictures of classic cars taped on the walls and deliberates whether his would be old or special enough to be included in the collection. Probably not. After a while the mechanic comes in and calls to him.

"You're the owner of the Ford Pinto wagon, right?"

"That's right. I'd like to know if you think the car is worth repairing."

"Well, with new transmission it's probably as good as it gets for a car that age."

"I know it's old. Thought I might turn it in and buy another. How much do you think this one's worth?"

"I'd give you three hundred bucks for it."

"That's all?"

"Well that's how it goes. You got 150,000 miles on her. Could last you a few more years but then maybe not."

Barnaby groans. "Do you have any others that are newer, with lower mileage, for sale?"

"Matter of fact, we do. There's a 2000 Honda Accord over there in the back lot. Those cars last forever. Eighty thousand miles. Got hit from behind, a fender bender, and has some dents, but she's okay."

"So how much would you sell it for?"

"Have to check with the boss. Repair'll cost you five hundred."

"Okay, let me think about it."

He strides to the back lot and checks the car. Inside, the upholstery appears as good as new. If it's in good running condition, this car could probably take him to California. After quick mental calculations he figures he still has some paintings he can sell, so that's extra cash, and he'll still have a thousand dollars left if he buys the newer car. It might be a good idea, especially if he can make a deal with the owner. He returns to the office.

"I'd like to talk to the manager," he says to the attendant.

"He's at lunch. Back around one."

"I'll stop by later, then. Thanks."

It would be a good time for a drink. A big decision like this calls for a little help. Barnaby is not used to having extra cash on hand, and the possibilities make his head swim. A drink would settle his mind. He turns in the direction of the bar at the end of the street. He opens the door, and the familiar aroma of stale beer emanates from the dank interior. Then he remembers. He wants to stop drinking. If he buys a newer car, he can realize his dream of getting to California, and even take Julia out in style before he goes. The thought gives him a jolt of pride. He closes the saloon door and crosses the street to a small café.

There are no free tables so he takes a seat at the counter next to a man wearing a tie.

The man nods to Barnaby. "Nice day for this time of year."

"Yes. A reprieve from winter."

The server behind the counter hands Barnaby a menu. "Soup of the day is French onion. Really good."

"It's delicious," the man beside him agrees. "All their soups here are good, but this one's special."

Barnaby has never eaten French onion soup, but it smells good. "I'll try it," he says.

"Comes with sourdough bread," the server tells him.

"I come here most days for lunch," the man beside him says. "Never seen you here before. Are you new to town?"

"No. Lived here almost all my life. I'm here to pick up my car."

"At Tom's Auto Body shop? What are we working on for you?"

"My 1980 Ford Pinto. Not sure it's worth repairing."

"I know the one. You're probably right, but if you like it and want to keep it running, what else can you do?" the man says, staring at Barnaby's torn overcoat.

"Actually, I'm thinking of trading it in, getting something newer." The server puts a bowl of steaming soup in front of Barnaby along with bread and a glass of water. He takes a spoonful. "Cheese on top is great," he says, blowing on the spoon to cool it.

"We have a few cars for sale on the lot. Got a nice Honda in last week. Owner didn't want it so we bought it."

"The silver one, year 2000? I saw it. Are you the owner? If so, they told me to talk to you about buying it."

"Yes, I'm Tom. So you'd want to trade your Pinto for that one?"

"Yes, I guess so."

"I don't know. As you said, yours is hardly worth repairing. It's not the best model Ford ever made. We'll have to charge you the return fee for the parts if you don't want us to do the work. Guess I could give you three hundred bucks for it. Sell it for scrap. I could sell you the Honda for five thousand."

"That's a lot of money, but I want to drive out West this year and I'm not certain the other car would make it. Could we make a deal? Do you like art?"

"What? I don't, but my wife does. Why do you ask?"

"I'm an artist, and I've recently sold some paintings to a gallery in New York. I know the owner will mark them up, and he gave me a thousand bucks wholesale for each of the larger ones. If I gave you one, would you take it and give me a break on the Honda?"

Tom shifts his head from side to side, pursing his lips. "Interesting idea. We have an anniversary coming up. What's in the painting? It's not one of those abstract things is it, that looks like a child did it?"

"Not at all. It's a seascape with a lighthouse."

"She might like that. I'd need to see it first, of course."

"Sure. I can bring it by."

"All right. Do that. Would you like to check out the Honda again?"

"Yes. Thank you."

They finish their meals and return to the auto body shop. Tom takes the Honda keys from a hook and hands them to Barnaby. "If you can show us some ID, you can take it for a drive," he says.

Barnaby hands Tom his driver's license, who copies it, then passes it back. Barnaby strides to the car. He likes the silver color and, compared to his station wagon, the car is sleek and stylish. He opens the hood and inspects the engine. It looks clean. Adjusting the driver's seat, he turns the key in the ignition, pleased with the way the dashboard lights up. The radio works, too. He backs into the street and drives around the block. The car doesn't backfire and responds well as he presses the accelerator and gathers speed. He smiles at the notion that he can actually afford such a luxurious vehicle. Now if he can get Tom to accept a painting to reduce the cost, he'll have made a good deal. After he parks the car in the lot again, he returns to the office.

"What do you think?" Tom asks.

"The car runs well, and I'd like to buy it," Barnaby says. "If you're still interested in the painting, I can bring it by. Will you be able to repair the back fender right away?"

"We can get to it within the next week. To be safe, let's say Tuesday."

"Sounds good."

"I'll need a deposit of a thousand bucks first," Tom says.

"Of course." Barnaby writes a check. "Thanks. See you Tuesday."

He waits for the bus, straightening his back and holding his head high. On his way home he makes two more stops. He buys a new coat at the men's store on High Street and flowers at the supermarket.

# CHAPTER 14

Julia drives to work feeling out of sorts. Her washing machine failed overnight, flooding the kitchen, and she'd spent the early morning mopping up. The cat, then, was not happy. Getting his paws wet, he padded through the living room, leaving prints everywhere. After placing Molière's bowl of Happy Cat Tasty Tuna on the floor in the hall, Julia stepped in it on her way out the door. Now she smells of fish. Damn it all. She'll have to call a repairman about the washer and arrange to be home for the service.

She runs into Lisa in the lobby of the New Haven County Social Services, Waterbury Division building.

"Good morning. How was your weekend?" Lisa asks.

"Okay. Washing machine's broken. I'll have to get it fixed, and I'm worried about the wooden floor because soapy water leaked all over it."

"Bummer. Look, I'd like your help with one of my cases. Could you stop by my office when you get settled?"

"Sure."

Julia feeds the coffee machine in the lobby with a dollar bill and watches while the black liquid drips into a paper cup.

That's never her favorite way to begin the day, but she'd been too rushed to stop at a coffee shop for a latte on the way in. She opens the door to her small office, sits down at her desk, and turns on the computer. While the blue screen flickers and springs into life she props her chin on her hands as she considers what to do about the washing machine and her ruined floor. She chastises herself for allowing the problem to distract her from her work until she remembers the last time this had happened. *Washing machines and ruin.* During her mother's illness, their washer had sprung a leak just as they headed out the door for an urgent doctor's appointment. Her father, dressed for work, watched them go without as much as setting down his coffee cup.

"Could you call someone about the repair before you leave?" Julia asked him.

"Call yourself. It's women's work."

Suppressing her anger, Julia hurried her mother out of the house.

❊❊❊❊❊❊❊❊❊

A string of email messages come into view in the computer, and Julia peruses them quickly. Nothing important. She takes a sip of the tasteless coffee and goes to see Lisa, who is rummaging around for papers.

"Have a seat. Can't find my notes," Lisa says.

Julia checks the room. Lisa has several framed posters of Impressionist paintings on the walls. She also has a large wooden sculpture of a pelican on a pedestal in the corner.

"Where did you get the bird?" Julia asks.

"Went to an art show in New York last weekend. I get to galleries once in a while. You should come with me sometime. It's fun."

"I don't really have money to spend on art."

"You don't have to buy anything. You can see what's going

on in the art world. Speaking of art, have you seen our local artist Barnaby recently?"

"No. He called to ask me out, but I said I was busy. Guess you scared me off him."

"Good thinking. Here's my file on the Hawkins case. I've had a few visits with the family, but I'd like a second opinion about what action to recommend. Would you go and see them and give me your thoughts?"

"I can do that. Where do they live?"

"Maple Street. Take the file and read up on the case, and thanks."

Back at her desk, Julia hopes the new project will distract her from her own petty problems. That's the good part about her work: there's always someone whose life is worse than her own, and she is glad to help. In fact, she'll use the opportunity of getting out to go by the hardware store at lunch to find out what materials she should use to treat her wet wooden floor.

After she reads Lisa's notes, she places a call to the Hawkins family.

A woman's voice answers the phone. "Elsa speaking."

"I'm Julia Morgan at New Haven County Social Services, a colleague of Lisa Nettler, whom you've met. She asked me to talk to you. May I stop by sometime today?"

"Sure. I'll be home. Come anytime."

"Good. I'll be there this morning, before noon."

Julia takes the file and lets the receptionist know she will be out until after lunch. She drives across town and parks in front of the small house on Maple Street where Elsa Hawkins and her mother Alma live. A woman in her sixties with tired eyes opens the door.

"You must be Julia," she says. "I'm Elsa. Come in."

Julia steps inside, noticing that the house appears neat and clean. Elsa offers coffee and Julia gladly accepts. They sit down at the kitchen table.

"I understand you may need some help with your mother," Julia says.

"Yes. She's at a doctor's appointment now. My sister Hannah took her. We share the caregiving, but it's becoming more difficult and we don't know what to do. Our mother is stubborn. She's had several falls and can't take care of herself, but she refuses to live anywhere else. Hannah and I are exhausted, dealing with her constant needs. Mother needs help with her leg brace, bathroom visits, and showers."

"Have you and she looked into places where she might go and have skilled care?"

Elsa grimaces. "We have, but assisted living facilities are either too expensive or not to her liking. She insists this is her home, and she belongs here with me, her daughter."

"Where does Hannah live?"

"In town. She's married and lives with her husband."

"How does your mother spend her time, and what's the state of her health?"

"Mostly she watches TV. She has no friends anymore. She's eighty-two and in good health except for her leg. Before this last fall, when she broke it, she would go out. We have to keep an eye on her because she has a history of shoplifting. She's sneaky. Takes things when no one's looking."

"Oh dear. That must make things difficult. What do you do about this?"

Elsa rolls her eyes. "When we find something she's stolen we try to return it, but we don't always know where she goes. Now her leg is healing, she's started going out again. We think she needs closer supervision. I have a part-time job and can't be here all the time."

Julia nods sympathetically. "Has your mother taken anything valuable, something that might get her in trouble with the police?"

"Usually not. She takes trivial things, like toothbrushes

or pencils. She's especially fond of crayons. There is one piece that may be of value, though. We can't figure out where she got it. It's a small painting."

"May I see it?" Julia asks.

"I'll fetch it. I locked it up, in a closet. She's furious with me for that. Claims it's hers, that it was promised to her years ago, and she wants it on the wall where she can see it. She says it brings back happy memories."

Elsa shuffles down the hall and returns with an oil painting, a seashore scene, depicting people wandering on the beach and children flying a kite under a cloudless blue sky.

"Nice picture, isn't it?" Elsa says. "We have no idea where she got it. Came back from a party on Christmas Eve with it. We asked the hosts if it belonged to them, but they said no."

"What party was this, and how did she come to be invited?"

"Former employers of hers, the Burtons, held the party. She used to clean house for them. They've always had a soft spot for her. They sent a car to pick her up. You know, they're rich folks who live in Hillside. She claims it was promised to her years ago by her employer, but that employer wasn't this family."

Julia wrinkles her brow. "It's clearly a difficult situation," she says. "What can I do to help?"

"Could you talk to Mother and explain that we can no longer take care of her? If you know of any nice place where she can go and we can afford, that would be fantastic. She's not safe in this house anymore. She wanders off and sometimes can't find her way back."

"I'll see what I can do. I understand my colleague Lisa has already talked to your mother."

"She has. That didn't go too well. They didn't hit it off. Mother has strong views about people. She either takes to them right away or can't stand them. She might listen to you. You have a kind face."

"I'll do what I can to help. I'll be in touch soon."

Julia sits in the car for a few minutes before driving off. She can see that Elsa is exhausted. Caregivers often are. She questions why Lisa failed to gain Alma's confidence, and she's not certain that she, Julia, can do any better. But it's obvious the family needs help, and a good assisted living facility or group home might be the right solution. Or, because of Alma's possible dementia, a memory care facility might be more appropriate.

She remembers Carano Hardware is nearby and that Barnaby works there. It would be good to see him again without the complication of a purely social visit. She drives the several blocks and parks the car outside the store. Inside, she sees a man at the cash register but no sign of Barnaby.

"Hello. I'd like to talk to Barnaby," she says.

"It's his day off. May I help ya?" Sal asks.

"I guess so. I wanted to talk to him, but I have a problem that can't wait. My washing machine flooded all over my floor, and I'm concerned that the wood might be ruined."

"Water's not good for wooden flooring. It can warp. First ya need to get rid of the water. Has the room been flooded for long?" Sal asks.

"Just since last night."

"It should be okay, then. As I said, ya need to mop the floors good. When they're dry, treat them with floor wax. I'll get it for ya."

"Thanks. Will Barnaby be at work tomorrow?"

"Yes. He's been real good at coming in lately. I've been sick, ya see. Couldn't get by without him. Do ya want to leave him a message?"

"No. That's not necessary. Thanks for your help."

Sal fetches the floor wax and deposits it on the counter. "That'll be eleven dollars and fifty cents."

She pays the bill and leaves the store. *Sounds as though Barnaby's a good employee*, she muses. *Perhaps there's some good in him.* She'll think about calling him soon.

Back at the office she finds Lisa talking angrily on the phone. "Yes. That's what I told you, sir," she says.

She catches sight of Julia, rolls her eyes, and motions to a chair.

"All right. I'll call you next week." Lisa hangs up the phone and glances at Julia. "Some days I wish I'd never gotten out of bed. You know, I'm getting sick of this job. I may be burning out, as they say. How did you make out at the Hawkinses' place?"

"I talked to Elsa. Her mother was out. The situation is troublesome for the two daughters, and it looks as though Alma would be safer living elsewhere. She'll need a formal evaluation, of course, but I told Elsa I would talk to her mother about moving."

"I already did that," Lisa says. "Between you and me, the old lady's losing it. Won't listen to reason, or can't. However, in my opinion she will be able to convince authorities that she has a sound mind, and if so, she'll have to agree before they send her to an assisted living facility. There are probably no grounds for committing her at this point."

Julia scrutinizes Lisa's expression, thinking her attitude unprofessional, but sees no sign of awareness on her co-worker's face. "Did they tell you she has a shoplifting habit, and that she may have stolen a possibly valuable piece of art?" Julia asks. "If she's caught, she could face charges of theft."

"I didn't know that. What kind of art? Did you see it?"

"I did. It's a painting of a beach scene. They don't know how she got it. Alma said her employer promised it to her so it belongs to her."

"Amazing story. Who was the employer?"

"They don't know. She came home from a party with the painting."

Lisa's eyes light up. "My God!" she says. "I wonder if it's Barnaby's painting, the one that got stolen. Let me think. I saw a woman going into his house. Come to think of it, she walked slowly, like an old person. She arrived in a green Mercedes. I don't know if she was the driver."

"Elsa told me the people who held the party sent a car to pick her up. Maybe Alma got the driver to take her to Barnaby's house, and maybe Barnaby's parents were her former employers."

"Good thinking. We'll have to talk to Barnaby," Lisa says, smiling. "I'll give him a call. He'll be happy if we've solved the mystery of his stolen painting."

"No, let me call him. I'd like to ask him some questions anyway before I talk to Alma Hawkins."

Lisa raises her eyebrows. "Are you sure? I thought you wanted to stay away from the man."

"But this is business, isn't it?"

"Be careful. You don't want to mix work with relationships. That can get complicated. I'll call him. It's my case, and I'm the one who's been talking to him about the missing painting."

"All right. Go ahead." Julia says, standing to leave. She hopes disappointment doesn't show on her face. As she returns to her desk, the thought crosses her mind that Lisa appears quite eager to get involved in the Hawkins case again. Now she wants to call Barnaby about a case she had happily handed over to Julia only a few short hours ago.

Something's not right.

# CHAPTER 15

Wearing his new coat and carrying a bouquet, Barnaby arrives home. He finds Popsicle in the kitchen, greets her, and reaches to scratch the back of her neck. She lowers her head in response. She always enjoys having her neck scratched.

"Good parrot," she tells him. She climbs up his arm to his shoulder, then nibbles tenderly on his ear.

"We'll go to O'Malley's for dinner tonight." he says, "But first I have to deliver these flowers to Mary, the kind lady who took care of you." He had told her he would think of a way to thank her for returning Popsicle and couldn't think of anything else to buy for her.

He knocks on her door. "Hi, Mary," he greets her.

She regards him uneasily. "Excuse me, but do I know you?"

He bows slightly and offers her the flowers. She takes them, and after a minute her face lights up.

"Oh, I didn't recognize you without the beard. You're Barnaby."

"I told you I'd give you a present for bringing Popsicle back."

"Thank you. That's not necessary, but flowers are always welcome. Come in."

"Well, for a minute."

He follows her inside. Her house is immaculate, with polished floors and a shiny black piano in in the living room.

"You must be a musician." he says.

"Yes. I play with the Waterbury Symphony. Not piano, violin. I'm surprised you haven't heard me practicing."

"I haven't, but then I usually keep the window facing your house shut to keep the parrot in."

"Right. How's she doing?"

"Well. I'm grateful to have her back, as you know."

"Have a seat on the couch. May I offer you a drink? A glass of wine?"

"No, thanks. Tell me more about the orchestra."

"It's small, but we've been around a long time. You should come to a concert. In fact, there's one this weekend. I can give you a couple of complimentary tickets, if you'd like. It's an all-Scandinavian program, Grieg and Sibelius."

"I don't know much about classical music, but I'd like to go."

"Great. Hang on and I'll get the tickets."

Barnaby watches as she leaves the room. Her hair is tucked into a scarf that reflects her cobalt blue eyes, and he notices again she's a pretty young woman. Too young for him, though. She returns a few minutes later with the flowers in a vase, which she sets on the piano, then hands him an envelope.

"The seats are the best, half way back. I hope you enjoy the concert."

"Thank you." He stuffs the tickets in his coat pocket and sits, twisting his hands. He has run out of things to say. It would be easier to talk if he had accepted the drink. "Well, I'd best be going. Thanks again for the tickets," he says.

"You're welcome. Let me know how you like the concert."

He stands up, and she lets him out the front door. As he enters his house, the phone rings.

"Barnaby? Lisa here. Good news. We may have found your thief."

"Really? Who?"

"Her name is Alma Hawkins. Does that ring a bell?"

"Alma. An unusual name. Sounds familiar . . . yes, now I remember. That's the name of the woman who used to clean house for my parents. I didn't keep her on when they died, and I understand she was furious."

"She was? So you do remember her. Any other details?"

"Let me think. Alma had worked for them for years and expected me to give her work. I couldn't afford her. Yeah . . . that's right. I might have promised her a painting but never gave it to her. It's coming back now. I had a phone call recently from a woman in the middle of the night, too. She sounded deranged."

"That could have been Alma. I hear she's not doing so well. I'm trying to help her and her family."

"Of course, now everything fits. She probably kept her key. The question is, why would she decide to come for the painting now, all these years later?"

"No idea, but I understand a family she used to work for, the Burtons, had a party on Christmas Eve. They're fond of her and sent a car to pick her up. We think she may have had the driver stop by your house to get the picture."

Barnaby plops down. "My God! Christmas Eve is when I saw my old friend Sylvester again. He came into the store to buy lights while he and his wife were in town visiting her parents. Could they be the Burtons? He said they lived in the Hillside neighborhood. If Alma attended that party and talked to Sly, she might have learned of his and my friendship and that could have triggered her memory about the painting."

"Aha. Sounds like we're unraveling the mystery."

"Maybe so," Barnaby says. "I half suspected Sly was somehow involved in its disappearance. He may not be directly responsible, but there's definitely a connection. I can't thank you enough for helping to solve this puzzle."

"Glad to help. This is one positive outcome of my challenging case. What do you want to do about the painting? Alma likes it a lot, says it reminds her of younger days. But we can ask for it back. Frankly, I wouldn't advise that you file charges of theft against her. She and her family are dealing with enough problems as it is."

"I've no intention of filing charges. Let her keep the painting, if she likes it. We all enjoy things that bring back thoughts of happier days. It may even be worth something, too, if she wants to sell it."

"All right. I'll pass this information on to Alma's family."

"Lisa, this is good sleuthing on your part. What made you connect the painting with me?"

"Well, let's just say you've been on my mind, and the beach scene echoed some of the other works you've shown me."

"This is cause for celebration, and it may let my friend Sylvester off the hook, besides. He bought some of my paintings and may buy more, and I'd like to keep the relationship friendly. Tell you what, I have tickets to the symphony for Saturday. Would you like to go? It's the least I can do to thank you."

"This Saturday? That would be lovely, but you don't have a car. Do you want me to drive?"

"Thanks for the offer, but I should have transportation by then. I'll pick you up at six-thirty."

"Wonderful. I look forward to it."

Barnaby sets the phone down. He's glad the mystery of the stolen painting is solved and vaguely remembers promising it to Alma. He had been drinking at the time. If she's having a hard time struggling with dementia, as Lisa implied, he's glad to help. He would prefer to take Julia to the concert, but she hasn't called and he doesn't know if she wants to see him, anyway. And he owes Lisa. His mind can hardly grasp how his life is changing right before his eyes: a fancy car, tickets for a concert, and an evening out with a woman for company. He almost sprints with Popsicle to O'Malley's for dinner. On his way out, he grabs his bag of sketching materials.

⁂

The regular crowd is there. Sean serves drinks, Charley plays pool with his teammates, and the professor leans against the counter perusing the newspaper, a glass of Jack Daniels at his side. Engrossed in reading, he hardly acknowledges Barnaby, who takes his place at the opposite end of the bar.

"Evenin', Barnaby," Sean greets him. "How's life?"

"Not bad. Not bad at all. I'll have the usual and a grilled cheese sandwich, please. And french fries."

"And a pickle for Popsicle?"

"Pickle," the parrot says.

"She's strange, that bird," Sean says. "Never heard of one that likes pickles."

"No stranger than people. Folks have different likes. Take Charley, for example. He only wants Bootleggers Beer. Won't touch Sam Adams, or plain old Budweiser."

"Yeah. Pain in the you-know-what, too. It's hard to get Bootleggers, and when we're out of it, he gets mad. But that's one reason he comes here. They don't serve Bootleggers over at his friend Horace's place."

"Is that so?" Barnaby asks. "Well, anything to keep the competition away."

"Sure. Horace draws a different crowd. Comes here to play pool when he can get away, though. Better players."

"I haven't noticed, but then I don't play. I'd rather talk to you here at the bar, Sean my friend." He doesn't add that after a few drinks he doesn't notice much of anything, definitely not who's at the pool table. But as he turns the thought in his mind's eye, a wonderful opportunity for a painting emerges:

Charley at the table, cue in hand. He pulls a sketchbook from his bag and twists on his stool to view the players.

Sean gives him the thumbs up, takes the order for the sandwich to the kitchen, and comes back with a scotch on ice.

The professor rushes over, eyes gleaming behind his glasses.

"You've got to see this!" he says, his eyes bouncing from Barnaby to Sean as he waves the local newspaper. "They've been running poems, and this one must have been written about O'Malley's. The uniform on the wall, the brass-edged counter, the pool tables—all are there. Who's the poet? Someone who comes here, but who? Ever heard of N. Staey? That's the author."

Barnaby shakes his head. "Nope."

"Here's how it starts," Professor Miller continues. "The title is 'At the Bar.'" He recites,

*"At close of day they come,*
*with their horses' eyes*
*focused blind, like steeds in a race."*

"Nice language, but it sounds as if the writer doesn't approve of the drinkers," Barnaby says. "Horses, and blinders? How does it go on?"

The professor hands the newspaper to him.

"You're right. The setting is right here, in the bar," Barnaby says.

"We've got to find out who wrote it. Do you have any customers who are poets, Sean?" the professor asks.

"Not that I know of. No one famous comes here, with the possible exception of yourself, Professor. This is a place for locals. Just everyday folk, not celebrities."

"Wait a minute, you're forgetting Brooke Taylor," Barnaby says.

"I don't think she's famous, though she could be," Sean replies. "No one knows much about her—though I, for one, would like to."

"Wouldn't we all," the professor sighs. "It's possible she's the phantom poet. The research is on! I'll take it as a personal challenge to find out whoever it is."

Barnaby smiles at the professor's enthusiasm. Then he sits at the counter until closing time, nursing only two drinks before heading home. He doesn't want to think of himself as a racehorse, blindly following the course.

# CHAPTER 16

Julia arrives at work exhausted. She spent the evening before waxing her kitchen floor, relieved to find the water didn't damage it. Now, she schedules a service call for the washer repair.

Lisa stops by her office.

"Hey. Did you talk to Barnaby yet about the painting?" Julia asks.

"Yes. He was thrilled, and invited me to go with him to a concert on Saturday."

"He did?" Julia feels a sudden pang of envy. "Are you going?"

"Sure. Why not? He's a nice guy."

Julia almost chokes. Barnaby, a hopeless drunk according to Lisa, is suddenly a nice guy?

"So what are you doing this weekend?" Lisa asks.

"Getting my washing machine fixed," Julia says slowly, fixing her gaze on Lisa.

"Oh. Sounds exciting." Lisa smirks, fumbles in her purse, and applies apricot-colored lipstick, smoothing her lips together. "Regarding the Hawkins case," she says, "since you're still assisting me with it, could you to talk to Alma soon?"

"Sure. I can call today to find out a good time."

"Okay. Let me know what happens. And by the way, Barnaby doesn't want to report the stolen painting or press charges. He said he probably offered her the painting at some point, anyway. She can keep it. As I said, he may have his problems, but he is a decent guy."

"That's what I think, too," Julia says.

"I'll see you later," Lisa replies as she turns to go.

*Bitch*, Julia says to herself, making a face behind Julia's back. Lisa warned her not to have anything to do with a man who she's obviously attracted to herself, and now she even has a date with him! Julia chastises herself for having turned down his offer for coffee. Now he probably thinks she's not interested. She can't go to the hardware store again with the excuse of asking for advice about the floor. He had invited her to call if she wanted to meet for coffee, though. She'll do that. Take the initiative. She can hardly accept that she might be in competition with a friend over a man, but Lisa isn't much of a friend these days. She's a colleague who mostly treats her with condescension, and she doesn't want to let Lisa gloat—or win.

During her lunch break, Julia calls the hardware store. "May I speak to Barnaby, please?"

"Sorry. Not here right now. Can I help ya?"

"No, thanks."

She hangs up. If he's not at work, he might be at home. She lifts the phone again. No answer. The phone rings several times. No voice mail. *He really needs to get with the times,* she thinks. No voice mail, no cell phone—his old-fashioned naivete. But that's part of his charm.

There's nothing more she can do for now. She calls Elsa Hawkins to schedule a time to talk with Alma.

"And I have some good news for your mother," Julia tells her. "Lisa figured out the artist's identity. She talked to him, and he confirmed that he had intended to give the painting to Alma years ago. She used to work for his parents, and he still lives in their house on Russell Road. Alma must have a key. She let herself into the house to reclaim her painting. Barnaby Brown, the artist, will not press charges, and if Alma likes it, he says she can keep it."

"Good heavens!" Elsa exclaims. "Glad to know the story. Thanks for telling us."

Julia arrives at the Hawkinses' later that day.

"Mother's in the living room," Elsa says. "She's looking forward to your visit. Today she's in a good mood and when she's happy she likes company."

Julia follows Elsa into the room and takes off her coat. Alma sits in an armchair with her braced leg propped up. She has gray wispy hair and watery eyes.

"Mother, this is Julia, the lady I told you about."

Alma smiles weakly and extends a skinny hand. Julia takes it and sits next to her.

"What a pretty shirt you're wearing, and I like that sparkly thing in your hair. It's nice to meet you," Alma says.

"Thank you," Julia says. "How are you feeling today?"

"Right good except for my leg. That's how it is at my age, you know, things break. I'm eighty-two. What brings you here?"

"I came to see you. There's some good news. The painting you have, the one in a closet, is yours to keep."

"Well, that's not news. I knew that. Elsa here won't let me hang it up. The young man who painted it promised it to me."

"I'll bring the painting out right away, Mother," Elsa says. "Where would you like to hang it?"

"In my room, where I can see it. It's a real nice picture. Reminds me of when I took you and your sister to the beach as kids. Long time ago." A flicker of a smile crosses Alma's face, and she closes her eyes.

Elsa goes out of the room and returns with the painting.

"Don't go to sleep now, Mother," she says, "we have a visitor."

She holds the painting up and the three women examine it.

"He's a talented artist," Julia says.

"Always was, spent hours in that studio of his, painting," Alma says. "Couldn't get in there to clean. Mrs. Brown always said not to worry about it. She was a fine woman, Mrs. Brown. Young Barnaby had his problems but when he was off the drink, he was okay. Kind. Liked to help carry my water bucket up the stairs. But he let me go, though the house could use cleaning. Wouldn't give me the work. I hated that." Alma stares past the painting toward the window.

Julia follows her gaze to the gray sky with its pale wash of pink where the sun sets. A winter sky. "Alma, I expect the painting would fit well in your new home," she says.

Alma sniffs and gropes in her pocket for a tissue. "What new home?"

"One that will be yours, and where they can take care of you. You know your daughter is tired and has to work. It's getting hard for her to look after you."

"Why's that? I never heard her complain."

"That's because she enjoys helping you and wants to keep you comfortable. But you might enjoy being in a place where you can have more visitors and people around."

Alma glances tearfully at Julia. "It gets lonely sometimes. I do like visitors some days. Don't see many here."

"Well, if you move to a group home, you could have a good life, and Elsa will visit you."

"I dunno. This is my home," Alma says glumly.

"We'll talk about it some more another day. You could visit some places soon to find one you like."

"I suppose so. Anyway, I'm glad my painting has come out of that closet. You're a friend, I guess."

"I'd like to be your friend."

"Anyone who can bring back the past is a magician, I think. Some want you to forget it all and you, as you once were, especially when you're old."

"I'm sure you're right, and I'd like to hear more about your life, Alma, though not today. I have to leave now, but I'll come again, and we'll have a long talk."

"I'd like that."

Julia gives Alma's hand a squeeze. "See you soon," she says.

Elsa hands Julia her coat and escorts her to the door. "That went well for a first visit. She likes you. What's next?"

"With your permission, I'll research some affordable places suitable for your mother. I'd suggest that you, your sister, and I check them out. You'll need to fill out some forms. All the facilities will want to evaluate your mother's state of health, medications, level of assistance needed, and financial position."

"I'm grateful to you for the help. I can talk more to Mother about the idea. She may come around in time. I know she'd enjoy having her own living space."

"Good. I'll be in touch."

Julia leaves, satisfied that the meeting with Alma had been successful. She feels sympathy for both women and will talk to Lisa about next steps. Again she questions why Lisa has shown such unprofessional behavior in her handling of the case.

She appreciates Barnaby's willingness to let Alma have the painting he promised her. *If only he could overcome the drinking.* From experience she knows how difficult that can be, especially for someone with a longtime problem, but if he can do so, who knows what he might become. She drives home from work in the darkening gloom. The weather channel forecasts snow for the next several days.

No point in calling Barnaby for coffee yet. She'll bide her time.

# CHAPTER 17

Barnaby can hardly wait for Tuesday, the day he will own a new car. The snowflakes fall thicker as he stands at the bus stop clutching one of his larger paintings wrapped in several layers of bubble wrap. He won't miss standing at the bus stop in the freezing weather. On his lunch break, he takes a taxi to the auto body shop with the painting. He finds Tom waiting for him in the office.

"Your car is ready for you," he says. "Looks almost brand new. I have the paperwork here, ready for your signature."

"Fine. I've brought the painting we talked about."

"Good. I hoped you wouldn't forget. Let's see it."

Barnaby unwraps the picture and sets it on a chair.

"I like it," Tom says, stepping nearer. "I think my wife will, too. The shine on the water and the clouds and lighthouse are especially nice. Blue is her favorite color. It'll make a fine gift. How much did you say you wanted for it?"

"A thousand dollars."

"I'll take it. Now that's settled, let's get this paperwork signed and the Honda will be yours."

Barnaby fills out the forms and writes a check. Tom hands him the key and title to the car.

"Be careful driving in the snow and don't go too fast. The Honda has a lot more pickup than your old Ford."

"I know. That's one reason I'm buying it. Thanks again."

Barnaby unlocks the car and slides into the seat. He adjusts the mirrors and turns on the windshield wipers. Then he backs carefully out of the lot into the street. The car moves smoothly, and he can feel the power of the engine. It's a terrific vehicle. His heart bursts with pride as he parks in front of the hardware store.

"What's this about? Ya win the lottery, or something? That's a good-looking car ya have there, man," Sal greets him.

Barnaby beams. "Just sold some paintings. Time I got rid of the clunker."

"I'll say. Good for you. Oh, I forgot to tell ya. A lady came in here askin' for ya yesterday. Wanted advice about a floor."

"Really? Do you know her name?"

"Didn't ask. Pretty, dark hair. Come to think of it, she paid by check. I can find out who she is." Sal goes to the till and pulls checks from the day before. "Julia Morgan," he says.

"Oh, Julia," Barnaby says excitedly. "Someone I used to know years ago. I met her again recently. I'm curious to know how she discovered where I work."

Barnaby can't fathom his luck. Would Julia like to go out with him after all? Too bad he's already invited Lisa to the concert. He might give Julia a call soon. He can afford to take her out to dinner now. Dinner would be preferable to coffee. He whistles as he gets to work arranging the paint supplies on the shelf.

At the end of the day, he hurries outside, eager to drive his new car again. The snow hasn't let up since morning, and there are six inches of soft powder on the ground. He wipes it off the windshield with his sleeve until he remembers he's wearing a new coat that he doesn't want to get wet and dirty. He goes back inside the store.

"I need an ice scraper and a brush," Barnaby says. "Forgot to keep mine when I picked up the new car."

"Sure. Help yerself," Sal says, "and drive carefully in this God-damned weather."

"I will. I'm going to take good care of this baby," Barnaby replies.

Soon the windshield is clear and he's on the road. He drives slowly, enjoying the purr of the engine. If it weren't January, he might just keep on driving west.

⁂

Next day the temperature rises, causing rivers of water to run into gutters. Piles of rutted slush line the roads, but the news predicts snow and Barnaby hopes it won't spoil his plans for the concert. What will he do if they can't get out, or if they cancel the performance? Will he still see Lisa? Will she still want to see him? She is a neighbor, so he could invite her over, but then he'd have to offer her something to eat. His anxiety reaches new levels as he considers his options.

On Friday evening he stops at the market to buy some fresh food, a good idea if he's going to be snowed in. He turns into the supermarket lot and parks the car. What should he make for Lisa? His cooking skills are limited, and he hasn't asked anyone over for a meal for a long time.

He takes a cart and wanders up and down the aisles. Perhaps he could offer spaghetti. That's easy and most people like it. He can make garlic bread and a salad as well. Ice cream for dessert. He buys hamburger meat, cans of tomatoes, pasta, onions, garlic salt, and a loaf of French bread, along with lettuce and a carton of vanilla ice cream. She might want some wine to drink. Actually, he'd like some himself, but then scolds himself that he's trying to cut down, and he decides not to buy any. He fills the cart with a few more easy meals for himself and goes to the checkout stand. The clerk titters as he checks out the pile of goods.

"Expecting company, are we?" he says. "Not your usual groceries, I see."

Barnaby nods.

"Different coat, too."

"Yeah. It's a new year, and I'm making some changes."

"Good for you. Maybe I'll see you at the next AA meeting. You haven't come in a while."

"When is it?"

"Tuesday night at eight."

"Okay, thanks. Maybe I'll go," Barnaby says as he picks up the bag of provisions.

Alcoholics Anonymous had been helpful to him in the past. He questions whether he still needs the program to keep his resolve of giving up. He hasn't had a drink for several days now. His happier state of mind makes it easier to resist temptation. Seeing Lisa tomorrow will help to reinforce his decision to stay sober, too. She's one of those people who won't let you forget. It's one of the annoying characteristics about her, even though he knows she means well. He drives the negative thoughts from his mind. She's a friend, and he looks forward to paying her back for her kindness.

At home he feeds Popsicle and stores the food. By the halo of the streetlight, he watches snowflakes whirling thicker. Maybe the concert will be cancelled and he'll have to serve dinner at his house. He moans. The kitchen floor and stairwell are the only places he has cleaned well, and he's supposed to work tomorrow. They should eat in the dining room, but he hasn't used it for that purpose in years. The surface of the table is barely visible for all the papers stacked on it. And he doesn't have a tablecloth or place mats. Damn it all. He's over his head, trying to entertain, and almost wishes he hadn't invited Lisa to the performance. Even that is cause for distress. He hasn't attended a classical music concert in years and knows he should dress up. He doesn't own a tie. Feeling overwhelmed, he peeks out again at the snowy scene and craves a drink to ease his worries.

As he contemplates the weekend with increasing dread, Lisa calls.

"I want to talk to you about our date," she says. "Looks like it's going to be a blizzard. If the concert is cancelled, how about coming over here for dinner? I'd love to cook for you."

He lets out a big sigh of relief. "That's good of you," he says. "I'd have you over here, except I'm not set up for entertaining. Let's talk about this again tomorrow, when we know more about the weather."

"Great. Until tomorrow, then."

Barnaby collapses onto a chair.

"Good parrot," Popsicle says as she flies onto the table.

"You are a good parrot, and I'm neglecting you. How about chicken for dinner tonight?"

"Good stuff," the parrot says.

Barnaby runs his hand along the bird's back. He's relieved not to have to entertain Lisa at his house and remembers that Popsicle doesn't like her. Had she called their outing a "date"? Yes, those had been her words. Good grief. His world has become bigger, but more complicated as well. And he wants to paint. His life, once again, is impeding his elusive goal of being an artist.

But at least he has a new car, and he can plan the trip to California as soon as winter's over.

# CHAPTER 18

On Saturday morning Barnaby shuffles barefoot to the window. The snow lies in white piles at least a foot deep. Plows have not yet arrived to clear the way for traffic; the neighborhood lies silent. Likely he'll stay home today. He can wait a while before he calls Sal and goes back to bed.

An hour later he turns on the television and hears the report: more snow expected, as much as three feet in some areas. Travel advisory: stay home. That settles it. He won't be going to work or to the concert. He calls the store, but there's no answer.

Barnaby dresses in his warmest sweater. It has holes, but it's wool. He fries some eggs and makes toast and coffee. Since the concert won't happen, he guesses he and Lisa will have dinner instead. Otherwise, he'll have a day to himself, a day to paint.

He goes upstairs and turns on the portable heater in the studio, then sets up his palette and mounts the sketch he made at O'Malley's on the wall. Finally he adjusts the canvas on the easel he'd prepared with the underpainting. Since it has been years since he's painted anything, this will be a preliminary study for a larger work he'll complete later. Or so he hopes. He'll soon find out if his skills have deteriorated, along with everything else in recent years. *But no use dwelling on that*, he tells himself firmly.

Dipping a narrow brush in turpentine and saturating it with Prussian blue, he blocks the architectural details of the bar, then draws a line on one side of the canvas to make space for a color chart. He works out the important elements of the painting: colors in the room, bottles shining in the background, the yellow light casting radiance on the patrons' heads and echoing in their drinks. Blue and silver mirrors reflecting figures will contrast well with the darker shapes.

Using different brushes, he mixes the colors on the palette and smears paint on the color chart. He begins the painting with big shapes—furniture and walls. As he works, he can feel the ambience of the bar, the low conversation, the tinkle of ice in glasses. He outlines the figures—Charley holding his pool cue in a menacing way, the professor reading a newspaper at the counter, Sean serving drinks. Working with such familiar subject matter, Barnaby hopes he can create a fine work of art. The composition shows promise, but it will need more details. Absorbed in his work, Barnaby paints until his rumbling stomach tells him it's past lunchtime. Standing back to examine the canvas, he notices his style differs from earlier paintings; it's now darker and bolder. His progress so far satisfies him, but this painting is too small to capture the magnitude of O'Malley's as he wants to portray it. It's not finished, but already he looks forward to attempting a larger painting as he gains confidence in his skills. He cleans his brushes, turns off the heater, and clatters downstairs.

After making a ham sandwich, he considers calling Lisa about the evening. No, he reasons. She might have thought the better of it, and he wouldn't be sorry. He'd prefer to go to O'Malley's, anyhow.

Lisa calls, interrupting his deliberations. "It's supposed to snow all day," she says. "Come over at seven."

"Fine, I'll see you then," he says, trying to sound cheerful.

But he's not cheerful. The thought of spending an entire evening with nothing to do but talk to Lisa without a drink to calm his nerves is daunting. He climbs the stairs to take another look at his painting. It's coming along, but needs more light. He could add liquor bottles of different shapes and colors lit from behind, and that means going along to the bar to sketch them. It's two o'clock. He has plenty of time before dinner.

Bundling up, he goes to O'Malley's.

"Well, hello stranger," Sean says. "Haven't seen you the last few days. How's things?"

"Pretty good. Actually, pretty complicated."

"How so?"

"I'm supposed to have dinner tonight with a woman."

"Well, why's that complicated? Are you seein' the woman you told me about, the one who used to come here?"

"No, someone else."

"Aha. The new Barnaby. Ladies' man."

Barnaby guffaws. "Hardly. I came here to do a sketch for my new painting."

"Okay. Want a drink to help you along, or are you still stayin' off it?"

"Haven't touched the stuff for a week now. How about a glass of water?"

"Whatever you want. In a martini glass, then no one will know," Sean says, winking. "Want an onion to make it a Gibson?"

"You always were generous to a fault, my friend," Barnaby says as he takes his place on a stool and pulls out his sketchbook.

As the afternoon progresses, more people enter the bar, the Saturday crowd. He knows most of them, and they greet him as they sit down. Charley claps him on the back. "Hey Sean, a drink for Barnaby on me," he says. "What are you drinking, man? Vodka?"

There's no fooling Charley. "Water. No thanks, but I appreciate the offer," Barnaby says.

"Whoa. Turning over a new leaf, are we?" Charley asks.

"Trying to," Barnaby replies, smiling.

"Have you got a bottle of Bootleggers there for me today, Sean, old buddy?" Charley calls.

"Sorry. No deliveries today because of the weather. How about a Samuel Adams?"

"Shit. I'm telling you, you can't get good service anymore. Sam Adams'll probably throw my game off."

Barnaby ignores him. He finishes several sketches and notes the color values. He always feels comfortable in the bar. He enjoys the sounds of chatter, the way people become cheerful after a drink or two, and the colors of bottles like the ones he'll have in his picture: ochre, burnt sienna, raw umber, cerulean. Without alcohol, he's aware of brighter colors and sounds, as though he's acquired a new pair of glasses with clear lenses to view a familiar scene. All the same, as he closes his book, he wishes he could have just one drink before he goes. One wouldn't hurt, and it would ease his increasing nervousness at the prospect of the evening ahead . . . but he'll be seeing Lisa, a woman who would notice if he arrived with even a hint of alcohol on his breath, and who would chastise him. And he's painting again. Art and booze don't mix well. With effort, he slides off the seat, grabs his coat, and hurries out the door.

❦

Back at home, he's proud he resisted the drink. Maybe he will manage the evening with Lisa just fine. He shaves and showers. His clothes, though worn, are freshly laundered. He's grateful not to have to worry about dressing up for the symphony. At seven he sets out for Lisa's.

"Come in," she says. "Take those boots off, please. They're wet and they'll muddy the floor."

He unlaces his shoes, pleased he's wearing fresh socks without holes. She's in the kitchen stirring a pot on the stove, and it smells like onions. She wears an apron over her black figure-hugging dress. "Make yourself at home," she says. "Would you like a soft drink or something else?

"Coffee would be fine," he says, noticing a pot on the counter. He sits down at the kitchen table.

"I'm making coq au vin. Hope you like it."

"Er, I'm sure I will," he says. He's never heard of it.

"Takes a long time to make, but it's worth the effort. I took a course in French cooking last year. You're not a guinea pig—I've tried this out on others before. We'll start with French onion soup. It just needs a few minutes in the oven."

"That's nice," Barnaby says. At least he's familiar with the soup.

"I'm finishing the dessert now. Chocolate mousse. It'll be cold by the time we're ready to eat it."

"Great. I love chocolate."

Lisa hands him a mug. "Here's your coffee. The soup needs a few more minutes before it's ready. Come over here and sit by the fire."

He moves to the couch, and she sits next to him. Barnaby shifts a few inches away from her. He has no idea what he's in for, with the unfamiliar food, and he'll have to make the best of it. She stares at the fire with an amused expression on her face. He's unsure what she finds funny.

"Too bad about the concert," he says.

"Oh, that's okay. It would have been nice, but there's not much time to talk when you're listening to music. This way we'll have a chance to get to know each other better."

He hesitates. "Uh, I wanted to take you to the concert to thank you for figuring out who took my painting."

"You're welcome. Quite a coincidence that the case I worked on took me to the family who used to employ Alma. Julia thought so, too."

"You mean Julia was involved in the case, as well?"

Lisa blushed. "Um, only a little," she stammers.

"Do you two work together often?" he asks.

"No, not usually. I've had a heavy workload lately, and I asked her to help out."

"So she met Alma?"

"We both met Alma. She loves the painting. It was good of you to let her keep it."

"How did you find out that she had it?"

Lisa avoids his eyes. "Uh, I don't remember exactly. It came up when we visited her."

"That *is* a coincidence, then. Strange."

"Oh well, that's how it is sometimes in my business. Strange things happen. I think the soup is ready now. Would you be good enough to light the candles on the dining room table?"

She hands him a box of matches. The table is set for two with flowers in the middle. He lights the candles and takes a seat. She brings in two bowls of steaming soup.

"Cheers," she says, raising a glass of water.

They concentrate on eating the soup.

"Very good," Barnaby says. "French onion."

"I always like it, especially in winter."

As she takes their empty bowls into the kitchen, he watches her prepare the next course for serving. So Julia had something to do with the discovery of the painting. He must thank her. When Lisa comes back to the table carrying plates of dark brown food, he peers up at her.

"Does Julia have a boyfriend?" he asks.

Lisa gasps. "Why do you ask?"

"Just curious. Does she?"

"I don't know. She used to. Not sure if she's still seeing him or not." She slams the plates on the table, splashing brown sauce on Barnaby's shirt. "Oh, I'm so sorry. The plate is hot. I'll bring a cloth to wipe you off."

He shrugs. "It's okay. I have a washing machine. Don't worry about it. I get paint on myself all the time."

She ignores him, fetches a paper towel, and wipes the stain from his sleeve. He catches a whiff of her perfume and holds his breath. Staring at her hand, he raises his eyes to her neck and face, and watches as she bends to throw the paper away under the sink. In spite of himself, he finds her attractive.

She sits down opposite him. Picking up a fork, he digs into the chicken.

"Delicious," he says. "Rich."

"It *is* rich. Cooks for hours."

"I'm not used to eating like this," he says. "When I make chicken, I roast it in the oven with salt and pepper. This sauce makes it taste completely different."

"Do you like it?"

"Yes. Very nice," he says.

In fact, he does like it. The flavors are complex, like a layered oil painting, where application of many glazes builds the depth of color. It's artistry he admires. She must have spent a lot of time preparing this dish. He watches her with new appreciation and notices her anxious expression. He struggles to think of something to say.

"You've been kind to me, Lisa, and I want you to know I value that."

Her face relaxes. "Thanks for saying so. As I keep telling you, I want to help you."

"Let me ask, do you like your line of work? It seems like you're always there, even when you're not."

"I did like it at first. Not so much anymore. I truly like helping people, but now I find I want more."

"In what way?"

"More for myself. More of a life for myself."

She peers up at him, and he reaches over and pats her hand. She doesn't resist the connection.

"We all want that, I guess," he says, "but most of us are more selfish to begin with. If I may ask, how did you get involved with your work in the first place?"

He lifts his hand. She sighs and takes a deep breath. "My husband was an alcoholic. We married young, and I didn't know about his problem until later. He died in a car accident. DUI. After that I got my master's in social work. That's probably why I'm so hard on you about the drinking."

"I see. Actually, it does help, to have someone pay attention. Thought about you this afternoon when I wanted a drink. I knew you wouldn't approve, and I resisted."

"I know how hard it is. Good for you!" Lisa says with a wide smile. "I could almost hug you for that."

"It's okay. The parrot approves as well."

She frowns. "Your parrot doesn't like me."

"Well, as I've said, you're competition."

She clears her throat. "Talk to me about painting. That's what you really want to do, isn't it?"

"Yes," he says at length. "I've had a stroke of luck with that, too. I've sold a few pictures."

"You have? Who bought them?"

"A guy I used to know, in fact, someone who Julia used to date. We all knew each other years ago. He has a gallery in New York."

"Right. I forgot. Julia and you knew each other before. What's the name of the place? I go to the city sometimes. I might pay a visit."

Barnaby scratches his head. "Goldstone Gallery, in the Village, I think he said."

"All right. I'll check it out," Lisa says. "If you're ready, let's have dessert,"

The mousse, silky textured, dark, and chocolaty, ends the meal. He spoons the spongy gel slowly into his mouth, scraping the dish. After they finish eating, Barnaby sighs with satisfaction.

"It would be easy to get used to this way of living," he says. "You've spoiled me. Thank you for the best meal I've had in years. I'm sure I enjoyed it more than the concert, not being a classical music fan."

"I'm glad you liked the food. Would you like another cup of coffee?"

"Yes, please. You know, you're a superb cook. You should open a restaurant."

After their coffee, he stands to leave. Lisa gives him a quick hug. He hugs her back, thanks her again, and reaches for his coat and boots. On the way home he judges the evening has worked out better than he expected. She knows how to entertain, and she's a fine cook. He's grateful he didn't offer her a spaghetti dinner at his house. But what had she said about Julia? Julia was involved in the painting's discovery. Now he has another reason to call her.

⁎⁎⁎⁎⁎⁎⁎⁎⁎⁎⁎

The next day he works on his bar painting adding background details like the walls and glasses on shelves, then slogs through the snow to O'Malley's for lunch. He again resists the temptation to order a drink.

"So how did your date go last night?" Sean asks.

"Well enough. That woman knows how to cook."

"Home cookin' is best. Do you like her? Are you goin' to ask her out again?"

"I do like her, but she's only a friend."

"So why not go out with her a few times, get to know her?" Sean asks.

"I don't have time for a relationship now. Trying to finish a painting."

"I wouldn't let that stop you, if you like her."

"Okay, thanks for the advice. I'll think about it."

"You do that. It'd be good to see you with a companion. You've been on your own for a long time, depressed, I'd say, and drinkin'. Lately you've been happier. Might want to take advantage, that's all I'm sayin'."

"I know you mean well, Sean, my friend. I need to go slowly. That's my style, and anyway, there's another woman I want to see. I came here to eat. What's on the menu?"

"Split pea soup. Beef stew."

"I'll have the soup. Got to get back home to work, and I don't want anything too heavy. I had a big meal last night."

"Well, you're sure changin' your style. The old Barnaby would have gone for the stew."

"Guess you're right."

Barnaby washes the bowl of soup down with a glass of water and trudges home. Working again on his preliminary study, he adds details and adjusts colors. He wants to create luminosity in the scene, atmosphere that he can replicate later. At day's end, flooded with relief and more than a little pride, he declares the study done. He's ready for the next step, a large painting of O'Malley's.

On Monday, the streets plowed, Barnaby deliberates going to work. He knows that Sal needs help and has lost business because of the weather. As if on cue, the phone rings.

"Barnaby, I know it's your day off, but I could sure use your help in the store," Sal says.

"All right. I can come in," Barnaby says, "but I'll need to clear my driveway first."

As he shovels, cursing all the while at the snow and hard physical labor, he decides it would be a good time to call Julia. He'd like to invite her to dinner at the Country House, one of the finer restaurants on the outskirts of town. She's probably at work now, but he'll call her that evening.

# CHAPTER 19

Julia drives slowly to work in the bad weather. She finds
Lisa waiting for her.

"How was your weekend? How's the washing machine?"
Lisa asks.

"Fine. Fixed. How did it go with Barnaby? Did you go
to the concert?"

"No. They cancelled it. We had dinner at my house."

"Did you have fun?"

"Yes. I like him. But we need to talk again about the
Hawkins case. I want to contact the family again, now you've
broken the ice with Alma."

Julia takes a step back. "Actually, I'd like to follow up,"
she says. "I told Elsa I'd investigate some appropriate living
places for her mother."

"Well, you can do that without seeing the family again."

"True, but Alma is going to need some convincing if she's
to move there. I've only recently made a connection with her."

Lisa frowns. "This is my case, and I'll handle it," she
says coldly.

Julia gazes at her in astonishment. "I don't understand. Last
time we talked, you acted only too happy to have my help."

"I've changed my mind and besides, I want to look at that painting. It might not be Barnaby's. Was it signed?"

"I didn't notice, but it's a beach scene, similar to ones he painted in Providence."

Lisa turns her back without another word. Julia shakes her head and drifts toward her office. *What is going on with Lisa?* Why would she doubt that Barnaby was the artist after he had confirmed it? She hadn't said much about their date, either. Perhaps—dare she hope?—it hadn't gone well, although since Lisa is such a good cook, she can't imagine that Barnaby didn't at least enjoy the meal. And now Lisa wants to re-involve herself in the case, precisely when she, Julia, is making progress.

Maybe Barnaby will never call now.

Some days she wishes she had taken more control over her personal life, with something to work toward, something more important than repairing a washing machine.

She'd had to arrange repair of the one at home in Boston, too. She cringes at the memory. After her mother's urgent visit to the doctor, waiting for test results, more whispers of "We're so sorry, Alice," the trip to the pharmacy, more waiting, and resettling of her mother in bed, the lapse of time caused the floor boards to warp. Meanwhile, her father quietly drank his bourbon within arm's reach of the telephone, grousing that the washer still needed fixing.

That incident seemed to change something in her mother. The following week, she asked Julia to fetch a journal from a chest in the bedroom closet. A rich leather-bound book with *Alice Lowell Morgan* embossed along the bottom lay on top of yellowing letters and folders beside several maps. Julia brought the book to the bedside. Alice took it, fondling the cover with wasted fingers.

"This is a history of our family I've been writing. I want you to finish it."

Stomach churning, Julia turned the pages filled with her mother's rambling script.

"Mama, I'm no writer. How can I do this?"

"You can. It's our family history. It's who you are. The documents you need are there, in the chest. I'm out of time, Julia . . . promise me, please?"

Alice reached for her daughter's hand, and Julia bent to kiss the damp forehead.

She promised. Then she let it drop from her consciousness. Twenty years ago.

❧❧❧❧❧❧❧

After lunch, Margaret Hill stops by, her expression stern.

"Julia, I just got a complaint from Elsa Hawkins. She's upset because Lisa went to visit the family this morning, and Elsa expected you. Why did you drop out of the case?"

"I didn't. I wanted to go back, but Lisa insisted that she be the one. I'm sorry to hear the family's unhappy."

"Well, I'd like you to make amends. There's another problem, too, something about a painting that Lisa said the mother stole."

"What's the trouble there? I thought we cleared that up. Something's amiss. I'll be happy to go along and talk to them but perhaps you need to make it clear to Lisa—and me—whose case this is."

Julia leaves Margaret standing with raised eyebrows in her office and heads for the Hawkins house. Things are going crazy. Lisa is behaving erratically, to put it mildly. Barnaby has already forgiven Alma for taking the painting and doesn't consider it a theft. Lisa's losing judgment. That's an important quality in a social worker, and something must be seriously wrong if Lisa is letting personal matters interfere with her work to this extent.

Julia rings the doorbell. Elsa's face appears through a crack in the door.

"Oh, it's you," she says. "Come in. I thought it was that other woman again. Lisa."

Julia takes off her coat and smiles at Elsa. "How can I help you?"

"I don't know if you can anymore. Mother was coming around to the idea of living somewhere else when your colleague Lisa showed up, the one she doesn't like. Lisa said she wanted to be sure the artist who did the painting was Barnaby Brown. Mother started crying. She thought Lisa was taking the painting away, and now she fears people are taking her life away as well."

"I'm so sorry about this. May I see her?"

"I guess so. She's in bed."

Julia follows Elsa into the bedroom. Alma is lying on her side, legs pulled up to her chest.

"Mother, Julia, the nice lady, is here to see how you're doing," Alma says.

Alma whimpers. "No more visitors."

"I just want to say hello," Julia says softly.

"Go away."

Julia catches Elsa's eye and motions they should leave the room.

"Best not to push her today," Julia whispers. "I'll come again later. Where's the painting?"

"It's here, propped against the wall. Mother screamed so much when Lisa took it off the wall that she almost dropped it."

"May I take a look at it? I'd like to see if it's signed."

"Sure."

Julia bends down to examine it. On the right side she sees the name in black paint: B. Brown.

"That's Barnaby Brown's signature, I believe." she says. "That's all I need to know. Please tell Alma not to worry. The painting is hers."

"That's a relief. Thank you very much. Please do come again and tell us what you find out about those senior living places."

"I'll do that."

Julia drives back to the office. What a muddle Lisa made of the case, so unnecessary. How did she fail to notice that Alma doesn't trust her?

"Did you see the Hawkins family?" Margaret asks when she sees Julia at her door.

"Yes. Elsa, the daughter, is fine. Her mother became distraught enough to take to her bed when she thought Lisa wanted to take her painting away. I explained we only needed to check the signature."

"I see. Well, was it stolen?"

"No. The artist allowed her to keep it. At least, I think so," Julia says. That's what Lisa had told her. She has not heard directly from Barnaby and does not know what he said to Lisa. Given Lisa's odd behavior, Julia's not sure she can trust her.

"Well, either it was stolen, or it wasn't," Margaret says. "Why was Lisa suspicious?"

"That's complicated. We need to talk to the artist. Would you be willing to do that?"

"All right. Give me the name and number. Is the case still on track?"

"I hope so," Julia says. "I'm sure we'll be able to help the family, but I'd like to request that you turn the case over to me. Just me."

Margaret raises her eyebrows for the second time. "Really? Is that necessary?"

Julia nods.

"All right. Let me think about this. Write up your notes so I can understand what's going on. I'll have to meet with Lisa as well."

Back at her desk, Julia again considers whether she should talk to Lisa first. She would do so without hesitation if she considered Lisa a loyal friend and ethical colleague. But this is business, and for now, the matter is out of her hands. She'll wait to find out what her boss has to say.

After work, she drives to a café to meet Nancy for dinner. Nancy, dressed in a black skirt and jacket, her boyish hairstyle shorter than usual, sits at a table drinking a glass of wine.

"Hey, Nance," Julia says, giving her a quick hug.

"Hey yourself. Will you join me? The Pinot Grigio's good."

"Thanks, I will. Let's eat right away. I'm famished."

They both read the menu and place their orders.

"We have something important to discuss," Nancy says.

"We do?"

"Your birthday. In two weeks, right? Your fortieth. Remember we agreed to celebrate this decade birthday together."

"So we did, with yours in March. What shall we do?"

"I'd like to say take a trip to someplace warm, but I'm too busy at work to take time away now. How about going to New York? We could see a show on Broadway."

"Great idea. What show, and when?"

"Let me find out. How are things going?" Nancy asks.

"So-so. I've been reflecting about my life. It's a bit dull these days and needs more sparkle."

"Uh-oh. Sounds like typical midlife crisis stuff. You shouldn't succumb. What happened with the man you met?"

"Barnaby? Haven't seen him. He asked me out for coffee, but I found out he drinks too much, and I said no. Probably a mistake."

"Why's that a mistake? I understood you wanted to avoid seeing men with problems."

"I do, but in the meantime, I've found out good things about this man."

Nancy grunts. "So call him."

"I may," Julia says, "but now he might be seeing Lisa."

"Oh, God. The plot thickens. Does he like her?"

"Don't know. She's acting strangely at work. I suppose she's attracted to him and is trying to keep me out of the picture."

"Oh. Competition." Nancy rolls her eyes. "Good luck there, but if you like him, don't be shy. Show some spirit, girl."

"Right. What about you? What are you up to?"

"Working, mostly. I plan to go hiking in the Catskills when the weather improves. Wanna come?"

"No, thanks," Julia replies. "But I like the idea of going to New York. We could have a party as well. What do you say?"

"Let's make a deal. I'll research the New York trip, and you arrange the party."

Their food arrives, and the women dig in.

"I want to comment on your professional appearance," Julia says after a while. "It always amuses me to see you dressed all in black for work. You wear such bright clothes at home. You seem like a different person."

Nancy laughs. "Appearances count. Lawyers always dress up, especially women. They have to, to be taken seriously. It's still a man's world in many ways."

"But the contrast in your case is extreme."

"Exactly. I can't wear black every day. Too depressing and serious."

Julia playfully raises her glass to Nancy, grateful to have a friend to celebrate with. Nancy is right. She's feeling middle-aged and isn't yet reconciled to turning forty. She'll think again about calling Barnaby.

※※※※※※※※※※

The next day Margaret stops by Julia's office.

"Let's clear up the confusion," Margaret says. "I talked to Lisa this morning. She's upset. I don't know what's wrong. She has always excelled as a competent, dedicated worker, but today when we spoke, she seemed distracted and asked for a few days off."

Julia nods her head. "She may need a rest."

"Yes. I assigned her another case earlier, a difficult one, and I'm guessing she's stressed. So the Hawkins case is yours. Oh, and I talked to the artist, Barnaby Brown. He confirmed that he's allowing Alma to keep the painting."

Julia is glad to know the truth of the matter, and even though she would like to have called Barnaby to talk about it, she doesn't want to make the mistake of mixing business with what she still hopes might be a personal relationship.

But what's going on with Lisa?

She casts her mind back to the early days of their friendship in New York. They had been such close friends that she had overlooked and forgiven any less appealing aspects of Lisa's character. Lisa had been supportive in the early days after Julia's divorce, having experienced problems of her own following the death of her husband three years earlier. His drinking, ending in his untimely death, had left her close to emotional collapse afterward, Lisa confided. She behaved like a crazy woman, she told Julia, adding how she needed extensive counseling to come to terms with her life, both past and present.

Julia twists a pencil on her desk, watching it spin. Is it possible Lisa is undergoing some kind of personal crisis now, one that affects her judgment, making her emotionally unstable? It might be time to have a chat with her old friend.

# CHAPTER 20

arnaby rushes home after work, eager to call Julia. The paper with her phone number isn't by the phone. Certain that he left it in the kitchen that morning, he searches everywhere, in his pockets, in the hallway, in the bathroom, but can't find it. He calls directory information and learns there's no listing for a Julia Morgan. He scratches his head. How can he can find her number? He could call Lisa, but that might be awkward. He may have to wait until the next day and call her at work. Disappointed, he goes over to Popsicle's cage with a handful of carrots. The bird sits on top, her head cocked.

"Don't you go staring at me so suspiciously," he says. "I haven't done anything wrong. Have you been a good parrot?"

"Good parrot," she says, pecking at the vegetables. "Heavens to Murgatroyd."

"I'm going to O'Malley's. See you later," he says.

"Bye-bye," Popsicle says.

He takes off for O'Malley's. He probably ought to make something for himself at home, but he wants the company. There's no room for him at his usual place at the counter.

After calling to Sean and ordering a Coke and pizza, he joins a bespectacled man of about his age at a table. The dim light makes his crew-cut appear like a closely cropped lawn.

"You're Barnaby, aren't you?"

"I am. Have we met?"

"Alan Nettler."

"Any relation to Lisa?"

"I'm her brother. I've been wanting to meet you and thought I'd find you here. She told me she's been dating you."

"She did?" *We've had one dinner together. That's not exactly dating.* But Barnaby lets Alan's comment pass and says, "How did you recognize me?"

"I attended Lisa's New Year's Eve party, and I've seen you here before."

Barnaby extends his hand. "Pleased to meet you."

"I understand you're an artist," Alan says. "Lisa says you're talented. She studied art history in college."

"Yes. She told me."

"Well, she probably missed her vocation," Alan continues. "She's creative."

"I guess so. She's an amazing cook."

"I agree."

"What do you do for a living?" Barnaby asks.

"Website designer."

Barnaby regards him with interest. "Oh, so you must know about computers. I don't own one, but I need to. Would you be able to advise me?"

"Sure. Glad to help a friend of Lisa's. She's always helping everyone, me included. For a while she thought I needed to meet women, so she hosted several dinners and invited single men and women. Great idea. Met my wife there. Are you one of her lonely heart cases?"

Barnaby purses his lips. "No. I hope not."

"Well, anyway. What sort of computer do you want?"

"One that will allow me to send emails and images of my paintings."

"That's easy. Go down to the nearest computer store and talk to them." He scribbles his number and some information on a napkin. "Here are some makes and models I'd recommend. If you need help learning to use it, call me."

"That's good of you. Thanks," Barnaby says.

Popsicle flaps her wings and squawks when he arrives home.

"You've been bad. I can tell. What have you done?"

He checks the room. On the floor, crumpled and a bit torn, lies a slip of paper. He picks it up and smooths it out. It's Julia's phone number. He sighs with relief, then shakes his finger at Popsicle.

"Bad parrot. You're not supposed to eat paper. No chicken for you tonight."

"Good parrot," Popsicle says.

"No, not good. Bad."

The parrot climbs into her cage and sits on a perch, eyeing him quietly. Then she picks up the peanuts in her food dish and drops them one by one on the floor without eating them. "What a mess," she says.

He sighs, picks up the phone, braces himself, and calls Julia. "Julia? Barnaby Brown here. I wanted to be in touch earlier but I've been busy."

"It's good to hear from you," she says. "How are you?"

"Fine. I understand you found my painting, and I'd like to thank you for that."

"Oh. You're most welcome. Quite a coincidence that my work took me to Alma Hawkins's house."

Barnaby takes a deep breath. "Er, the reason I'm calling is to ask if you'd like to go out to dinner this weekend, on Saturday. If you would, I'll make a reservation."

The line goes silent. He waits with bated breath.

Finally she says, "That sounds great. What time?"

"How about seven? Where do you live?"

"31 Mulberry Street."

"Fine. I'll see you then."

He hangs up the phone and straightens his shoulders, drawing himself to his full six feet. He has a date with Julia. And this time, it's a real date.

# CHAPTER 21

On his lunch break, Barnaby gets a haircut.

"I remember you," the barber says. "You haven't been here in years. Looks like you've been cutting your own hair."

"You're right, Jed. I need a proper haircut."

"Do you want me to tidy it up some? Or are you going for the clean-cut look?"

"Not too clean. Just cut."

"So what have you been up to, all this time?" Jed asks, swinging a cape over Barnaby's shoulders.

"Nothing much. Working, mostly."

"Still live on Russell Road? Your dad used to come in here from time to time. I liked him."

"Yes, I'm still living in my parents' house. Now it's mine."

The barber snips away. "Your dad could sing. Had a fine baritone voice. Have you inherited his talent?"

"I used to sing in musicals years ago. Haven't even seen a show for a long time, though," Barnaby says.

"Well, you should. They're calling for tryouts for *Carousel* at the renovated Palace Theater."

"I'll consider it," Barnaby says. "Nice to know they're renovating this town. I hear they've raised funds to restore City

Hall, too. Beautiful building. Wouldn't mind doing a painting of it. It helps businesses when there's a thriving downtown, don't you agree?"

The barber nods. Fifteen minutes later, Barnaby's hair is shorter. He peruses his reflection. Not bad. Makes him appear more confident.

"Good job, thanks. I'll come again," he says. He leaves a generous tip.

Back at work, the hours fly by. Only three more days until he sees Julia. Sal asks if he can stay late to reorganize some items on the shelves, and he quickly agrees. With the overtime pay, he can splurge when he takes Julia out.

***

Later that week Lisa calls.

"Barnaby, I have exciting news. I've been in New York, and I stopped by your friend's gallery. Your paintings are for sale for between two and four thousand dollars each! And the salesperson said two have sold already!"

Barnaby sits down. "What? Are you sure those were my paintings?" he asks, hardly able to take in what he's hearing.

"Definitely. You're going to make a lot of money."

"Maybe so, though not with that group of paintings."

"How so? Aren't you selling them on a commission basis?"

He runs a hand through his hair. "No. Sylvester bought them outright. I didn't figure they were worth much, and was grateful that he bought them at all."

"Oh, that's terrible. Do you think he cheated you?"

Barnaby hesitates. "Hard to say. He's a friend. I didn't ask how much they would sell for, and I knew he would mark them up, but this is much more than I expected."

"Well, perhaps he's not such a good friend, and you should talk to him and ask if he will share the profits."

"I doubt he'd do that. We made a deal. But I could ask if he'll take more on a commission basis."

"You need to make more paintings. There's obviously a market for your work."

"I'm trying to. Just finished a new one."

"Good for you. Are you staying off the drink?"

He bristles and ignores her question. "How are you, Lisa?"

"Took a few days off. That's why I went to New York. That place's energy always improves my state of mind. I may take a cooking class there."

"You don't need one. You're already an accomplished chef."

"Thanks for saying so, but there's always something new to learn."

"By the way, I met your brother. He offered to help me use a computer."

"He's a good guy. Very protective. I'm sure you will have expert advice."

"I expect so."

"Nice talking to you," she says. "We must get together for dinner again soon."

"Sure. Thanks for telling me about the paintings."

He hangs up, uncertain if the news is good or bad. Good, if his paintings are worth something in today's market; not so good, if Sly deliberately lowballed them. He must call him.

On Saturday after work Barnaby prepares for his date. His stomach feels fluttery. He contemplates going to O'Malley's for a drink to calm himself, but reminds himself it has been eleven days since he had a drink and he doesn't want to slip back into old habits. But he might have one glass of wine at the restaurant, especially if Julia does. He spies Popsicle opening and shutting her beak, as if tutting, warning him to behave himself. He feeds her a banana and leaves the house. Fifteen minutes later, he knocks on Julia's door.

"Hi, Barnaby," she says as she comes out. She's wearing a brown coat and tall black boots, and her hair is tucked into an Irish cable-knit cap. His heart sings. "New haircut?" she asks. "You look good. Happy."

"Happy to see you, and yes, I am more cheerful these days. Things are going well."

They take the path through the garden to the car, and Barnaby opens the door for her.

"Where are we going?" she asks.

"To the Country House. I haven't eaten there for a long time, but I remember it fondly."

"I've never been there. It's a luxury, going to a fine restaurant."

After a half-hour's drive, they reach their destination on the outskirts of the town. The restaurant is in an old farmhouse, a clapboard-faced building painted white. The lights in the parking lot illuminate patches of snow and dim shapes of cows grazing in an adjoining field.

"Good choice, Barnaby," Julia says, grasping his arm as they move toward the entrance. "It's a change to be out of the city. I love nature."

"Me, too," he says.

He's enjoying the feel of Julia's hand on his arm and has an urge to hold her hand. Too soon, he thinks. Inside the building, the maître d' asks Barnaby if he has a reservation. He's proud to give his name.

"Ah, yes, Mr. Brown. Seven-thirty. Come this way."

Their table near the fireplace is set with a white cloth and a vase of snowdrops. A server greets them and asks what they would like to drink.

Barnaby glances at Julia. "Would you like a glass of wine?"

She hesitates before answering. "Are you having one?"

He hesitates in turn. "No. Just water for me. But if you'd like a glass, please go ahead."

"Then I won't," she says.

Barnaby sees the relief on her face. He has made the right decision.

They spend some minutes examining the menu.

"What do you think? Does anything appeal?" he asks.

"It's a great selection. I'll go for the trout almandine."

"Sounds good. Same for me."

He's not familiar with most dishes on the menu and is willing to follow her lead. If he eats fish, it's fish and chips. After they order, he relaxes and gazes across the table at Julia. Her red sweater perfectly matches her lipstick, set off by a sparkling clip in her hair. She's lovely. He smiles at her.

"Tell me about yourself," he says.

"What do you want to know?"

"Everything. What have you been doing all these years?"

She takes a deep breath. "Let's see. I think I told you already that since we knew each other, I've been married and divorced. Single for the past fifteen years. I moved to Waterbury after I earned my social work degree, and I've worked in my present job since then. I own my condominium and make a decent living. That's about it."

"Don't you perform any more on the stage? You were such a good actress," he says.

"No, though I'd like to."

"I learned recently that there's a new production of *Carousel* in the works here in town. You could audition."

"Good idea. How about you? Will you try out?"

"No. I want to concentrate on painting. Indoor scenes."

She raises her eyebrows and meets his gaze. "Are you painting now?" she asks.

"Yes. What do you mean, *now*?"

"Nothing. Lisa told me you had given up."

"Oh, Lisa. I don't know why she would say that."

"Well, she's not herself these days. Something's wrong. I haven't seen her at work all week."

"She's been in New York. She called me last night to let me know several of my paintings have sold in a gallery there."

"Did she? So she went to the city. I'll have to talk to her."

"Let's not talk about Lisa. Tell me more about yourself."

"Later," she says. "I'm glad you sold some of your work."

Their dishes arrive and for a few minutes they both concentrate on the food.

"The trout is perfect," Julia says.

He agrees. He likes the delicate flavor of the fish decorated on top with grape halves and almonds. "Do you still hunt for four-leaf clovers?" he asks.

She smiles. "Oh, clovers—I had forgotten. I used to find them all the time in Providence, in grassy areas by the beach. Good luck charms."

He smiles. "You found several for me. I think I sold a painting every time you gave me one."

"That wasn't luck. That was because your work had merit. Now it's your turn. What have you been doing?"

"Not much, I have to admit. I let myself go for a long time. But that's changing. As I've told you, I'm painting again, using new subject matter. I like depicting people in ordinary pursuits of life—having drinks in a bar, a drink in a coffee shop, that sort of thing."

"You mean, interior scenes like Edward Hopper's?" she asks.

"Not like Hopper. Not as gloomy. Lively, with a lot more hope."

She smiles up at him and their eyes meet.

His heart flips. "It's like being in a field of clover when I'm with you," he says.

She flushes. "That's a lovely thing to say. But there's no clover here, only snowdrops."

"Well, it's winter. Those are brave flowers, blooming in blizzards."

"Yes. Full of hope. But speaking of clovers, I like the old memories, too."

He gulps. "That's because they remind us of our younger selves. All the years in between don't count, somehow."

"I agree," she says.

He reaches across the table for her hand. "I'd like to know more about you, about all those years in between."

She pauses before speaking. "I had a rough time of it, myself, for a while. My husband became unstable, but I didn't know that at first. Bipolar. So we never had children, and the marriage broke up. I really wanted a baby."

She lowers her gaze, and he squeezes her hand. "I guess we've both had our problems," he says, "but I'm so happy we've met again."

"Me, too."

His heart expands. He meets her glance, and a grin creeps to the corner of her eyes, crinkling her face. He allows his eyes to linger.

After dessert and coffee, they walk hand-in-hand back to the car. When they reach Julia's condo, Barnaby accompanies her to the front door and kisses her, and his heartbeat doubles. He catches the scent of coconut in her hair and enfolds her in his arms. She feels right in his embrace, and he wonders why it has taken so many years for him to find someone like her.

"I had a wonderful time. Thank you," Julia says.

"I did, too," he says. "I'll call you soon."

# CHAPTER 22

On Monday, Julia sees Lisa back at her desk.

"Where were you all last week?" she asks.

"I took a break. Went to New York. Checked out a cooking school. I might take classes."

"That's a good idea."

"I'm thinking of quitting this job and opening a restaurant. Tired of trying to help people who won't help themselves. It's tragic when children are at risk."

"I agree. Sounds like you have your hands full. Perhaps you would find the hospitality business more to your liking. I can tell you're losing patience with the work here. Speaking of that, Margaret told me I'm solo on the Hawkins case now. Hope that helps you out."

"Maybe," Lisa says, wrinkling her brow. "Perhaps that's as well. Listen, don't say anything to Margaret about my plans. I want to be sure I know what I'm doing before I give notice."

Julia pauses. This would be the opportunity to sit down with her friend and find out what's going on. "Okay," she says. "It's a big decision. Would you like to have dinner and talk about all of this?"

"No. I have a lot of thinking to do first. How was *your* weekend?"

"Good. Unusually good, actually."

"What did you do?"

"Had dinner at a restaurant."

"Oh. Which one?"

"The Country House."

"Very nice. Did you go with your friend Nancy? Your birthday's coming up."

"Not with Nancy. Another friend."

Julia moseys to her office. It might be good for Lisa to change careers, but clearly she doesn't want to discuss this touchy issue. There's no point in telling her about her date with Barnaby. Better to let things run their course first.

Her mind keeps skipping back to the magical evening she'd had with him. She's relieved that he appears to be living his life responsibly, avoiding alcohol, selling paintings, and taking care of his appearance. He looked downright handsome on Saturday. He had a shiny car and gave every indication of being successful, not at all the loser Lisa had warned her about. She would like to have a good man in her life.

But now she needs to focus on her online search for senior living facilities. By noon she has checked some reviews and Department of Health ratings and compiled a preliminary list of suitable accommodations. Three offer flexible room options for different budgets, are close to the Hawkinses' house, and have space available. She picks up the phone.

"Elsa, Julia here. I've located some places for you to consider—"

Elsa interrupts her. "Oh, Julia. Alma's gone missing. She must have left the house early, before I got up. I've called the police. I'm so worried."

"Of course you're worried. Is there anything I can do to help?"

"I don't think so. The police have a description, and they're driving around the area."

"Do you have any idea where she might have gone? Anywhere she talked about going?"

"She usually goes to the drugstore. That's where she gets toothbrushes to bring home. The police have already checked there."

"I'm so sorry. All the more reason for finding a safe place for her. Do let me know when you find her."

Julia heaves a sigh and turns her attention to other tasks. At one o'clock, Lisa sticks her head in the door. "You'll never guess what's happened. Barnaby called me. Turns out Alma Hawkins found her way to the hardware store to thank him for letting her keep the painting."

"That's great! So Alma's not missing."

"What do you mean, missing? He didn't say anything about that. He called because his boss told him Alma had come by and looked lost, or something. He knew I was handling the case. I don't know if she's still there, or not."

*Except you're not handling the case*, Julia thinks. "I'll go to Carano's and find her." she says. "Better still, I'll phone first and tell the owner to keep her safe until Elsa or I can get there."

"I'll go with you," Lisa says.

"That's not necessary, thanks all the same."

Julia calls the hardware store. "Mr. Carano, Julia Morgan here. I came by your store the other day about my flooded floor. I'm a social worker, and I'm working with Alma Hawkins and her family. It's my understanding Alma came to your store today, asking for Barnaby. She's an older woman, gray haired, and has dementia. Is she still there?"

"Don't know. She was looking around. Hold on and I'll check."

A few minutes later he comes back on the line. "She's not here. I saw her, must've been ten minutes ago, so she can't have gone far."

"Thanks. I'll be right there. The police are searching for her, too. If she comes back, please call them."

Lisa appears at Julia's office, dressed to go outside. "Let's go," Lisa says.

"Are you sure you want to come?" Julia asks. She observes Lisa's face, crumpling at the jaw. "All right, if you insist. We should notify the police and Elsa. Perhaps you can do that while we're on the way."

Julia grabs a coat and hat and they hurry to her car.

# CHAPTER 23

Barnaby dreams of Julia every night. She sits beside him in her red dress in the Honda as they drive out West to California, the windows down, her hair scattering in the summer wind. He wants to ask her out again soon, but he has work to do first and tries to stay focused.

He starts a new painting of customers buying wooden shelving in a hardware store. After working on it for a while, he remembers he needs to contact Sylvester about the price he's charging for the paintings at the gallery. He also needs to go to the store to check out computers. It will be a busy day with not much time for housecleaning. Although he promised himself to do more of that, it's a daunting task. Besides, Popsicle will tease him and tell him with good reason that it's a "helluva" job. He can't accomplish everything all at once.

He picks up the phone and punches in Sly's number. A recording comes on the line saying Goldstone Gallery is closed on Mondays and messages can be left after the beep. Barnaby hangs up. He doesn't want to leave voice mail. In the meantime, he can have lunch and go to the computer store.

As he's leaving, Sal calls on the phone. "Barnaby, glad I caught ya, What's going on with ya lately? Another lady came in asking for ya. This one was older. Said she wanted to thank ya for letting her keep the painting she took."

"Well, that's nice of her. Must've been Alma. How did she look?"

"To tell ya the truth, not too good. Seemed confused. I had to tell her how to find her way out. She was wearing bedroom slippers, too."

"Oh dear. Thanks for telling me."

He stares out the window considering what to do. He'll call Lisa. It's her case. Perhaps Alma needs help. After talking to Lisa and learning that Alma has just recently gone missing, he decides to go and find out for himself. At the store, he tells Sal that Alma has dementia and might have wandered away from home. "Did anyone else come with her, and what was she wearing?" he asks.

"As I said, bedroom slippers. I think she had on a blue coat. No hat. Didn't see anyone with her."

A police car arrives at the parking lot, and Barnaby goes out to meet it.

"We're searching for a woman wearing a blue coat. Have you seen her?" one of the two officers asks.

"I'm searching for her myself," Barnaby says.

"Okay. We'll check inside first."

Another car pulls up. Julia steps out. Barnaby's pulse quickens.

"Julia!" he says, approaching her. "What a surprise, seeing you here. You've been on my mind . . . I meant to call you." He hesitates briefly, then dashes toward her and gives her a hug. Her eyes light up, but she pushes him away. At that moment, he catches sight of Lisa.

"Hello, Lisa," he says.

Lisa's face turns ghost white. She stares from him to Julia and back again. Loud voices echo from inside the store, and two police officers come out with Alma, followed by Sal.

"I can find my own way home," she screams, "Go away."

Julia steps from Barnaby toward Alma. She gently takes Alma's hand.

"Oh, it's you, Julia," Alma says. "I don't like these big policemen pulling me along. Can you take me home?"

"Of course," Julia says. She turns to an officer. "Where did you find her?"

"She was in the basement. Looks like you're a friend of hers. Do you want to take her back?"

"Yes. She lives on Maple Street."

"We'll need some ID from you first."

Julia reaches into her purse and hands the officer her business card.

"Okay, thanks. We'll follow you to be sure the lady gets back safely."

"Hang on a minute," Sal says. "You caught her in the basement, did you say? I usually keep that door locked. Must have forgotten. There's valuable stuff down there."

Julia's throat tightens. "Oh, dear. I hate to say this, but we should check Alma's pockets to be sure she didn't take anything." She whispers to the officer, "She has a habit of taking things. It's a common symptom of dementia."

"Well, then. We'd better check," the officer says. "I saw a lot of antiques there. Amazing things."

"All brass and copper," Sal says proudly. "Clocks, light fixtures, cartridge cases, bird cages, locks. Made right here in Waterbury."

"All right," the police officer says. Turning to Julia, he asks, "Can you assist us here?"

Julia takes a deep breath while she considers what to say. "Alma, do you have some gloves in your pockets? It's frosty outside."

Alma gives her a soft smile.

"Let me help you," Julia says.

She searches the old woman's pockets and finds one glove.

"Here you go," she says, pulling out the piece of clothing. A button falls to the ground.

"What's this? Did you lose a button?"

Sal bends to pick it up. "Hold on. This belongs to me. It's brass. These are collector's items."

"You're sure this one was in your basement, sir?" the officer asks.

"Absolutely. You've probably heard of Chase Brass and Copper Company. They made brass buttons, among other things. I have dozens of 'em. This one has an engraving on it of a centaur, the City's logo. You'll probably recognize it."

He opens his palm to reveal the button.

Barnaby chuckles. He'll tell the professor, who might be interested in this.

"She didn't take anything else, apparently," Julia says. "Let's get Alma home. Could you please call her daughter to let her know we've found her?"

"Will do," the officer says.

Julia places her arm around Alma's shoulders and escorts her to the car. Barnaby watches them go. Alma turns to glare at Lisa, still holding Julia's car door open.

"I don't want her going with us," Alma says.

Barnaby sees her lurch as though she's going to lunge at Lisa, and he steps forward to restrain Alma, who pulls back, but pays no attention to him and continues to leer at Lisa with fire in her eyes. Lisa moves out of reach and slams the car door shut.

"Can I catch a ride with you, Barnaby?" she asks. "Clearly I'm not wanted here."

"Sure," he says.

Lisa surveys the parking lot.

"I don't see your car," she says to Barnaby in a strained voice.

"It's right here. It's new."

"Oh, I didn't know. Going up in the world," Lisa says as she climbs in.

"Poor lady," Barnaby says. "I remember her well, but I never would have recognized her. She was always such a strong, energetic worker when she cleaned our house. She sometimes walked all the way to the hardware store to buy supplies."

"Well, she's eighty-two now."

"Hard to imagine. Where to? Guess you want to go back to work, right?"

"No. I'm bushed. This business gets you down, sometimes. Let's have a cup of coffee. My treat."

"Uh . . . I have a lot of things to do. Another time," he says.

He turns the ignition on, then twists his head to observe her. She's hunched over, wiping a tear from her face.

"All right. Guess I have time for coffee," he says. *What harm could it do*, Barnaby thinks, *to return her kindness when she's feeling sad?* He never considers himself someone who could help a woman out of trouble—lately he's always the one needing assistance—but he likes the idea of being gallant. "Where to?" he asks. The donut shop is hardly her style.

"There's a nice little place around the corner. Rick's Coffee House. They make good lattes."

He doesn't drink espresso, but says, "All right. Lead the way."

They take seats by the window in the small café. Barnaby orders and pays for two lattes. He's impressed by the thick foam at the top of the cup and slurps it down. Lisa reaches with a napkin and wipes the white bubbles from his face. *Just as though I'm a child*, he thinks. Offering a friendly shoulder for her to lean on might be more difficult than he guessed. He swallows loudly. "Nice drink," he says.

"Yes. Comforting. Guess I need a little TLC."

"Ah. Well, if you want to talk, I can listen."

"It's hard to explain. My work hasn't gone so well lately. I've had some challenging cases. A different family, not Alma's."

Barnaby frowns. "I think I can understand that. You're in the helping profession, right? And after a while that must get tiresome."

"More than tiresome. Things happen. A child disappeared. Domestic violence. I didn't do enough to intervene. I'm so ashamed. Don't tell anyone." Tears stream down her cheeks, and her narrow shoulders shudder.

Barnaby jerks back, too shocked for words. He reaches for her hand.

She raises her eyes. "So I've had enough. I'm getting out of this line of work."

"It's a lot of responsibility, I guess," Barnaby says soberly. "So what are you going to do instead?"

"Don't know yet. Maybe if I met a good man . . ."

Barnaby withdraws his hand, uncertain what to say. *Does she mean me?* He can't tell her he's interested in Julia, not her. And he's at a loss to explain to himself how he, a recovering drunk, living a reclusive life for years and preferring his parrot's companionship to others, is suddenly, unbelievably, of interest to not one, but two women.

He rubs his chin. "They're expecting sleet. When winter's over, I'm getting out of here. Tired of the Waterbury winters," he says gently.

She drains her cup. "Well, I guess we'd best get going," she says, rising and wiping her eyes. "Thanks for the coffee."

He watches her while she slowly draws her arms into her coat. "Please allow me to drive you home," he says.

They're silent in the car, and as she waves good-bye at the gate, he feels his eyes soften with sympathy.

# CHAPTER 24

After delivering Alma home and arranging with Elsa to meet the following day, Julia returns to the office. It's only three o'clock, but she's exhausted. She switches the radio to a classical music station and makes herself a cup of tea using hot water from the coffee machine. She wishes Lisa had not gone with her to find Alma. Lisa will eventually learn about her relationship with Barnaby if things progress further. And she's not sure about that, especially since she saw Barnaby and Lisa leaving the hardware store together. What a muddle.

Margaret appears at her door. "Got a minute?"

"Sure. Just got back from finding Alma Hawkins, who went missing this morning."

"Oh, dear. How's the case going?"

"Well enough. It's now more urgent that we find a suitable home for Alma, one where she can have more supervision. Speaking of that, I thought you planned to tell Lisa she's off the case."

"I haven't talked to her about that yet, but I will. She's fragile, and I don't want to upset her. Do you want her back to help?"

"She's never actually left, but I need to manage this by myself. Wires are getting crossed, and the family doesn't like it."

"That's what I wanted to know. Thanks."

Julia spends the next hour making appointments to see memory care facilities with Elsa. She's irritated with Margaret. Telling Lisa she's off the case would make Julia's job easier and might help Lisa make difficult decisions about the future. And if she's going through an emotional crisis, Lisa needs all the help she can get. Julia considers talking more to Margaret about Lisa's disturbed emotional state, but decides to wait. She doesn't want to damage her friend's professional reputation without cause. It's all so confusing.

At home, Julia draws a hot bath. She's too tired to eat and wants an early night. The phone interrupts her plan.

"Hi, Julia. Nancy here. I want to talk to you about our party. Do you have a venue yet?"

"Oh, the party. It completely slipped my mind. The birthday, too, for that matter."

"It's next week, January twenty-sixth, right?"

"Yeah. Forty. Let's forget the celebration."

"No way. I thought you were up for this. What's changed?"

"Things have gotten complicated. I don't want a party, and I can't possibly plan one in a week. People need more time to get things on their calendar. Let's go out to dinner, the two of us, or to a movie."

"You sound down. Let's not make firm plans now. Are things okay with your new boyfriend?"

"Not my boyfriend. Not yet, anyway. We've only had one date."

"How did it go?"

"Fantastic. Look, I've had a hard day. Let me rethink this."

"Okay. Talk to you soon."

Julia collapses on her bed. She speculates how things went between Lisa and Barnaby. They left together. Lisa didn't return to work, and Barnaby didn't call as Julia hoped. She expected by this time in her life she would have sorted out problems like boyfriends that seemed insurmountable when she was younger. But here she is, almost forty, still trying to figure things out. She needs to get a grip and grow up.

# CHAPTER 25

"Morning, Barnaby," Sal greets him. "Quite a drama yesterday, with the police and all. I take it the old lady got home okay. Who was she, anyway?"

"My family's house cleaner many years ago. I let her have one of my paintings."

"So yer painting again?"

"Yes."

"I hope that doesn't mean yer going to quit the job. I'd sure miss ya."

"Don't worry. It'll be a while before I have a body of work. It's hard to make a living as an artist. Say, Sal, are you interested in selling any of those brass buttons of yours? I know someone who might buy some."

"Sure. Have the person stop by. I'd appreciate the extra income."

During his morning break Barnaby calls Julia at work. "Sorry I didn't call sooner. Things have been busy. I was happy to see you yesterday. Did Alma get home safely?"

"Yes, thanks," she replies softly.

A little too softly, or is he imagining that? "I'd like to know if you're free to see me this weekend." He hears her inhale and waits anxiously for her answer.

"Yes, I am," she says at last.

"Great! Pick you up at six on Saturday for dinner."

"I wasn't sure you'd call. I look forward to it."

He smiles to himself. Where shall he take her this time? He must give it careful thought. He has time to make one more call, to Sylvester. After the usual pleasantries, Barnaby says, "I understand you've sold some of my paintings already."

"Yeah. Three. Not bad, for an unknown artist."

"Would you mind telling me how much you asked for them?"

"Fifteen hundred each for the two larger ones. A thousand bucks for the small piece."

"That's not what I heard," Barnaby says.

"Oh, really? Who told you something different? Well, perhaps I forgot the numbers. I can check my records. Any others you want to sell?"

"Not for that price. I might consider selling them at your gallery on a commission basis, though."

"Well, send me some images online, and I'll make you a deal."

"I might do that. Thanks," Barnaby says.

His so-called friend isn't honest. *Damn him*. Barnaby will have to consider another venue for selling his work. Thanks to Lisa, he knows the truth about Sly's profits. *But is she telling the truth?* It's possible she got the information wrong. He shouldn't rely on Sly for sales, anyway. He can send his work out to other dealers on a computer. It's time to buy one.

The week passes quickly, and on Saturday evening he knocks on Julia's door.

"Where are we going?" she asks as she climbs into the car.

"We'll have a quick bite to eat and then go to see *Cats* at the Palace Theater. We have tickets. Does that sound good?"

"How exciting!" she says. "I'd love to see that show. It's set to T. S. Eliot's poems about cats. I have one, you know. Molière."

"It's good to have a pet. I have a parrot, Popsicle."

"I don't know much about birds. Does yours talk?"

"Does she ever! You must meet her sometime."

"I'd like to. But speaking of the Palace, I haven't gone there since it reopened three years ago. I heard Tony Bennett. Do you know he sang there at the last performance before it closed in 1987 and again when it reopened four years ago? Almost puts Waterbury on the map, doesn't it?"

"For me, Waterbury has always been on the map. I just wish it wasn't so cold."

"The winters are long, I agree."

"Well, how did your week go? Did you sort things out with Alma?"

"I did. We found a good place for her to live. Her daughter can't manage her anymore."

"You do good work," Barnaby says. I saw how beautifully you handled Alma at the store."

"Thank you," she says.

The restaurant is small and cozy with red and white checkered tablecloths. It's full of people like themselves, most likely theater-goers having dinner before the show. They examine the menu and choose lasagna.

"You look great," he says. "Green's a wonderful color for you, though I associate you with red. You wore a red dress when we met at the New Year's party."

She smiles. "Green's my favorite, actually."

*Green like Popsicle*, he thinks. *And the color of Anna's eyes.*

Julia says, "What's your color?"

"Blue. There are so many shades of it: cerulean, Prussian, cobalt, ultramarine."

"Of course, you like blue. The color of sky, and dreams," she says.

"Speaking of dreams, tell me one of yours."

She props her elbow on the table and rests her head on her hand and meets his gaze. "Marriage, someday."

He sits back, at a loss for words. His chest tightens, and his head spins. Both odd sensations. *Is marriage all these women want?*

"Now I've scared you. Sorry," she says. "How about you? What's your dream?"

"I want to move to California. Leave all this chaos behind and drive there."

Her eyes widen. "You mean, go away from here, for good?"

"Yes. It's been my dream for years. I've always wanted to go where life is gentler, where there are palm trees, long beaches, soft winds. And no Waterbury winters."

"Oh," she says, dropping her eyes.

He can see she's not happy with his scheme and considers telling her that in his recent dreams she is part of the plan, too, that he wants her beside him on the drive out West. But it's too soon, and he shouldn't have spoken so frankly. And she wants marriage . . . that's too soon as well.

The lasagna arrives. It's hard to talk against the noise in the small room and, preoccupied with their thoughts, they stop trying. On the way out, he puts his arm around her shoulders as they stroll down the street to the theater.

The production is lively, and they giggle at the witty lyrics. When the aging cat woman sings "Memories," Barnaby swallows a lump in his throat and steals a glance at Julia. A tear trickles down her cheek. They remain in their seats as the audience exits the rows.

"What is it about memories?" Julia asks, wiping her eyes. "They bring nostalgia and yearning. Why can't we appreciate the present with the same intensity of feeling?"

Barnaby gazes toward the stage, now closed from full view by velvet curtains. "Good question. Maybe because we can view the past with a clearer perspective, like a painting that recedes into the distance. But it's not good to get lost in that distance." He places his hand on hers. "I'm enjoying *this* moment, even though that performance brought back powerful reactions."

"Me, too." He feels the warmth in her voice before she goes on, "You know, there's nothing like a live stage production to heighten reality. I've never felt so alive as when I'm acting. Do you remember when I forgot my lines in *South Pacific?*"

He laughs. "Yes. The prompter from behind the curtains spoke for you, and her tone was at least two octaves lower than yours. I forgot my lines once, too. It didn't matter. We kept going."

"Yeah. Faking it is part of the business. The show must go on."

"Easier on stage, isn't it?" he says.

As they rise to leave, she turns as if to reply, but remains silent.

"What?" he asks, looking at her, but she just shakes her head.

"Nothing."

"It's still early. Would you like to go somewhere for a drink?"

She hesitates. "Why not? If you're sure."

Soon they're sitting at the counter at O'Malley's.

"Hey there, Barnaby. I see you have company tonight," Sean says.

"Yes. This is Julia."

"We've met, I believe," she says. "Hello, Sean."

He gives her a twisted grin. "Always pleased to see old customers. What'll you have, Miss Julia?"

"Not sure yet," she says, and looks at Barnaby. "What are you drinking?"

"A Coke for me. If you want something stronger, go ahead."

"Are you sure?"

"Absolutely. Have a glass of wine."

"All right. Chardonnay. It's my fortieth birthday next week, and there's no reason I can't celebrate early."

"Absolutely," Barnaby says again.

The place is crowded, and Barnaby speaks into her ear so she can hear him. He loves the scent of her hair, like coconuts, the way it smelled when they danced together on New Year's Eve. She makes him want to celebrate.

Sean sets two glasses down in front of them.

"To you," Barnaby says, meeting her eyes as she turns toward him.

"And you, too,"

They clink glasses. The wine gives Julia's cheeks a pink glow. She shifts in her seat. "How is Lisa?" she asks.

"Okay, as far as I know. Why do you ask?"

"As you're aware, she's had some problems lately. I could tell Alma's reaction to her offer of help at the car bothered her."

"Yes. She was upset about that."

"Oh. How do you know? Have you talked to her? Or seen her again?"

"Not since we found Alma on Tuesday." He takes her chin in his hand and turns her face toward him. "I'm not interested in Lisa, if that's what you're thinking. She's a friend, that's all."

Julia's blush deepens. "I don't mean to pry. The last few weeks have been hard for her. Our boss recently let her know she's no longer on the Hawkins case. I heard she's considering changing careers."

"She told me. It must be challenging, facing other people's serious problems every day."

"Yes. She's burned out. Do you know anything more?"

He starts to reply, then stops. Lisa had asked him not to tell.

A man with spiky hair sits down heavily on the stool next to Julia.

"The usual, Sean," he says. Then his eyes settle on Julia. "Hey," he says. "Haven't seen you here in a while. How's it going?"

"Fine," she says.

"Hey," he says again, "you still seeing Mike?"

"No. This is my friend Barnaby."

The man reaches across her to shake hands. "Horace Holmes. This your girlfriend? Better watch out for her. She's a hottie. You should see her at the pool table. She's a regular shark." He throws back his head and guffaws, displaying a chipped front tooth.

"Thanks for the warning," Barnaby says. Turning to Julia he says, "I didn't know you played pool."

"I don't, now."

Charley Carson stops by. "Well, look who's here. Lady Pool Shark herself. Up for a challenge? Sharpen your teeth, lady."

"Let's go," she whispers to Barnaby. "I don't like the way the conversation is going, if you get what I mean."

"Okay." He leaves some money on the counter and helps her on with her coat.

"Nice meeting you, Barnaby. Catch you later," Horace calls as they leave.

"What was all that about?" Barnaby asks as they drive away.

"I don't want to talk about it. Horace Holmes is not a friend."

"He isn't?" Barnaby says. "I guess there's a lot we don't know about each other. We'll have to take things slowly."

She nods her assent and sits with her head resting against the window until the car stops outside her condo. Barnaby escorts her to the door.

"I like you a lot. You know that." He puts his arms around her. She pulls away from him, avoids his kiss, and fumbles in her purse for a key.

"Thank you for the show and dinner," she says and shoves her key in the lock.

After she goes inside, Barnaby stands for a few minutes staring at the closed door. What went wrong? It may have been a mistake to go to O'Malley's, but he wanted to introduce her to part of his life, a place where he's comfortable. Too late he remembers that Sean had told him about Julia's visits there with a man who he'd had to throw out. Hopes sinking, he revisits his earlier insight: they don't know each other well, she's secretive, but so is he about his past wrongdoings. They do need to take things slowly. She mentioned marriage as a goal, too; he's not at all sure about that, either.

⁂

The next morning, Barnaby gets up late, deeply disappointed, both with Julia and himself. He replays in his mind the course of their date and how his desire to show her how he has changed went so badly awry. O'Malley's clearly has memories for Julia as well, not good ones, and he wonders why she accepted the invitation to go there in the first place. Will she want to see him again? Perhaps not.

Popsicle has already greeted him and waits in the kitchen. When he comes in, she flaps her wings on top of the cage, flies down to the table, cocks her head, and regards him silently.

"Top of the morning?" she asks at last.

"Not the top, not this morning. More like the bottom. Guess you're hungry. How about nuts and an apple, you silly bird?" He puts them on the table and the parrot sidles over to them.

Actually, she's not a silly bird. He's often amazed at how well she picks up on his emotions. He runs his hand down her feathery back. Birds are less complicated than people, and Popsicle is a fine companion, besides.

Three hours later he returns from the store with a new laptop computer and printer. He hopes he has bought all the right software. Next, he calls Lisa's brother to find out how to use the equipment. Alan is happy to come over the following day.

"Don't know how to thank you," Barnaby says after their training session.

"No need to thank me. I've told you, anything for my sister Lisa. I'm so glad she's met you."

*What has Lisa told him?* Barnaby wants to clarify that they're not romantically involved, but says nothing. *Stay focused on the computer*, he reminds himself, as he shows Alan out. He can't help wondering about Alan. Something doesn't seem quite right, but Barnaby is grateful for his help and has no desire to get drawn into personal discussions.

Pleased with his accomplishments, he hauls out supplies to continue his house cleaning project. He works on the windows, then vacuums the floor. Sneezing from the dust, he lets the fresh air in, taking care to keep the kitchen window closed. He doesn't want to lose Popsicle again.

"Don't even think about it," he says to her, eyeing her sideways.

Soon the house smells fresh. He's amazed how much more light streams through the windows now. Working in the house reminds him of his mother, a careful housekeeper. He conjures a mental image of her setting the table and calling up to the studio that dinner would be ready in ten minutes. He'd just enough time to clean his brushes. She cooked simple meals. Where did she keep her recipes? He should find them and attempt to recreate the dishes. Be more domestic. He especially liked her chicken pot pie. He's momentarily ashamed how he has let the place decline, surely disappointing his parents. It's another reason to keep pulling himself up. He can shop for food and cook a nice dinner for himself. He rummages in a kitchen cabinet for her recipe book, recalling it has a picture of an apple pie on the cover.

After pulling out the contents of the cabinet, he finds the book. As he turns the pages, an envelope falls out. It's addressed to him. His throat constricts as he sees the familiar curves of his mother's hand and unfolds the letter.

*June 11, 1988*
*Dear Barnaby,*

*Your father and I are thrilled to hear of your engagement. Anna is a lovely young woman and a suitable partner for you. We're sure you will make a good life together. She believes in your talents, as we do. Please let us know what we can do to help with your wedding. We're so proud of you, son.*

*Love, Mom*

Barnaby sits at the kitchen table and buries his face in his hands. How could he have let his promising young life slip away? He failed his parents, especially his mother. He lost his wife and his art and allowed drinking to overtake his life. But the awful truth is that he can't face life without it. Too many ghosts. He finds his coat and heads for O'Malley's.

Sean's not there. Robert, the new assistant bartender, takes his order for a drink and sets it in front of him. Barnaby reaches for it, and as he does, senses a hand on his arm.

"You don't need it."

He turns his head to find Brooke Taylor's eyes on him. He sets the glass down.

"I've seen it so many times," she says. "Lives ruined by the bottle. You have a gift to offer the world. Don't squander it."

He's so taken aback he can't come up with a response. The beautiful woman regards him with unblinking steel-gray eyes. He gulps. "Too late. I've already ordered it."

She hands him a newspaper clipping, then turns and leaves. He gapes after her, as though she's a mirage. Then he reaches across the counter, dumps the drink into the sink, drops some money on the counter, and goes home.

# CHAPTER 26

Brooke's words echo in his mind. He has not thought of his painting as a gift to offer others, but he appreciates the concept. He doesn't want to let anyone down—his parents, his friends, or himself, and it's not too late to redeem himself. Brooke did him a favor by reminding him that drinking and defeating his artistic impulse isn't the way to live.

There's no time like the present to start the new painting of O'Malley's, the place that has recently been the cause of both his demise and inspiration.

He ascends the stairs two at a time to his studio and places his largest primed canvas on the easel. He sets his earlier study of the O'Malley's scene on a chair beside him along with some sketches, then chooses his base color of raw umber mixed with turpentine to complete the underpainting. The familiar aromas raise his temperature, chasing coldness from the room. He's often feverish when he works on a painting that arouses his interest, and it has been a while since he felt the sensation. It feels good. Spreading a thin wash over the surface, he tries to match the values in the composition. The lights over the bar call for almost no pigment, but the rich mahogany of the counter requires a heavier application. Using a rag to wipe the surface, he lightens some areas. Once he has covered the entire canvas with the raw umber wash, he stands back to appraise it. The compositional elements of the painting are clearly outlined, and he's content with the result.

Adding color will develop the painting, but in small steps. He starts at the top, loosely outlining bottles on the shelves. He'll only tighten the shapes in the final stages of the painting. Working his way downward, he fills in figures, their backs visible as they straddle the stools beside the bar. The bartender stands prominently behind the counter holding up a cocktail glass. Barnaby squeezes beads of burnt sienna, cobalt blue, and alizarin crimson onto his palette, then mixes them to create the mood and shades he wants. He completes the first rough version of the bar scene before stopping to allow the paint to dry. He'll continue in a day or so as the pigments allow.

Once again, he steps back to appraise his work. So far, so good. It's the first large painting he has attempted in years. There's nothing to compare with the feeling of satisfaction in completing a work that's in harmony with his surroundings. *It's only possible to do this when things have a certain order,* he thinks. For so long his life followed a pattern of disorder. Now he can create the illusion of a new life and perhaps make it a reality. His favorite college teacher's advice comes to mind: the transformative value of art is in making the ordinary extraordinary.

He has found the right subject. He can almost spring from the studio into this painting, the rediscovered world of his art.

# CHAPTER 27

J ulia wakes with a headache. She hasn't slept well. The evening with Barnaby had started out okay, but things went downhill after she stupidly told him about her dream of getting married someday. Of course, she didn't mean to. It was far too early for such discussions. She scared him off. He said as much when he'd told her they need to take things slowly. And then running into Horace Holmes at O'Malley's. Why did she agree to go there, anyway? She must be losing perspective. Rebuking herself for her foolishness, she runs a hot bath and submerges herself, her hair floating around her face like frayed nerves. Afterward she paints her toenails a hot pink, for extreme embarrassment.

As she mulls over their date, she replays their conversation about memories. She enjoyed the recollection of youthful times in the theater and notes the shared poignant feeling that life now appears flat, somehow lacking in passion. Her more recent memories are only ones she would rather forget. Surmising that indigestion is causing the uncomfortable feeling in her gut—the acidity of tomatoes in lasagna—she downs some Tums.

She drifts through the morning doing laundry, watering the plants, tending to the cat. Molière, a gray mound in a patch of sunshine, lounges on the living room floor. She brushes his fur. He stretches and allows her to work on his white front. He purrs softly as she rolls him around to reach his other side.

"Let's watch TV tonight," she says to him. "We can have dinner and a movie. I'll steam some fish," she says, scratching him behind the ears.

*I could learn a lot from this cat,* she says to herself. *He knows what's good for him, unapologetically, something I have trouble with. I make mistakes, and I may be about to make another one, getting involved with Barnaby. Sure, he's a nice guy, but he's afraid of marriage, and he's planning to move to California soon.* "I don't want to waste valuable years on a hopeless prospect," she tells Molière. "I'll be forty in two days." She twists the pearl ring on her right hand. The cat rubs his head against her arm, purring loudly.

But she knows she has far older mistakes to remedy, ones she has pushed away, hoping to bury them out of sight and mind forever. As she views the flickering TV, she can almost piece together scattered scraps, pieces of a fabric quilt, not yet sewn. *Alice Lowell Morgan's unfinished history.* The uncomfortable notion bursts in her mind like a patient learning a diagnosis after years of suffering.

With a flick of her finger, she shuts off the television.

She needs to settle the old business, the promise she made to her mother. Now the task she has put off for years calls her with new urgency. She needs to clear the debt with herself as well as the one she owes her mother. She must complete the family story.

Julia's pulse races as she contemplates the task before her. She's not accustomed to writing long stories and wonders again, as she told her mother earlier, if she has the skills to do so. What will she learn that might disturb her? She has no idea what Alice has written so far and knows little of those old relatives. It's a daunting prospect.

Exhausted from the force of her revelation, she falls asleep on the couch. But when she wakes in the early hours of the morning, she knows at once she must make arrangements to fulfill her mission.

The next day, Nancy calls.

"Hey. Are you out of the doldrums yet? Can we talk about New York?"

"Oh, Nancy. Something's come up. I have to go out of town."

"Really? What's going on?"

"I have to go back to Boston to see my father."

"Have you taken leave of your senses? I thought you and he didn't get along."

"We don't—he's as appealing as garlic ice cream—but I have a reason for going back. I have to talk to him."

"If you say so. I don't want the birthday to pass you by. Let's talk when you get back. How about dinner?"

"All right, but no fuss. No card with jokes about getting old and over the hill."

"Agreed."

*There's no time like the present.* This mission will be a birthday present to herself. To find her mother's materials, she'll have to go to the family's home. She hopes they're still there. And first she has to call her estranged father to arrange the visit. That will take all her resolve. There's her father's wife to consider as well. Will she want to allow a long-lost daughter into the house? But Julia is determined to succeed and to pack the remnants of her immature years in boxes, where they belong, at long last.

She makes a cup of tea, steels herself, then lifts the phone.

# CHAPTER 28

arnaby stands and stretches, stiff after spending several hours using his new computer. He's happy he can remember how to type—the last time he'd used that skill was on an electric typewriter in college. As a studio art teacher, he'd never needed to provide handouts, as many of his colleagues had. His speed improves as he practices. He enjoys researching information on the internet and sees that this new link with the world will present opportunities, and not only for selling his paintings. Alan Nettler had shown him how to scan small images on his printer and send them to the computer. Larger ones would have to be scanned by a professional copy service.

He wants to go along to O'Malley's for lunch. Thinking of the bar reminds him of the newspaper clipping Brooke passed to him. What had he been wearing? He pulls a pair of pants out of the laundry basket, rifles through the pockets, and draws out the piece of newspaper. He flattens the wrinkles.

## ARTS COMMISSION ANNOUNCES
## CONTEST FOR NEW MURAL

Artists should submit drawings and dimensions for a mural honoring Waterbury's history by February 14. Winner will receive a $10,000 commission to paint the mural. Visit the City's website for details.

✻✻✻✻✻✻✻✻✻✻✻

He reads the words twice. *What an opportunity!* It might be a longshot, but he'll enter the competition. He ought to thank Brooke. Almost skipping to O'Malley's, he rushes to Sean at the bar. "Do you know how I can contact Brooke?" he asks, catching his breath.

Sean stops polishing a wine glass and narrows his eyes. "Why? You're not interested in dating her, are you?"

"What? No. Of course not. I'd like to thank her for passing me some useful hints. That's all."

Sean shakes his head. "I only see her when she comes in here. Never asked how to contact her."

"All right. Guess I'll have to wait until I see her here, then."

"Speaking of women, nice young woman, that Julia," Sean says. "Saw you left in a hurry Saturday. Did Horace bad mouth her, or somethin'?"

"Not really. He did say she played pool well. That surprised me. I didn't know she was the type to hang around pool halls."

"She had friends who used to play here with Charley all the time," Sean says. "Horace was one of 'em. They got into a nasty fight once, and Horace got arrested."

"What was it about?"

"I don't know. You'll have to ask Julia."

"She got involved in a fight? Hard to imagine."

"Not directly, but she was there. I think I told you, but perhaps you don't remember. I had to call the police; things got so ugly."

"Ah, so that's why she wanted to leave. Probably embarrassed and afraid Horace would talk."

"He's an ass. A gambler, and a bad loser."

"I see. I don't know him, only met him here with Julia. He mentioned a guy called Mike. Do you know anything about him?"

"Julia's former boyfriend. I think I told you about him already. Nice enough until he got drunk, which he did quite often."

"Now I remember. Well, who am I to judge?"

"Speakin' of drinks, what'll you have today?" Sean asks.

"Coffee. How about a chef's salad to go with it?"

"My goodness. Still on the wagon and you're turnin' into a health nut, besides. *Salad?*" Sean eyes him suspiciously.

"As I told you, I'm turning over a new leaf. Salad is part of that. *Leaves*, you know?"

"I get it. Okay."

This is a new side of Julia, Barnaby muses. It's not necessarily bad, but he wants to know more about the incident and this group of people she had known. She was clearly embarrassed. Is that the reason she dismissed him at the end of the evening? He decides not to worry. He has other problems calling for attention.

Sean brings him the salad and coffee. "Say, Barnaby, what are you doin' the rest of the day?"

"Nothing much. It's a free day. I'll probably work on my new painting. Why?"

"Would you like to go fishin' with me?"

"Fishing? It's winter, man. Freezing out there. Surely you don't mean outdoor fishing."

"I do. Ice fishin'. If you've never tried it, you should. Cold, but fun."

"I don't know, Sean. Not really my kind of thing."

"Aw, come on. I've got a man to cover for me at the bar this afternoon. It'll be good for you to have a change of scene, do somethin' different."

*A change of scene*, Barnaby thinks. Yes, it would be that. He could use it for a new painting, his new series of people at work, ice fishing. As he considers it, the idea grows more appealing. "Okay. When, and what do I need to bring? I don't have any gear."

"Put on the warmest clothes you have. I've got everythin' we need. It'll be good to have some company. Finish your meal first. How about if I see you back here at one o'clock? That'll give us time to finish before it gets dark."

⁂

Sean is waiting for him in his pickup truck when Barnaby arrives back at the bar. A stark sun shines brightly in the scarred winter sky, causing Barnaby to squint. He should have brought sunglasses to lessen the glare, but it's too late now. He climbs into the truck with his backpack containing a sketch book and pencils and an extra pair of gloves.

"Where are the fish?" he asks.

"Crescent Lake. The top is frozen solid. The fish are underneath."

"Hard to believe I've lived this long and never knew about ice fishing."

"Well, my friend, if you don't mind my sayin', you've been livin' in a bit of a fog for a while now. Nice to see you're comin' out of it."

"Yes. Amazing, all the things I've missed."

"Oh, forgot to tell you. There's a contest. Whoever gets the most fish wins. There's another prize for the biggest fish. I wouldn't mind winnin'."

Barnaby laughs. "I'll do my best to let you win. What kind of fish are we looking for?"

"Lake trout, bass, and catfish. The biggest ones are often trout."

"Will we keep the ones we catch?"

"Sure. Eat 'em, too."

*Well, this might not be so bad*, Barnaby reflects as they rattle along. Freezing temps, though. He shivers, despite the blast of warm air coming from the truck's heater. "How did you learn to fish, anyway?" Barnaby asks.

"My dad taught me, and he learned from his dad. They both fished in Ireland. River fishin' mostly, for trout. They never went ice fishin'. I learned that myself. My dad thought it was a stupid idea."

*A man after my own heart*, Barnaby thinks.

"He always ended an outin' with a visit to a pub," Sean goes on, smiling. "He liked good company, beer, and Irish Whiskey. That's why, after he lost his job in the '70s when the brass factory closed, he bought O'Malley's. We enjoyed fishin' together in good weather, though, and tendin' bar."

Barnaby looks at his friend with envy. He wishes he'd had a father who shared his interests. His father worked all his life as an accountant and never understood Barnaby's passion for art. It was his mother who'd persuaded him to pay for Barnaby's studies in art school. But he couldn't fault his father, who came around in the end and expressed admiration for his son's talent.

When they arrive at the lake, Sean pulls equipment out of the truck bed. Barnaby can already see that his friend is better prepared for the weather. He has boots with thick soles and a heavy jacket. Barnaby wears only his overcoat on top of several layers of sweaters. His stomach rumbles, and he wishes he had eaten a more substantial lunch. Perhaps this adventure is a mistake. Several other fishermen are already scattered on the ice.

"Give me a hand, would you?" Sean says, handing Barnaby an ice chest. "Let's set up over there." He points to an open area, and the two men trudge across the frozen lake. As they organize their things, they hear a voice booming from several yards away.

"Hey, Sean. You competing?"

Barnaby turns in the speaker's direction. Even though the hefty man wears loose clothes almost obscuring his face, Barnaby can easily recognize him.

"Sure, Horace. You, too?" Sean calls.

"Yeah. Well, may the best man win. Is that Barnaby with you? The one who Julia's dating these days?"

"Yes. Barnaby."

Barnaby follows Sean back to the truck, wincing at the mention of Julia and his befuddled situation.

"Damn him, Horace would show up," Sean says. "He's such a sore loser it almost makes me not want to compete. He still resents me for callin' the police on him in the bar that time. Takes all the fun out of things, havin' him here."

"Don't worry. Enjoy the fishing. It doesn't matter who wins."

"Suppose you're right. Here, take these." He hands Barnaby two folding chairs, and they return to their spot on the ice. He holds up the hand ice auger, a tall metal pole with a handle on top and screws below. "First, we need to drill holes. You can help by removing the ice and slush while I make the hole."

He cuts through the first layers of ice, then stops to allow Barnaby time to scrape the shards away. After a while, he has bored a hole about eight inches wide.

"Almost ideal conditions today," he says. "Some days it's so frosty you have to use a heater to keep the holes from freezing up. Today they might just melt."

Barnaby privately considers the conditions far from ideal. "I hope we don't fall through the ice, then," he says. "What's next? When does the contest begin?"

"At two o'clock. We'll fish for an hour."

"So you'll start fishing right away, then. I'd like to do a sketch while you do."

"What? You're going to draw? That's crazy! And not why you're here. No, man, you're goin' to fish. I'll make you another hole."

Barnaby shrugs. Too bad. He could do a good painting of the scene. He likes the soft gray clouds on the horizon and the blue shadows cast by the fishermen on the ice. It would make a fine monochromatic painting in bluish gray. Well, he can fish for a while and do a sketch later.

Soon Sean has made an identical hole. He demonstrates how to bait the small fishing rod and lower it into the water. "You have to keep movin' the pole now and then to attract the fish," he says. "When you get a bite, pull the rod in. He may fight, so lower the pole until you can get the head through the hole."

"Thank for the explanation, but I don't expect to catch anything," Barnaby says as he looks around. He sees several contestants lifting bottles of beer out of coolers. "Say Sean, where's the beer?" he asks.

"Back at the bar."

Barnaby figures it's just as well, but beer would go a long way toward making the fishing expedition more pleasant.

They take their seats on the chairs and lower the poles. Ten minutes later, a gunshot sounds, signaling the start of the contest. Barnaby's feet already feel numb. *It's going to be a long, cold hour*, he thinks.

Almost immediately, Sean pulls fish out of his hole. Barnaby forgets to tug the pole and hopes he can get away with sketching his companion without him noticing. He reaches for the backpack lying beside him. As he does so, he jerks his pole. All of a sudden, it almost twists out of his hands.

"Help! I've caught something!" he shouts.

Sean rushes over and grabs the line. "It's a big one. Hold

tight." He lowers the rod into the ice-frozen water. It thrashes around, and both men grasp it tightly. Sean cautiously pulls it up, then pushes it down, then up again, until the fish head appears out of the hole.

"Quick, fetch the chest." he says.

Barnaby reaches for it, sets it down, and opens the lid.

"He's a beauty. Must weigh nine pounds, at least. You did it, Barnaby! Caught a big fish! You might even be a winner!"

Barnaby throws back his head and roars with laughter.

Sean thumps him on the back. "Well, keep goin'. There's still half an hour."

"Thanks, but I've had enough. You keep going. I'll draw you."

"You're not a fisherman, I can tell. But go ahead."

Barnaby sits back on the chair, changes his gloves so he can control the pencil, then pulls out his sketchbook and draws. He barely notices his numb feet and hands now. The gunshot signals the contest's end, and the participants collect their gear and drift across the frozen lake back to their cars. Horace passes by them. He holds a large fish suspended from a line.

"Ain't he a trophy? Might win this time," he says, then regards Barnaby. "What are you doing? Making pictures?" He sniggers. "Takes all types, I guess."

After he leaves, Sean checks the fish in the cooler.

"I think yours is bigger," he says, beaming. "Let's go weigh it."

They pick up the equipment and edge gingerly over the ice to a table in a tent at the edge of the lake. The line of competitors waits for results. Horace stands by the entrance, swinging his fish. It's wriggling, and its eyes are wild.

When it's Barnaby's turn to weigh the fish, the man in charge greets them. "Hey there, Sean. How did you do?"

Sean places the fish on the scales. "My friend Barnaby here got a big one."

"Yep. Looks like a winner. Six ounces more than yours, Horace."

Horace growls. "Whatta you mean, his is bigger? Let me see. This nerd here's a painter, not a fisherman, for Christ's sake."

The man shows Horace the numbers he's written on a chart.

"Goddammit," he says under his breath as he stomps away. "Can't believe I'd lose to a rank amateur, a *Sunday painter*, besides."

Barnaby frowns. He knows he's a newcomer at fishing, but how dare Horace attack him as an artist.

"What does he mean, a Sunday painter?" Sean asks.

"He means someone who's a dilettante, amateurish. It's an insult."

"So I guess you've made an enemy. Wouldn't wish that on anyone," Sean says. "But you've won five hundred bucks!"

"Are you kidding? There's money? Beginner's luck, I guess."

He takes the envelope and whistles, shaking his head in disbelief as he counts the cash. They load the truck and drive back to the bar.

"Let's split the winnings, and you keep the fish," Barnaby says. "It's too big for me to eat by myself and anyway, I couldn't have pulled it in without your help. I'll be happy to exchange it for some of the smaller ones you caught."

"Thanks. My mother sure will appreciate that. Good that you came along. And congratulations."

On his way home Barnaby feels chilled and expects a hot shower and fish for dinner. He can't help chuckling to himself at his luck. He can use the money, but can't imagine he has made an enemy simply by winning a fishing contest. It has been a good day. He has the beginnings of a good painting, and a chance to compete for a mural contest. He doesn't need a woman in his life. Too complicated, and he wants nothing to interfere with his plan of moving to California. He has bigger fish to fry.

# CHAPTER 29

"Hello, Father? This is Julia."

A long silence ensues. Then a gruff voice resounds. "Julia. A surprise, after how many years?"

"Twenty, I believe. I hope you're well." *Of course he doesn't remember my birthday this week*, she thinks.

"Well enough," he grunts. "Never expected to hear from you again. I take it you have a reason for calling."

"I do. I'd like to come to Boston."

A deep inhalation reverberates through the line. "I see. Well, I suppose I can't deny my only daughter a visit. I take it that's what you want."

"If it's convenient for you and your wife."

"Edna. She died five years back. I'm alone now."

"Sorry to hear that. I was hoping to come soon, this week. The weather's all right for driving. I'll be driving up from Waterbury."

"Guess that's okay. Let me know when you expect to arrive."

"How about tomorrow, around noon?" *Before I change my mind.*

"All right then." The line clicks off.

Julia's shoulders relax. She doesn't recognize her father's voice, but he has aged and must be close to seventy. He had always been a domineering man, one who wouldn't let others talk until he finished what he had to say. As a lawyer, he could assume that authority, or at least, he did. Conversations at home had rarely been two-way.

It would take all her courage to face the man again after all these years. But he's the gatekeeper to her mother's legacy, and she has no choice.

After calling into work saying she needs a day off, Julia fortifies herself with an extra shot of coffee, tosses a bag of snacks on the passenger seat of her car, and sets off along Interstate 84 East toward Boston. She expects a two-hour trip, depending on traffic. After a while, the road becomes Wilbur Cross Parkway, a well-designed four-lane highway that prohibits commercial and other large vehicles. She always enjoys driving this stretch, appreciating the curving stone bridges and corridor of well-groomed trees which, even in winter, hug the road, softening the thrust of swishing cars.

After Hartford and the Interstate 90 interchange, the traffic volume increases. The emergence of trucks, trailers, and buses causes cars to slow down, crawling like reptiles along multiple lanes, red tail-lights flashing and brakes squealing as they stop and start. A siren wails from behind, and drivers pull over to the right. An ambulance streaks past, and the sluggish vehicles resume their forward roll.

Julia punches the radio button, wanting distraction from her mounting anxiety. Beethoven's Fifth Symphony blares from the dashboard. She shuts it down. Too dramatic. She slips a CD into the slot and soon the airy sounds of Enya float inside the car. The gurgling in her stomach subsides.

As she approaches Boston, her trepidation and dread increase. After a gas station restroom break, she approaches her old neighborhood. Somehow the two-hour journey has taken on almost epic proportions. In fact, she has already extended the time she had allocated—she wanted to be finished with the visit, its purpose accomplished, and back on the road before dark. Despite the cold, her hands sweat on the wheel and the knot in her stomach tightens.

Within minutes of entering the city limits, she turns onto her father's street, which is exactly as she remembered it with proud old townhouses. Her family's home stands in the middle of the block. Its exterior appears unchanged, the white paint of the window frames setting off the dark brick façade. *Traditional, tasteful, and thoroughly intimidating.* She parks the car and mounts the front steps. A brass plate by the door reads JULIUS MORGAN, ESQ. Her instincts tell her to turn and run, but she stands firm, and after a few moments rings the bell.

A middle-aged woman wearing a scarf around her hair opens the door. "You must be Julia," she says. "Mr. Morgan told me he expects you. Come in."

Julia steps into the oak-paneled foyer. The familiar scent of lemon oil polish permeates the air.

"He's in his study. May I offer you a cup of coffee or tea?"

"No, thank you," Julia says. She's afraid her stomach might not tolerate any refreshment, and her knees shake as she advances along the hallway to the office on the left side. She knocks on the heavy door.

"Come in."

She cracks the door slowly at first, then widens it as she peeks round to face the desk. Her father sits in his usual place almost enveloped by a leather executive chair. She hadn't remembered him as small, but as he rises to greet her, she sees that he stands not more than a head taller than herself. He extends his hand across the desk as she grasps it. His steel-gray eyes glint behind horn-rimmed glasses as he scrutinizes her. She draws herself to her full height and meets his gaze.

"Well, well, well," he says at last.

"Hello, Father. How are you?"

"Good enough, considering. You look older. What age are you now?"

"I'm about to turn forty."

"Ah yes. Take a seat. I'll have Mrs. Hall bring us some tea. Or would you prefer something stronger?"

She shakes her head. "Nothing for me, thank you."

"Well, I could use a drink about now, myself." He pushes a button on the desk and the housekeeper appears at the door. "A bourbon on the rocks, if you please." Turning to Julia, he asks, "So to what circumstance do I attribute the pleasure of your visit?"

"Some forgotten papers. I should have taken them years ago. Now I have a use for them."

"What kind of papers? School reports?"

"Nothing like that. Materials my mother wanted me to have."

He grunts, shifts in his chair, and steeples his hands on the desk. "What makes you think they're still here?"

"I don't know if they are. They were in her closet, in a chest."

"Cleared all that stuff away. Could be in the attic, though."

"Yes. I expected that. Would it be possible for me to look?"

"I suppose so. Why do you want them, after all this time?"

"Let's just say I'm recovering history."

"Ah, yes. We all need to remember the past. I've spent my career basing decisions on past precedent. An important concept. So what do you do with yourself? Are you still married?"

"No. I work for the County of New Haven. Social work."

"Interesting. Do they pay you well? Hate to think of that fine education you had going to waste."

"It's not about money. Listen, I'd like to start the drive home before dark. May I take a look in the attic for those papers?"

"Don't see why not. You've never asked for anything since you left home. I'll have Mrs. Hall bring you the key."

Julia watches as he lifts the drink in a cut-glass tumbler from a tray offered by the housekeeper. In all these years, he hasn't changed. He quaffs his afternoon cocktail, sitting at his desk in his big chair, perusing files and winning cases, solemn and unforgiving. His face reflects it all. Not a different face, but more entrenched lines. She waits for the key while he sips. The winter sun streams through narrow windows onto the polished wood walls. The grandfather clock chimes three muffled tones.

When the housekeeper returns, she hands Julia the key. Julia rises and inclines her head. "Good-bye. Thank you for seeing me," she says, turning to leave.

"You remind me of your mother," he calls.

She doesn't reply. She knows. She has photographs.

Julia spends a half hour rummaging through items in the attic. She finds relics of her past: her old dolls, a dollhouse, and stacks of books. Remembering she last saw the papers in a wooden chest, she continues her search until she finds it buried under a pile of blankets. She pries the dusty lid open. Inside, piles of notebooks, envelopes, and photographs lie in disorder. *Easier than I expected*, she sighs. She drags the chest to the top of the attic stairs, then gently allows it to slide down, holding the handle on one end. On the third floor, she finds an elevator, a new installation. She enters, presses the button and stops at the first level. Mrs. Hall helps her carry the trunk to the street and load it into the car.

"Thank you for your help," Julia says. "There's something else I'd like to take home, but I can bring it by myself."

She runs back upstairs to the attic. Her old dollhouse. She wants to retrieve it, with its miniature furniture and figures, an ideal family, the one she had always dreamed of having.

She had kept the card her mother had written to accompany that Christmas present: "To Julia, who makes an old house young. Enjoy yours, sweetheart, and fill it with love and kindness." Julia understands now, as she didn't then, how her presence as a child in that dreary home must have comforted her mother, giving her hope.

⁂

*Definitely easier than expected*, she thinks, as she drives away. Easier for her now to manage her father, anyway. He'll remain unchanged, but she is growing into her true self, the person Alice Morgan would have wanted her daughter to be.

As Julia turns south on the interstate, she allows memories of her mother to flood back. Alice had dealt with Julius the best way she knew, brushing him aside and attending to her own interests. As long as she kept a clean house and good table, he didn't usually complain. Julia doubted he ever noticed her gentle, artistic soul, her extraordinary garden filled with shining plants, her intricate knitting, or her well-crafted writing. The butterfly lightness of her garden never penetrated the dark recesses of the house. He'd given her a comfortable lifestyle, but no companionship. Sympathy for her mother's lonely illness drove Julia to leave school and hasten home to care for her during those last months of her life, a decision Julia never regretted.

On the drive home, she reaches for chocolate, then turns on the radio and sings to the catchy refrains of songs from *The Wizard of Oz*. "Over the Rainbow" strikes her as a fitting end to the day she dreaded. She'll likely never see her father again. She will live more comfortably, free of the crushing burden of unfulfilled promises, and finally honor her mother by writing the family history.

# CHAPTER 30

Back at work, Julia resolves to talk to Lisa. She wants to clear the record, doesn't like the tension between them, and hopes to find her in a happier frame of mind.

Lisa stomps around her office cleaning out files.

"I submitted my resignation this morning," she says icily. She avoids Julia's stare as she stacks a pile of folders on her desk.

"Oh. That's good, isn't it?"

"Probably. It's important to know when you're done."

"True. Look, I want to apologize if I've caused you any trouble," Julia says.

Lisa slams a file on her desk and regards her with an expression of incredulity. "You tried to take over my case. That was bad enough. Then you tried to steal away my man."

"You handed me the case," Julia says in exasperation. "And I didn't steal Barnaby. He doesn't belong to anyone."

"Oh no? That shows how little you know."

Julia flushes. "I came to find out how you're doing, not to get an update on your love life. I'm sorry you're so bitter, and I wish you the best of luck in your new career, whatever that is," Julia says as she backs out of the room, not wanting to hear any more.

January twenty-sixth. *You're forty*, Julia says to her reflection in the bathroom mirror. Are these lines in her face she hasn't seen before? She smooths moisturizer on her cheeks and forehead and brushes her long hair. Maybe she should cut it. It's still thick and shiny without a trace of gray, so not yet. She chooses a gray wool suit to wear for work and a bright green scarf to brighten it for her dinner with Nancy later.

"Happy birthday," Margaret says, handing her a card. "I want you to know how impressed I am about your management of the Hawkins case. Elsa called me and told me her mother has come around to the idea and will move next week to her new home. Elsa gives you credit for that. Excellent work."

"Thank you," Julia says, "but just curious—did you ever explain to Lisa in no uncertain terms that I was in charge of the case?"

"I did, but she resisted the idea—couldn't accept the fact that she wasn't performing up to standard. Anyway, as you may know, she resigned from her job, says she's enrolling in cooking school in New York intending to open a restaurant someday. I've assigned you a new case, but we can talk about that later. Have a good day, and feel free to leave early."

Julia feels a great sense of relief. She sits for a while at her desk savoring her success, but can't help worrying about what on earth is going on with Lisa.

After work Julia meets Nancy at Bistro, a new French restaurant in the historic Municipal Center. They've agreed having dinner in Waterbury suits them better than a longer trip to New York in the uncertain weather.

"Nice restaurant, Nancy," Julia says. "Have you eaten here before?"

"I bring clients here sometimes. My wealthier ones. The food's excellent, and they have an extensive wine list."

They peruse the menu.

"Champagne?" Nancy asks. "My treat. And oysters for an appetizer?"

"Champagne, thank you. Not fond of oysters. I'd prefer a salad. Then the artichoke quiche."

Nancy places their orders. The champagne arrives immediately, and she proposes a toast. "To your next decade. I predict great success and happiness."

"I don't think I share your boundless optimism, but thank you all the same."

They clink glasses and sip.

"This is a luxury, Nancy. Thank you."

"Is it? I thought Barnaby took you out wining and dining."

Julia grimaces. "I've only seen him twice. Not sure I'll see him again after that disaster at O'Malley's. Let's not talk about him. I'd like to enjoy myself tonight. How are things going for you? Don't you miss having someone in your life?"

"Not me. Happy as I am. I wouldn't mind a few more clients, but I enjoy my work. I still want to go to New York. Let's plan to go for my birthday in the spring."

"All right."

"How was the visit with your father?"

"Okay. I retrieved some important documents I needed." She leaves it at that. The task before her needs attention, but not advice from well-meaning friends. Nancy won't pry.

"So how's work going?" Nancy asks.

"Well enough. I keep hoping I can make peoples' lives better. I may not succeed, but I try."

"A worthy goal. Here's to you, my friend!" Nancy says.

The two women finish their meal and bottle of champagne. They chat about their fitness goals for the year. Not unexpectedly, Nancy's expectations are much higher. They order crème brûlée for dessert.

Julia forces Barnaby out of her mind. She has a new project, one to occupy heart and soul for months to come.

# CHAPTER 31

Barnaby spends weekday evenings learning to use his new computer. The amount of information he can learn on the internet continues to amaze him. After researching the best route to California and the mileage to various cities, he checks the price of rental properties in Santa Barbara and Santa Cruz. They're exorbitant. He's uncertain what to do about the house and what it's worth in the current depressed market. Putting that question aside, he considers the possessions to take along. The fewer the better. Best to keep things simple in his new life. He needs money for the move and living expenses when he arrives and quickly decides the best way of raising the funds will be through his art. He'll apply for the mural competition and sell more paintings—to Sly, or online, or both. Though not certain he can trust Sly, he wants to explore all possibilities for earning money.

His possessions will fit into a small trailer that he can haul with the Honda. U-Haul offers several trailers to hold his painting supplies. He can transport Popsicle in the back seat of his car in a new, smaller cage. She won't like it, but he can't do anything about that. He'll take his summer clothes. As he makes plans, his spirits rise. It'll be a new adventure—one he has dreamed about for most of his adult life. Anna had been equally enthusiastic about the idea. He'd like to fulfill at least his side of their shared goal. But he's getting ahead of himself. He has to make money from his art first.

By Saturday, he's ready to launch his online business. He has already scanned some paintings and now needs to post them online to capture some sales. Alan has designed a website and, following his instructions, Barnaby sets up the listing. He prices the paintings at $2,000 each and uploads the images. It's easier than he expected. Buyers will send him an email to confirm the sale, along with mailing instructions. Pre-payment is required, with the final payment due once he knows the shipping costs. This will be a good way to build a following, and much simpler than going to galleries to install the work.

On Sunday morning, he checks his email. There's a note from a Steven Michael.

> *Hello. I'm writing from Oregon. My wife has been look-ing at your website and loves your work, especially the beach scenes. We'd like to know more. We're especially interested in any larger paintings you have. Could you send more images and the dimensions? Thank you, and we hope to hear from you soon. Steven.*

Barnaby is impressed. A sale, so quickly? This is the way to go. He hasn't thought about including larger paintings, partly because of the higher prices, insurance, and shipping costs, but if someone wants one, it's okay. The larger paintings will have to be scanned by the print shop, though, and that will take time. He writes back.

> *Dear Steven, Thanks for your interest in my work. I have larger paintings, measuring 40 inches by 23 inches but it will take me a few days to scan them into the*

*site. They are also more expensive, $3,000 plus shipping. Please let me know if you're still interested. Regards, Barnaby Brown.*

He presses the send button. He hopes he hasn't priced the paintings too high, but that's about what Sly is selling them for, so why can't he?

Almost immediately, he receives a reply.

*Hi again Barnaby. We're interested. Please let us know when the postings are up. Cheers, Steve.*

Elated at the quick response from a complete stranger, he adds three paintings with beach scenes onto his website. He emails Steven Michael and once again, receives a quick response.

*Love all three big paintings. Want to buy ASAP. Wife's birthday coming up. I'll send a cashier's check for $13,000 to cover the shipping costs. Expect it within the week. THANKS. Steve.*

The check arrives. There's an extra $4,000—more than enough to cover the shipping costs. He'll have to refund the extra amount. This sale is too important to wait, and he calls Sal to explain his need to take a day for personal reasons. He buys bubble wrap, boxes, and tape. Then he wraps each painting and takes all three to the post office. He writes a check for the difference in shipping and sends it in a separate envelope to the address in Oregon.

After finishing his business at the post office and depositing the check at the bank, he concludes it would be fitting to celebrate his first online sale with a drink. He'd like to tell Sean about his second run of good luck, and a stiff drink has been his first reaction for years—but then he remembers he's given up alcohol. He understands it's hard to break an addiction but very easy to slip. He's shivering, though, and a drink would warm him up. Perhaps it's all the excitement. Happy he has the rest of the day to himself, he drives home. By the time he arrives, he's boiling hot. Popsicle greets him as he opens the kitchen door.

"One, two, three, four, five, once I caught a fish alive," she says.

"Six, seven, eight, nine, ten, then I let him go again," he replies. *Only I didn't let him go.* Felt sort of sorry for him, actually, that big fish—he'd fought hard to resist his capture. It hadn't been fair. Fishing through a hole in the ice had been a tricky invasion of the fish's space. Barnaby gives Popsicle a treat, then sits down at the table. He feels his forehead. Sweaty. Maybe he's coming down with something. He drags himself to the bedroom and lies down.

⁂

Dull light bathes the room when he wakes and reaches for the clock. Friday, a work day, and he has overslept. He sits up. His head aches—his whole body aches. He sneezes, hauls himself out of bed, and pads to the bathroom. Glassy eyes squint back at him from the mirror. *Not a time to get sick, with so much going on*, he groans. He can't miss work again. He takes a couple of aspirin, gets dressed, and goes to work.

"Sorry I'm late," he tells Sal.

"What's with ya these days, anyway? I thought ya laid off the drink. Hope yer not slipping." Sal casts a wary eye at Barnaby, who is leaning against the wall. "Hey, ya don't look so good. Are ya sick?"

"I'm never sick."

"Well, ya don't exactly act like the cat's meow. Let me take a look at ya." Sal holds his hand against Barnaby's forehead. "Yer burning up. Got a fever. Go home, take care of yerself."

Barnaby curses to himself. He has never felt so weak. He heads back to his car. Why is he sick? He doesn't know anyone else who is ill. Then he remembers the wintry day fishing. He hadn't dressed warmly enough. Ridiculous, catching fish in a frozen lake. At home, he peels off his clothes and flops into bed.

# CHAPTER 32

Barnaby sleeps all day. When he wakes, the clock reads four o'clock. *Is it still Friday?* He's not hungry, but his throat is parched, and he stumbles to the kitchen for a glass of water and to check on Popsicle. He gives her a handful of parrot food and a carrot.

Slowly, he climbs the stairs back to bed. He's dropping off to sleep when the phone jars him awake.

"Is this Barnaby Brown? Vince Olivetti from the Bank of Boston here. I need to talk to you about a check you deposited here recently."

"Uh, yes. Look, can I call you back? I'm sick."

"Sorry to hear that. But please call soon."

He slams the phone down. He's too ill to deal with anything right now.

───────────

By Monday, he's better. Not well yet, but the aching has lessened, and he's no longer feverish. It must have been the flu. Either that, or a bad cold. He has enough energy to take a shower. It'll help, and he can go back to work. He vaguely remembers there's something else he needs to do . . . the bank.

He needs to return the call to the bank. After making a cup of coffee, he dials the number, and asks for Mr. Olivetti.

"Ah, Barnaby. Thanks for calling," he says. "We wanted to inform you we're unable to cash the check you deposited here for $13,000."

"But it was a cashier's check."

"Yes. But a bad check all the same. You can find anything on the dark web these days. If I may ask, who sent it?"

"Someone I don't know, by the name of Steven Michael."

"Is Steven the first or last name? Sounds like a scam, my friend. Those people often use two names that sound like first names."

Barnaby groans. "I should have guessed. Is there anything I can do?"

"Well, if you think the guy is honorable, you can ask him to send another payment."

"Right. Thanks."

Barnaby hangs up. He doesn't have the address. He'd sent the paintings to a post office box in Oregon. Stupid of him to get taken in. But who has scammed him? Someone trolling the internet, or someone he knows? He's lost the paintings and the few thousand dollars he sent to the man. It might not be too late to cancel his check. He redials the bank number and asks for Mr. Olivetti.

"Barnaby here again. Is there any chance I can cancel my last check? I sent it to the man to reimburse him for shipping costs."

"Wait a minute. Let me see. What was the date of the check?"

Barnaby thinks for a minute, then replies, "Must have been four days ago."

"For $2,050?"

"That's the one."

"Too late. Cashed yesterday."

"All right. Thanks," Barnaby says miserably. Now he's lost the money he sent to the fraudulent buyer, and he's in debt again.

The online sales weren't such a good idea. He'll ask Alan to take down the website. His temperature rising, he reminds himself he's not fully recovered yet and needs to take it easy. His head feels congested. Sudafed might help. He coughs and makes a strangling sound with his throat as he downs two tablets. A visit to Sean is the tonic he needs. He might allow himself a shot of brandy for medicinal purposes.

Barnaby drives to O'Malley's to preserve his strength and heaves himself up to his usual post. Sean comes over to him right away.

"Hey, champ. How's it goin'?"

"Brandy," Barnaby mumbles. He watches Sean narrow his eyes as he pours the drink.

"What's up, fella? You don't look so hot."

"Got sick and lost a lot of money."

"But you just won a lot of money," Sean says, frowning. "Did you lose it already? Or spend it?"

"Lost it. Got scammed online. Someone sent a bad check to buy paintings."

"You don't say. Bad luck, huh? And here I was thinkin' how your luck's changed. By the way, remember that guy Horace? He got really sore about not winnin' the fishin' contest. Came in the other day, wantin' to know all about you."

Barnaby blinks. "He did? What did he want to know?"

"You know how he is, disrespectful and all. He couldn't get over you drawin' at the fishin' contest. Had some colorful words to say about that. Asked if you were a talented artist. I told him yes, of course."

Barnaby takes a few sips of the brandy. It burns his throat but feels good. "That's strange," he says. "Why would he care?"

"I already told you. He hates losin'. And I think he likes Julia."

Barnaby remembers Horace's insult on the ice. *Sunday painter.* Perhaps he's also a rival for Julia's attention. He dismisses that unwelcome thought and leans across the counter. In a low voice he asks, "When did he come in?"

"Right after we went fishin'. Tuesday, maybe."

"Hm. Could he be the scammer? Sounds far-fetched, but he clearly resents me for winning and who knows what else." He downs his drink. "Do you know where he lives?"

"In town, on Water Street."

In his weakened state, the strong beverage makes Barnaby's head spin. *Maybe Horace is the one.* "I might drive over there and find him, then. See you later." He slips off his seat.

"Hey, are you sure you're in condition for drivin'?" Sean calls.

"Sure am," Barnaby says, giving him a wave as he sways out the door and makes for his car.

He'll find the culprit himself. Remorse matches his agitated anger about the scam for his own foolishness. He's trying to build respect and hates the idea of becoming an object of ridicule. On his way, the thought strikes him that he might find Horace's address online. It would be good to know where he's going instead of driving around in circles. He parks the car in his driveway, screeching the brakes to avoid hitting the garage door. At home, he turns on the computer. He hates the way emails always appear first after the machine boots up. Impatient to find the information he needs, he deletes the messages, then types Horace's name and street into the search engine. A site called whitepages.com gives him the address and phone number. Adrenaline pulsing through his medicated and inebriated veins, Barnaby climbs into the car again and heads for Water Street.

He parks a few houses away from number 72, a four-story apartment building. Damn. He hadn't considered that. He had hoped to peer through the windows of a *house* to find some paintings or evidence that the man collects art. The door to the lobby is unlocked and a list of occupants with buzzers to the units hangs on the wall. The name Holmes appears next to the buzzer for apartment 303. What's he going to do now? He can't confront the man without evidence. Crestfallen and sobering up, Barnaby drives home. This is a matter better handled by the police. He hates dealing with authorities, but if he's to reclaim his paintings and money, he may have no choice.

Sitting at his computer, he searches for the local police number and places the call. "I'd like to report a scam operation."

"All right. Name, please, first and last."

"Barnaby Brown."

"Address?"

"55 Russell Road, here in Waterbury."

"I recognize that name and address. Aren't you the guy who called earlier to report a stolen painting?"

"Yes."

"I have you on file. Is this another stolen painting, or the same one?"

"Three paintings. Different ones. But as I told you, this is a scam. No one came into my house to take them. The culprit discovered me on the internet and passed me a bad check."

"Any idea who?"

"I have my suspicions. It might be a local guy, here in town."

"All right. We must take a report from you in person. Can you come down to the station? Bring all the evidence you have."

"How soon can I come?"

"Soon as you like. We're here all night."

Exhausted by his efforts, Barnaby lies down. The report can wait until later. He doesn't want to deal with the police anyway. He soon drifts into sleep.

⁂

Next morning, he wakes up, irritated with himself for his rash behavior the day before. He was acting foolishly, trying to catch Horace, who may not be the man who cheated him anyway. He'd slipped as well, fallen off the wagon. At least he'd only had one snifter of brandy. His head feels heavy with shame and remorse. But he wants his paintings back and the money he lost. It's still a good idea to report the crime on the chance that the police can discover the identity of the culprit. He stuffs his computer into a bag. The bad check would be good evidence, but the bank has it. Perhaps he can bring a copy of that later.

He drives straight to the police headquarters and straightens his shoulders as he passes through the entrance. They frisk him before they allow him through the metal detector. Officer Turner, a burly man with a protruding stomach, ushers him into a small room and they take seats around a table.

"So when did this happen?" he asks.

"During the past two weeks. I've opened an online business to sell my paintings and this person was my first customer. He calls himself Steven Michael. I have the emails he sent in my computer. Mind if I show you?"

Barnaby boots the computer and the screen flares into life. The emails appear, new ones first. Steven Michael had sent notes recently and should come up quickly. He scrolls all the way to the bottom of the list, but he can't find them. Then he remembers. In his impatience to find Horace Holmes's address he had deleted several lines of email. Steven Michael's must have been among them.

"Goddammit. They're not here," he says, slapping his fist to his forehead.

The officer grunts. "Well, do you have any other evidence?"

"Yes, a bad check, but it's at the bank."

"Not much to go on here. Why don't you come back when you can provide more information. Where did you send the paintings?"

"To a post office box in Oregon."

"A post office box? In Oregon? And you say the guy you suspect lives locally? You need to get your story straight, Mr.

Brown. Also, if he lives out of state, this would be a case for the FBI. Assuming there *is* a case, of course."

"I swear, I'm not making this up," he says, but his words sound hollow, and he knows the meeting is over. He can hardly speak for anger and humiliation. Without proof that Horace tricked him, there's nothing for the police to investigate.

He has failed once more, and heads for O'Malley's before he stops to remember he'd had drinks there the day before. *I can't slip again.* He'll attend the AA meeting that evening.

# CHAPTER 33

With Molière in her lap, Julia settles in to read the beginnings of her mother's story. Her great-grandmother Emma Hampton had arrived in Boston from England in 1882 to marry into one of Boston's most prominent families. She became a society matron, living in a fine house on Beacon Hill. Surprised to learn her ancestors had names of buildings and streets familiar to her, she wonders why her mother never spoke of these relatives. *There must be a reason, perhaps some scandal.* Engrossed in the story, she barely hears the telephone ring.

"Hey Julia. Charley Carson here." His gruff voice over the phone causes her to hold the receiver away from her ear. "Remember me?" he asks.

"Sure. What can I do for you?"

"I've been thinking. Seeing you the other night at O'Malley's reminded me of your badass skills at pool. I'd like to invite you to a game—uh, challenge you to a game, is more like it. What do you say?"

"It's a while since I played, and I'm out of practice," she says warily.

"We can play for money or not, as you wish. I thought it'd be fun. There have been no other women who can shoot like you for as long as I can remember. Most of them are amateurs. You're almost professional, I'd guess. A real star."

Julia chortles. The man is chatting her up. "I'll think about it. When will you hold the contest? Will others be part of it? Not Horace Holmes, I hope."

"No. I remember what happened last time. Just the two of us."

Julia recalls how much she liked the smooth feel of the cue in her hands, the way she could glide it over the table with a sure hand, stroking a ball into a pocket. Though rusty, she could probably regain her skill fairly fast. It would be an adventure, a challenge unlike others. "Tell you what. I accept your offer," she says.

"Great. How about Friday, at seven?"

"See you then."

*What has she agreed to?* She'll be going to O'Malley's, Barnaby's hangout. That might not be a smart move. But the bar is a public place, and she has as much right to be there as he has. She likes the challenge and knows she is—or was—a skillful player. She will go, and win. But she's out of practice. Best to warm up first. She searches her mind for out-of-the-way bars where she could shoot a few balls. Certainly not Horace's Joint, but there's another place round the corner. Not the best neighborhood, but if she goes during the day before happy hour, she might be able to slip in and out without anyone noticing or bothering her.

She leaves work early on Wednesday. Wearing black clothes, she hopes she's inconspicuous. She cautiously opens the door of the saloon, stopping momentarily as her eyes adjust to the dark interior. The stench of sweat and liquor almost cause her to retreat, but she stiffens her resolve and enters. She approaches the bar.

"Okay if I shoot a couple of rounds?" she asks the bartender.

He regards her with furrowed brows. "By yourself? Sure, but you'll have to order a drink first."

"Sure. Diet Coke, please."

Loud rock music plays, lending pulsing life to the ugly place. He hands her a tumbler and after paying and telling him to keep the change, she drifts to the rack on the wall to choose a pool cue. She places balls into the triangular shape on the board, then stands back and checks her position. Leaning forward, she strikes, shaking the balls loose.

A tall man wearing a T-shirt and worn jeans enters the room. "Hey, Jimmy, who's the pool player?" he shouts to the bartender.

Jimmy grins. "Guess we're going up in the world. Classy lady."

Julia ignores them and concentrates on sinking the balls into pockets. The *smack* of the cue is barely audible over the loud music. The blue-jeaned man laughs. "I'd join you, but I see you're good. Ever played with my buddy Horace? He's a crack shot."

"Not recently," she says. She has finished her practice and wants to get out of there. She hangs up the cue, and trying not to appear afraid, heads out the door. It's a scary place, but the practice has been worthwhile. She's confident she hasn't lost her touch.

❊❊❊❊❊❊❊❊❊❊❊

On Friday after work, Julia rifles through her closet and chooses black pants, a white tank top, and a bright red sweater for her game against Charley. Sweeping her hair off her face, she anchors it with a shiny barrette. She needs minimum distraction and maximum flexibility for the game.

The bar hums with the usual Friday crowd. As she pushes her way to the table, she runs into Charley.

"Atta girl. You made it! I knew you wouldn't back out. This is going to be fun. I've already announced the contest to Sean, and there's a crowd of fans."

She raises her eyebrows.

"You do have your fans, you know," Charley says. "People remember you."

"I hope they won't be disappointed," she replies.

Peering through the crowd, she doesn't see Barnaby. That's fine. He might upset her equilibrium. Not a good thing when you need a steady hand.

"I'll grab a beer, then we can get started," Charley smiles, heading for the bar. "Can I get you anything?"

She shakes her head.

"A pint of Bootleggers," he calls.

"Sorry, all out. Budweiser okay?" Sean says.

Charley scowls. "Dammit." He takes the mug and returns to the pool table. "Choose your weapon, Julia," he says, taking a cue from a rack on the wall.

Julia has brought her own cue. She removes it from a bag, assembles it, twists it in her hands, then grinds a piece of chalk against the tip. She surveys the scene and recognizes several of the men.

"Listen up, everyone," Charley shouts. "This here's the greatest woman champion ever to enter these premises, Julia Morgan. She has accepted my challenge. We'll play three rounds. Winner takes all."

He takes several swigs of beer, and people throw bills into a can on a bench. The crowd forms a circle around the pool table. "Good luck, Julia!" someone calls. She bows slightly and tightens her grasp on the cue.

Charley tosses a quarter and she calls heads. "You win, you break." Charley responds. "We'll play by the usual house rules."

She holds the cue with her right hand, then slips it between the fingers of her left, forming a bridge on the table. She carefully aims at the cue ball, then strikes it with full force, scattering the balls. None fall into pockets. Charley steps to the table, places his hand near the cue ball, and prepares to shoot. He sinks two solid balls into pockets but misses a tricky combination shot. *He's made a good start*, Julia observes. She aims at two balls blocking access to the pocket. If she can hit the first ball at the right angle, it will bounce off the other and go in. *Definitely a low percentage shot, but worth a try*, she thinks. She pulls it off.

"You go, girl! Great carom shot!" a man cries.

"She knows what she's doing. Tough competition, Charley boy!"

Julia misses the next shot, but the cue ball rolls behind others denying Charley an unobstructed view of any solid ball. Charley grimaces, reaches for his beer mug, and swallows a deep draught. He takes a stance, reaching toward a ball on the rail. He shoots, but the ball nicks the side of the pocket and veers away.

The room becomes strangely quiet as the game continues. Both players land their balls until only the eight ball remains. Several people stand on chairs to gain a better view. Julia focuses on the ball, leaning forward to aim. She strokes, not too hard, and the ball rolls slowly toward the pocket, then drops in. The crowd applauds.

"Hold on a minute!" Charley shouts. "Foul play! You didn't call the pocket!"

A collective groan echoes around the room.

"Sore loser!"

"Hey Charley. Give the lady a break! That's not a house rule."

"It is today," he shouts.

"Julia, he's cheating you. Ask for a replay."

"It's okay. There are two more rounds," she says. "It was a house rule when I played here before. I forgot."

Patches of sweat creep from Charley's armpits, staining his shirt. Red-faced, he holds his stick with white knuckles and breaks the rack to start the second game. He shoots too hard and knocks a ball off the table.

"Cool it, man! You lose a turn!"

Someone returns the ball to the table. Julia effortlessly sinks several balls.

"You're doing great, Julia. Keep up the fight!"

Charley takes another shot, nicking the top of the ball. "Shit. Can't believe I scratched," he says.

Julia notes his lack of poise. Now she needs to focus and hang onto every shred of confidence she can muster. She peels off her red sweater. Her white tank top shines in the subdued light. She wants to win.

The game progresses until only the eight ball sits on the table. Again, it's her turn. This time she calls the pocket, aims for the target, and sinks the ball. The crowd roars.

"Two down, a tie. One to go," the large man yells.

Julia breaks this time. They continue the game, skillfully sinking shots as they clear the board. Julia gains the upper hand by completing a dazzling variety of shots. Charley, now sweating profusely, can hardly contain his composure and misses some easy shots. Julia, increasingly confident, pockets the last striped ball until she only has the eight ball left. Several solid balls lie between it and the cue ball. Julia faces a formidable shot. The rules require hitting the eight ball before any other. But she's blocked. *I can do this*, she tells herself. Gathering courage, she slowly chalks the tip of her cue stick, places a knee on the table, leans forward, and positions the stick almost vertically over the ball.

There's hardly a breath in the room as viewers observe the unusual move.

With a downward thrust, Julia strikes the ball. It curves in a perfect arc around the crowd of solid balls and hits the eight ball, which rolls squarely into the pocket on the other side of the board.

The crowd claps and whistles.

"Wow! Amazing massé shot!" someone yells "She's a true champion!"

Charley throws his hands up and tosses his cue against the wall. The game is over, and Julia has won.

Julia pulls away from the table and holds her head high. Her face flushes as she acknowledges the compliments of the observers. People shake her hand. As she glances toward the bar, she catches sight of Barnaby. He's standing on a chair, applauding and smiling. Knees buckling, she grasps the table.

"A drink for the lady on the house!" Sean calls.

Julia glances at Charley. He's sitting down, head lowered. She goes over to him.

"Thank you for the game. You're a fine player," she says, offering her hand.

He takes it reluctantly. "Thanks," he replies. "Wrong beer. Never liked Bud. I would've played better drinking Bootleggers."

She nods briefly. She pities him, a sore loser, blaming it on beer.

Barnaby pushes through the throng. "You played brilliantly, Julia. Absolutely amazing. It's so good to see you. Let's talk."

Her stomach flutters. He takes her hand and leads her to a table in the corner.

"However did you learn to play like that?" he asks.

She sits, allowing time for her pent-up emotions to subside. "I'll tell you in a minute, but I'd like a drink first. It's a long story, and embarrassing."

"Embarrassing? Can't wait to hear. I'll get your drink. Chardonnay?"

She has to admit, she enjoys winning. She used to take pride in her skill at the game and is overjoyed she can still compete. Charley was a worthy opponent, but he allowed his emotions to hinder his performance. Pool takes a steady hand and steadier nerves. When Barnaby sets the glass of wine in front of her, she's immediately aware of her pleasure at seeing him again and grateful for the opportunity to set the record straight about her pool playing experience.

She sips her wine.

"So tell me," he says.

She crosses her arms on the table. "You may remember last time we came Horace Holmes asked if I was still seeing Mike, my last boyfriend."

Barnaby nods.

"I met Mike while I babysat for his son, Robbie. Mike was divorced, and had visitation rights with his son, but he often had to work. The little boy was about eight, and in trouble. His mother became ill, and I could give him some stability at a hard time in his life. He was a lovely child and liked pool. His dad had a pool table at home, so I spent many hours playing with him. It turned out I had a knack for it and became quite skilled."

She glances at Barnaby and observes she has commanded his unwavering attention.

She continues. "One day, when Mike and I were at O'Malley's, Horace came in. He boasted he was a great player, so Mike told him I was, too. Horace challenged me to a game.

Things escalated when several of his friends came into the bar and Horace, who's a habitual gambler, took bets on who would win. They threw quite a lot of money into the pool. We played three rounds, and I won each one."

Julia pauses for a sip of wine, then goes on.

"Horace had gotten pretty drunk by the time we finished. He got angry and went after Mike. I guess he didn't want to strike me, a woman. Mike was drinking as well, and the two of them came to blows. Sean tried to pull them apart, but finally had to call the police. They arrested Horace, who witnesses said instigated things, for assault and disturbing the peace. He never forgave me for winning, and Mike and I never went to O'Malley's again after that."

"Aha. Now everything makes sense. Thanks for explaining it all. But you weren't to blame for what happened, so why all the embarrassment?"

"I should never have been with a man like Mike. It was one of my less successful relationships, and I thought you would think worse of me for even being around people like him and Horace."

"Well, I'm relieved to know this. Why should I judge you? I've had problems of my own and done things I'm not proud of. It's good you never knew me when I was a heavy drinker. I can tell the difference, now that I'm sober again."

She reaches over and touches his arm.

"It's really so good to see you," he says.

Sean approaches the table. "So, we have two winners here."

"Only one, I believe," Barnaby says.

"Two." Sean turns to Julia. "Barnaby won $500 in a fishing contest."

"Well. I'm impressed. Didn't know you liked fishing," Julia says.

"I don't. It was a fluke."

"Go on."

"There's nothing to say. What's strange about it is Horace Holmes competed as well. He got mad when I won."

Julia laughs. "Serves him right."

"That was some game you played, Julia," Sean says. "May I bring you another drink?"

"No, thank you. I have to leave now. I've had enough excitement for one day. This place wears me out."

"That's the whole idea. It's another world. Congratulations again."

Julia turns toward Barnaby. "I really have to go. Great seeing you."

She stands up, flings on her coat, and strides toward the door, blowing Charley a kiss. *He'll never know how big a favor he did me tonight.*

# CHAPTER 34

B arnaby stares after Julia. He's not sure if she wants to see him again or not. He's surprised at his powerful attraction to her and feeling of pride when she won the pool contest. It would all be easier to understand if he'd had more experience and knew what to expect from a woman's mixed signals. Seeing her pushed recent unpleasant events out of his mind. *She's magnificent.* As he sits in the bar's corner, he considers what he can do to please her. Then his eyes light up: flowers for her birthday. It's late, but that's okay.

The following day, he calls a local florist and arranges delivery to her home.

She calls him right away. "Thank you for the flowers. They caught me completely by surprise. Red tulips. Lovely."

"Happy birthday and congratulations again on winning the game. I was hoping you'd like to go out with me this weekend."

"I'd love to."

"Wonderful! I wasn't sure you'd want to see me again."

"Sorry if I gave you that impression. I needed time to think things through, and the flowers came at just the right moment."

Barnaby smiles with satisfaction. The flowers *were* a good idea.

Meanwhile, the troubling business of the lost paintings haunts him. He can't reconcile himself to the idea of letting the scammer go. Preoccupied on his workday, he vacillates, blaming himself for foolishly eliminating the emails and then forgiving his errors because of his inexperience at using a computer.

But then he remembers he had sent them to Oregon. So probably Horace wasn't involved, though the timing pointed to him. *Who else could it be?* Sly? But he doesn't think Sly would engage in such shady dealings when he has a business reputation to consider. It's puzzling that the shipping address was Oregon—although if someone were trying to hide their identity, that would be a good way of doing so. He scolds himself. *Face it, Barnaby. You're in over your head, too new in the online business to understand how to protect your interests— and drowning underwater, as you will be soon if you don't keep up with your house loan payments.*

He's at a loss for what to do, but talking to Julia couldn't hurt. She's smart and competent and might have some suggestions. Calling her at work, he explains that he'd like her to help with a thorny problem regarding his online painting business.

"How so? I wasn't aware you had one."

"Only recently started it. Without going into many details, it's possible Horace Holmes stole three of my paintings. Is there any way you could see him and talk to him? I need to find out if he has any connections in Oregon."

"Barnaby, I'd like to help, but without understanding all the details, there's not much I can do. Besides, how would I approach him? He's not a friend."

"Right, but you could call him up and ask him for coffee or something as a pretext. He'd hardly refuse a meeting with a pretty woman. I think his ego is big enough that he'd be flattered you asked."

"But he saw you with me at the bar. He might guess I'm on your side and get suspicious, especially if he's guilty of theft. Talk more about that."

He explains the details of how he got scammed.

"Good God," Julia says. "What bad luck. So you lost the paintings. Did you lose a lot of money as well?"

"Two thousand actual cash loss and nine thousand in paintings."

"Oh dear. Have you called the police?"

"Yes, but I can't give them much to go on." He continues to explain the series of events leading to the possibility that Horace had something to do with the theft. "I know there's only a slight chance he's the scammer, but I'd like to satisfy my curiosity," he says.

"My God," she says. "I suddenly remembered. He has a pretty impressive art collection. Look, it wouldn't work if I talked to him, but I could ask my lawyer friend Nancy what to do. You might need her services, anyway. Let me talk to her. We'll try to work something out. I'll tell you when I have something to report, but it may take a while."

Barnaby hangs up the phone and paces the kitchen. He can only wait and see now he's left things in Julia's hands. His head buzzes from all the fretting.

# CHAPTER 35

"I need some advice," Julia says to Nancy on the phone. "Would it be a conflict of interest if you did a little sleuthing?"

"Possibly. It would depend on whether I'm providing legal services for the party involved. Who are we talking about?"

"Barnaby. Someone scammed him, and he wants to find out who."

"And how, exactly, am I supposed to do that? Does he want to take legal action?"

"No, nothing like that, at least, not yet. Let me get straight to the point. He sold three paintings over the internet and shipped them to a man called Steven Michael before the check cleared. It turned out to be a bogus cashier's check. There's no hard evidence, but he and I suspect Horace Holmes. You remember what a creep he is. Barnaby wanted me to talk to him and find out if he's a suspect. I can't do it because Horace saw me with him recently, and so if he's guilty, he wouldn't talk freely. But he doesn't know you. All I'd like you to do is casually sit down with him and ask him some questions. You'd need to feel your way so you don't arouse suspicion."

"I can't do that," Nancy says, "but it looks as though your friend could use some legal advice for protection in the future. This might be a case for the police, or FBI if it's an organized scam out of state. How are things going between you and Barnaby, anyway?"

"We have a date this weekend. Meanwhile, he asked for help with the tangle he's created as part of his new online art business."

Nancy smirks. "I've heard about cases of scams aimed at artists. I don't mean to stereotype, but those creative people are often clueless and easy victims."

Julia shifts uncomfortably in her chair. "He's not really clueless," she says, uncertainly. "Only luckless."

"Well, has he reported this scam to the police?"

"Yes. But as I've said, he has no factual evidence. Just a strong hunch. The police can't act on that."

"What makes Barnaby think Horace is a criminal? It could have been someone else, anyone who saw the website."

"True, but the timing suggests him. The website had only been up for a couple of days, and right afterward Barnaby went ice fishing. Horace was there. He made disparaging remarks about Barnaby, who apparently sketched the scene. What got him hopping mad was Barnaby's winning the fishing contest."

Nancy snorts. "Barnaby won a fishing contest?"

"So then shortly afterwards Horace showed up at O'Malley's and started pumping the bartender for information about Barnaby, asking about his skill as an artist."

"Hmm. Okay, that could seem like circumstantial evidence. Barnaby shipped the paintings to Oregon, to someone called Steven Michael, right?"

"So I understand."

Nancy groans. "What can I say? It's classic. That's often how scammers work. They give false names, a distant address so the shipping costs are higher, and pass a fraudulent check."

"Oh dear. Didn't know this was so common."

"More than you'd think. Makes me mad. The victims usually don't protect themselves by obtaining legal advice first. I understand they can't afford it, but it often costs them in the long run. Actually, I'd consider doing some pro bono work for artists for this reason."

"Great. Perhaps you could start with Barnaby."

"For your sake, I'll consider it. Your Barnaby sounds like a good man, despite his troubles."

"You're a true friend. Thank you."

Relieved that her sensible and knowledgeable friend would help Barnaby, Julia turns her attention to the immediate task, her family history project. When she brought her beloved old dollhouse home, she set it on Alice's chest containing documents in a corner of her bedroom. Now she lifts it up. The wooden house, sliced open to display the rooms, feels light in her arms, and the miniature figures and furniture shift as she tips it onto the floor. She kneels beside it and delicately restores the pieces to their original positions. How many times had she done that, wanting to restore order, even as a small child? Maybe now she's moving into a new adult phase of her life, at last.

She lifts the musty books from the chest and examines each one before placing it in a pile by chronology. The earliest letters, dated 1882, involve correspondence between Alice's great-great grandmother Emma Hampton and her English family about her sea voyage to America. Several more letters to her family describe her happy marriage to Thomas Lowell. After 1890 Julia can't find any further letters from Emma but discovers a divorce agreement giving custody of her child Robert to her husband. *This must have been a scandal in 1890.* She hopes later documents and photographs will tell the story, but fears her ancestor had suffered in marriage, as Alice had. And as she had. Julia doesn't believe in curses handed down from one generation to another, but even if true, the curse will end with her. She's sure Alice would have wanted that, and she knows it's within her power to do so.

# CHAPTER 36

Barnaby reviews the newspaper clipping Brooke gave him, then visits the Waterbury Arts Commission website and scrolls down to find details about the mural competition. A private donor is financing the project to honor Waterbury's industrial past. Images of historic buildings in the National Register District are especially welcome. Artists are required to submit drawings as part of the application. He'll enjoy preparing them, using the new subject matter.

Saturday arrives, the day of his date with Julia. They have agreed to go to the Country House again, for lunch this time, when daylight will allow them to see more of the countryside, something they both appreciate. They wear heavy coats and snugly fitting hats, and their spirits soar skyward as they reach the old farmhouse. The hazy winter sun throws purple shadows on the snow, and thickly forested hills stretch into the distance, bare limbs softening in the gray mist.

Barnaby inhales the chilly air. "So pure, like spring water," he says, exhaling a thin cloud of breath. "Let's walk around and see the animals before we go inside."

The black cows stand with bent heads in a field near a rust-colored barn. As Barnaby and Julia approach, they look up, their dark eyes serene.

"It must be a good life for these cattle," Julia says. "They're in a lovely place, are well fed, and they have a barn to go to in bad weather."

They watch a flock of crows fly overhead, their loud cawing fading as the birds become black flecks vanishing in the sky.

"I've always wanted to live in the country," Julia says. "I grew up in Boston, and we usually got out of town in summer."

"I've lived in a city all my life, but I like it here. Freer. More expansive. Like the ocean."

He takes her hand. They stroll to the restaurant, their footsteps crunching on the frozen snow.

"Mr. Brown. Welcome back, sir," the maître d' says as they enter the dining room. He shows them to their table next to a window. Barnaby shivers as the outside air penetrates the glass and observes Julia, who sits hunched, arms hugging her chest.

"Are you comfortable here? Shall we ask for a table next to the fire?" he says.

"I'd like that."

Barnaby flags the server's attention and asks for different seating. Soon they're placed in a warmer spot, ordering their food. They both refuse wine.

"I wasn't aware you grew up in Massachusetts. There's still so much to learn about you."

"Well, I was born in Boston and I've lived in New England all my life. I planned to teach, but I never completed the training because my mother became ill and I moved out of the dorm to look after her at home. She died of leukemia the summer after my junior year of college."

Barnaby remembers how he had watched Anna die. "I know how sad losing someone can be, especially when it's slow."

She nods, sniffing. "Anyway, soon after I graduated, I got married. Too soon. I still missed my mother. My father remarried, I felt lonely, and I wanted my own family. But as I've mentioned, the marriage wasn't a success. My husband became violent when in the manic phase of his condition."

Barnaby touches her arm. "Excuse me for asking, but did he hurt you?"

"Sometimes." She moves her arm and fiddles with her napkin. "Anyway, after the divorce, I moved to New York and earned my master's degree in social work. That's where I met Lisa. She had already qualified and was working in the field. When she took the job in Waterbury, she suggested I move as well, and I've lived here ever since. She's a longtime friend, although lately she's not been as friendly."

"So that's how you ended up here. As you know, Waterbury's hardly the garden spot of New England."

"True, but it has its character. Hard to explain how a place weaves itself into your heart, but it does."

Barnaby blinks. The thought had never occurred to him, but it makes sense.

Their food arrives. Barnaby takes a sip of soup and puts down his spoon. "Too hot."

"Better hot than cold. That's true of relationships, too," she says, smiling.

He gulps. She's flirtatious! How can she mirror his own feelings, stating them so boldly? "Uh . . . I understand colors more. Cool colors versus warm. Blue versus red."

"And I'm red?" she asks.

"Yes." He beams at her.

She gives him a shy smile. "Okay, I'll take that as a compliment."

They finish their soup and wait for the next course.

He leans forward. "You know, comfort is important. Things have to fit, like elements in a painting. Works of art are like homes. When they're a refuge, the colors are warm."

"Makes sense, but cool colors make beautiful paintings, too. Take blue, for example, your favorite."

"True, but I've been thinking lately that I've spent too long allowing the cold to seep the warmth from my life. It's no way to live . . . and you know what?" He smiles. "I think that we're fine, and we should go back to O'Malley's." He regards her solemnly. "Neither one of us has anything to apologize for, and it's long past time for forgiving ourselves."

"You're right," she says.

"We also need to come here again, to this valley. I'd like to see the place in summer, when everything's green."

"Agreed."

They finish their lunch and drive back to Julia's condo. They talk easily until midnight. As he puts his arms around her and kisses her—a long, lingering kiss—the thought passes through his mind that he could quite happily spend the next forty years at her side.

# CHAPTER 37

O'Malley's is empty but for Professor Miller. Barnaby wants to have an early dinner and a Coke and go home. Sean hands him a drink, and Barnaby walks to his usual seat. As he passes the professor, he asks, "How's the investigation going? Have you uncovered the identity of our mystery poet yet?"

"Still no clues, but whoever it is keeps publishing. Today's poem is a limerick, though it doesn't fit the traditional format. Quite silly, but then limericks are. Want to hear it?"

"Sure. Silly poems are always welcome."

"There's no title, but it's signed N. Staey again." He recites the poem.

*"The young beauty appears*
*At all times of the year*
*All eyes are upon her. It's true.*
*But she sits at the bar*
*With a smile from afar*
*And the men have found others to woo."*

"I guess we know who this one's about. So that eliminates Brooke from the list of possible authors," Barnaby says. "Any other ideas?"

"I've been asking around. No takers,"

"Keep at it. I'm sure you'll succeed."

"There's another poem. Want me to read it?" Before Barnaby can reply, the professor picks up the newspaper. He reads aloud:

*"The professor comes in*
*Takes a place with his gin*
*And a nod and a wink in his eye.*
*'There's a story, says he,*
*If you'll listen to me'*
*But his voice just gets lost in the din."*

The professor takes off his glasses. "That one's about me, I suppose, though I don't drink gin."

"Rhymes with din, though. I'm no expert, but in my opinion, these aren't very good poems."

"They're light, with a grain of truth. There's another, though it may not be one *some people* would want to hear," the professor says, stealing a glimpse at Barnaby.

"Out with it. We're all open to poetic license."

"Okay, since you ask, here goes," says the professor, replacing his glasses.

*"The man with the beard*
*Has already been feared*
*For his talent. But when will he learn?*
*He's forsaken his brush*
*For the drink. He's a lush*
*And his life, like dry tinder, will burn."*

Barnaby splutters, almost spilling his Coke. Who would portray him this way? No friend of his, that's for sure. Raising his hand to flag Sean's attention, he orders a bowl of soup with bread and butter. He only wants dinner, not conversation, and has an important mystery of his own to solve. The professor and he share one characteristic, he muses drily—both are sometimes objects of ridicule. An unsettling thought.

*Dry tinder?* He does not want to think his life will burn, leaving a pile of ashes in its wake, before his time.

As though reading his mind, Professor Miller taps Barnaby on the shoulder. "Don't take it too seriously. Getting older requires humility and a good dose of humor. I should know," he says, thinning his lips. "Here's another poem. Different style. Unsigned. Not like the others."

*The professor has a point*, Barnaby thinks. *I do take offense sometimes.* He swings round on his stool to face the older man.

"It's called 'Sean's Place.'" The professor begins reading.

> *"Like birds at a feeder*
> *they flutter low*
> *for a safe landing.*
> *Each seeks a kernel*
> *from the font—*
> *a clip of kindness,*
> *a wink of words,*
> *their secrets locked*
> *under the soft-strong beam*
> *of the barlight."*

"What do you think? Pretty good, I'd say."

"I like it. Puts us in a more literary light, wouldn't you say? Everyone here has a secret, perhaps even you, Professor."

Professor Miller smiles. "Well, this one has me completely baffled."

Barnaby racks his mind, trying to think of a way to retrieve his paintings. He's left the investigation in Julia's hands, but he doesn't expect her findings to provide any evidence. Though he's willing to let the money go, he wants the paintings back. They're three of his finer works, and he'd prefer to consign them with Sylvester, as long as his friend will agree to an acceptable commission arrangement. It would be a good idea to talk to him anyway to rule out the possibility he was the scammer. He lifts the phone.

"Sylvester, Barnaby here. How's it going?"

"Hey there. Thought about you. A client would like to view more of your work. She likes beach scenes. Have you got a website yet?"

"Actually, I do, but I'm probably taking it down. I may not want to continue online sales."

"Yeah, I get it. A lot of artists get scammed. Well, I'd like to buy a few more of your works on a commission basis."

"Okay, I hope we can work something out. What are you offering?"

"Fifty percent commission. Your stuff is good and sells well. I think I can ask $5,000 for the larger paintings."

"Sounds good. Unfortunately, I only have two left. Want to come by and pick them up?"

"I'll swing by soon. Perhaps we could have a bite to eat as well."

*So that likely puts Sly out of the running*, Barnaby thinks. He's offering a decent deal now, and if he was the culprit, he did a good job of hiding it. If he can continue to sell, Barnaby can give him the new series of paintings as well. Then he, Barnaby, will be on his way to making a successful career as an artist, a dream he'd given up on a few years ago. And Julia is still working to find the identity of the scammer. He hopes she'll have something to tell him before long.

Barnaby spends some time looking up the details of City Hall online: "Artfully designed by Cass Gilbert, who won a contest in 1910, the marble and brick City Hall building exemplifies Georgian Revival style. Bas-relief sculpture on the third story represents 'Industry' as a workman." Barnaby likes that—the theme perfectly fits his new series of paintings of the ordinary working man. The building's lines appeal to him as well, and perhaps for the first time in his life, he feels proud to be a resident of this historic city, his hometown. He might even listen more closely to Professor Miller's lectures from now on. He has dismissed the professor's knowledge in the past but now realizes the man possesses a depth of knowledge that might be useful as he, Barnaby, reexamines familiar buildings with his artist's eye.

Armed with newfound information, Barnaby is ready to sketch buildings for the mural contest. Though he dislikes standing for hours outside, he'd rather work *plein air* than from photographs. Something always gets lost when he paints a subject viewed through the camera's lens. It might be the way a shadow falls across a window, or a curve that needs sharpening—details that make the artist's rendering unique.

He concentrates on two subjects, City Hall and Union Railroad Station, both grand buildings with clock towers. One bay on the City Hall façade displays Waterbury's motto: QUID AERE PERENNIUS ("What Is More Lasting Than Brass"). As he completes his drawing, he's gratified by the recent community preservation efforts. But for those, the old buildings would be like sandcastles waiting for the tide, scenes he had portrayed countless times in his beach paintings.

Now he knows. There's comfort in a respectful recognition of history, even his own muddy-hued past.

# CHAPTER 38

A week goes by before Nancy talks to Julia again.

"What's going on with your friend's scamming dilemma?" Nancy asks. "Any new information?"

"No. Barnaby's pretty sore about it all, but he recognizes he needs to pay more attention to security on the internet."

"Glad to hear it. I have some time this week. Perhaps I could sit down with him and draw up some contracts he might use with potential buyers. I can refer him to a colleague as well, someone with expertise in internet fraud."

"That would be wonderful. I'll talk to him about it. Thanks a million. How about dinner? On me."

"Sure, though you don't owe me anything."

Happy she has news to report, Julia calls Barnaby.

"Did you find out more about Horace, enough to investigate him?" he asks immediately.

"No. Nothing new. But my friend Nancy has offered to give you legal advice."

"I appreciate that. I could use some. But I've reached a conclusion. Even if I don't recover them, those paintings represent my old life. Every artist has to learn to let things go. What's important is to keep producing new work. I had stopped doing that and almost lost myself. Now that I'm painting again, it makes all the difference."

"Good insight," Julia says, "but I'd love it if we could find the thief. People shouldn't take advantage of others illegally, with no consequence."

"You're right, but I need to learn how to accept responsibility, too. I made a mistake, trusting a complete stranger. I made another mistake suspecting Horace with no evidence. Guess I wanted an easy solution to my problems. An old habit I'm trying to break." After a moment's pause, he continues. "We may never find the culprit, and I'm willing to let this go. But you know what else I've discovered? We have to demand responsibility from ourselves as well as others to earn respect."

"You just sunk the eight ball," she tells him.

# CHAPTER 39

As Barnaby turns into his driveway after work one day, he notices a FOR SALE sign posted beside Lisa's house. So she's leaving town? He ought to stop by and wish her luck. The old dilemmas confront him: should he buy her a present, flowers, or send a note? He doesn't want to send the wrong message to Lisa, but he does consider her a friend. He'll think about it later.

As he's finishing dinner, the doorbell rings. He opens the door to find Lisa standing on the doorstep.

Before she can speak, he blurts, "Lisa, I've been thinking about you. I saw your 'for sale' sign and hoped you wouldn't leave without saying good-bye. Would you like to come in?"

She steps inside, brushes past him, and heads for the kitchen. Startled, he follows.

"Helluva woman," Popsicle says from the top of the cage.

"Perhaps she's right," Lisa says. "I hardly know myself anymore, sometimes. But I've done a lot of thinking and plan to move to New York."

"So I heard," Barnaby says. "May I offer you something to drink?"

"Bourbon, with ice, please."

"Sorry. I don't keep alcohol in the house now."

She nods. "How about a Coke, then?"

She takes a seat at the table and pulls her coat a little tighter around her neck. Barnaby pours her drink, sets it in front of her, and clears his dinner dishes.

She takes a sip, then a gulp, and twirls the ice in the glass, viewing it intently. "I came to talk to you about something important."

Barnaby eases himself into a chair opposite her. He's not sure he wants to hear this.

"I feel awful. I really had nothing to do with what happened. Well, not directly."

She swallows another mouthful, then pushes the tumbler to the side. He waits, eyeing her as she fiddles with the cuff of the sweater peeking from under her coat. Finally, he asks, "What happened?"

"I know who the scammer is, the person who stole your paintings."

Barnaby's mouth drops. "Really? Who?"

"My brother Alan."

Barnaby gulps, feeling his mouth dry. "I had no idea," he says slowly. "Alan's the last person I'd suspect. Whatever caused him to commit such a crime? He was so helpful, so thrilled to do anything for you, his sister."

"That's the problem. He got overzealous. He wants nothing so much as my happiness, and when I met you, he thought I'd found a partner at last."

Barnaby's throat constricts, and he stands to fetch a glass of water. "I'm sorry. Never meant to lead you on."

She holds up a hand. "It's okay. You didn't, and I don't blame you. I won't deny I had hopes, but deep down I knew your heart was elsewhere. I never told Alan. He thought we were on the road to marriage."

"How could he think that?" Barnaby asks. Then he remembers. It's true he had never disabused Alan of the notion that he and Lisa were dating, but really, all Alan had said recently was that he was glad they'd met.

"Well, he did think that. Then when he learned we weren't a couple, he went ballistic. An over-reaction, of course. But he wanted revenge. He thought you broke my heart, and that I was falling apart over that. But it wasn't only that. I had problems at work, too. I'm all right now, though."

Barnaby sighs. "My goodness."

"So you can guess the rest. He had all the means for setting you up. We have a cousin in Portland who received the paintings."

Barnaby lets out a long whistle and stretches his legs. His mind feels numb from the strangeness of it all. *How can everything have gone so horribly amiss?*

Behind him, Popsicle echoes his thoughts. "What a mess!"

He regards Lisa sadly. "I'm grateful to you for telling me this."

"I'm afraid we can't return the paintings. They've been sold. But Alan asked me to tell you that he's committed to returning every penny of your money, including the profit he made on the sales."

She grabs her glass again, and seeing it's empty, stares vacantly at it. Barnaby moves quickly to refill it.

"Thank you," she rasps, taking a mouthful. "Barnaby, we're hoping you might consider not pressing charges if Alan makes full restitution. We know you're fully entitled to do so, and we understand the gravity of what he's done. But . . . we're hoping."

Barnaby shuffles in his chair. *Theft. Fraud. Felony. Police. Lawyers, so much unpleasantness . . .* his mind whirls. Then he faces Lisa.

"I think that would be okay," he says. "No charges, if full restitution within thirty days. Let's look at it this way. I've learned a hard lesson. I won't make the same mistake again."

Lisa's eyes water and she passes a hand over her forehead. "Thanks for understanding. My brother means well, but was really misguided this time. He's never been a criminal."

"I believe you. But I'll have someone else handle my website from now on," Barnaby says, a twinkle in his eye.

"Of course. And, again, I'm so sorry for the trouble I've caused. It's a family affliction. I'll go home now."

She stands, and Barnaby gives her a hug. She pulls back.

"One more favor," she says. "Please don't tell Julia. I'm so embarrassed. I'll write to her myself later."

"Of course not," he says. "I'll see you before you leave town."

After she goes out, he collapses on the couch. Just when he's reconciled himself to his losses, things change. *Things change, even me.*

# CHAPTER 40

Sean leans across the counter, looking Barnaby in the eye. "Out with it, Barnaby. Did you tell the professor I wrote those poems?"

Barnaby jerks forward. "What? No, of course not! *Well . . . did you?*"

"He figured it out. I couldn't deny it. He's been accusin' everyone in sight, and people started complainin'."

Barnaby rolls his head back and laughs. "So the professor solved the riddle! I had a hunch it was you, but I understood you wanted to remain anonymous. If you'd wanted us to know, you would have published under your name."

Sean raises his finger to his lips. "Here he comes, now."

"Evening, Professor," Barnaby says.

The old man dips his head, hoists himself onto his post, and deposits a can on the counter. "You've heard the news? I've solved the mystery of the phantom limerick poet."

"Yes! Congratulations! How did you figure it out?"

"It wasn't hard. Remember when Sean quoted the line from Yeats a while back? I asked him then if he was a poet, and he said his father used that expression. That threw me off, until I realized the poet's name Staey is Yeats, spelled backwards."

Barnaby laughs and settles his eyes on the bartender who is busily engaged wiping glasses with a dishcloth. A flush rises to Sean's ears.

"Why didn't you want us to know you're a poet?" Barnaby asks. "It's nothing to be ashamed of."

"Come on now, how could I let it be known I was writin' silly poems about my customers?"

"They're not silly," the professor says, "or even if they are, we need more nonsense in our lives."

"My sentiments, exactly," Sean nods.

"Most artists suffer from fear of failure when they throw their work into the world," Barnaby says. "So you get credit for publishing."

"But I didn't publish. My mother did, without my knowin'. After the first time, I begged her to stop, but she wasn't havin' any of it. She worked out an arrangement with the paper. They even paid for the poems. She's proud of me, you see."

"As she should be." Barnaby says. "Are there any more to come?"

"I've got hundreds, some better than others."

"This is splendid news, cause for a celebration. Another artist in our midst!" the professor says. "Pour me a jigger of gin!"

Barnaby examines the can sitting on the counter. "What's this, Professor? More secrets?"

Professor Miller lifts the lid and displays the contents. "Brass buttons. Bought them from your friend Sal. A treasure trove, an impressive addition to my collection."

Barnaby claps the older man on the back. "Well, bless my buttons, as Popsicle would say."

***

Two days later, Barnaby strides into the bar with his latest painting. He props it on a lighted table.

"What've you got there?" Sean asks. He strolls over. "What do you know? I recognize those figures! You've got the professor exactly right. He always looks like he's about to fall off the stool. I like the way you've painted the bottles, too. And what's this? A red rose on the counter?"

"Of course. She brings you one each time she comes in, doesn't she?"

Sean steps back, raises his eyebrows, and throws up his hands. "How do you know?"

Barnaby winks. "You're full of surprises and secrets, my friend, but anyone can tell you're smitten with Brooke. And it appears it's mutual."

Sean guffaws. "What can I say? Between you and the professor, my life is now an open book."

"Tell us more. We're all dying to hear about the mystery woman," Professor Miller says. "What does she do?"

"She writes poetry. She's an English teacher. We're no Yeats, but we've had fun writing about the bar here," Sean says, eyes glowing with pride.

The professor nods slowly. "Aha. So she's the other poet, the one who eluded me."

"Yes. She confounds us all," Sean says.

Barnaby points to his painting. "Well, what do you think? Do you want it?"

"Of course I do!" Sean smiles. "I'll hang it right here." He points to a space on the wall where the framed uniform hangs. "How much do I owe you?"

"Nothing. It's a gift. O'Malley's is a service to the community, and we're all grateful."

"O'Malley's is more than that," Professor Miller adds. "It's the next *salon*, right here in Waterbury."

Everyone laughs.

"Come on now, Professor," Sean says. "We're just plain folks here. Plain folks, with ordinary lives."

Barnaby nods. "Exactly. As one of my art teachers told me, the purpose of art is to make the ordinary extraordinary."

"Well said," the professor agrees. "Even Yeats wrote poems about everyday life. In his words: 'Think like a wise man but communicate in the language of the people.'" He raises his glass. "To artists everywhere."

# CHAPTER 41

Barnaby begins the week with two goals: to complete another bar painting and finish cleaning the house. He'll then have three additional works to sell, and he can invite Julia over. They talk every night on the phone.

"When are we going to celebrate?" he asks at last.

"What's left to celebrate? We've already celebrated my birthday, my victory at pool, and your winning the fishing contest. You've given me flowers, taken me to lunch . . ."

"But you haven't heard the latest. I won the Art Commission's mural contest. They've commissioned a mural downtown and will pay me $10,000."

"Wow! Now that's something worth celebrating. Congratulations!"

"Thank you. I'd like to have you over for dinner. You can meet Popsicle. Will you come?"

"I'd love to."

After he hangs up the phone, Barnaby swallows hard. Why did he make such a bold offer? He worries about whether things are clean enough. He appraises the kitchen. The oven needs cleaning, and the sink could use scouring. He needs to run a newly repaired dishwasher. He needs to buy some place mats and new glasses at the hardware store. Sheets for the bed. And new pillows.

On the morning of Julia's visit, he turns up the heat. When she arrives that evening, he helps her out of her coat and ushers her into the kitchen.

"It's cozy in here," she says.

He smiles.

Popsicle sits on top of the cage, peering sideways at Julia. "Good parrot," the bird says.

Julia gapes. "Sounds like a human voice. What else can she say?"

"Lots of things. Sometimes she comes up with words that surprise you. You'll hear her, I'm sure. She always speaks her mind."

"She's an honest bird?"

"I'd say so. More than many humans, anyway."

Julia crosses the room to Popsicle's cage. Using her beak, the bird claws her way lower down and views Julia intently.

"Heavens to Murgatroyd. Good stuff."

Julia giggles. "I haven't heard that expression in years. What does she mean, good stuff?"

"It's a compliment. She likes you."

"May I touch her?"

"Let's see. She's usually wary of new people." He offers Popsicle his arm. After a few moments, she steps onto his sleeve. "You can try stroking the back of her neck like this," he says, demonstrating.

Julia caresses the feathers. Popsicle lowers her head and rubs her beak against Barnaby's arm.

"She does like you. She doesn't let just anyone get close. Let me get you a drink."

"One for the road," Popsicle says.

Barnaby and Julia laugh.

"Is this a signal I should leave?" she asks.

"I don't think so. She responds to the word *drink*. I sometimes take her to O'Malley's with me."

"That makes sense. She's your companion. Most people talk to their pets, I guess, but yours talks back!" Julia says.

"True. She has opinions of her own, too. Probably that's why she likes O'Malley's. Everyone's opinionated there. No shortage of conversation, ever."

"With Sean, you mean?"

"Not just Sean. Professor Miller as well."

Barnaby rises and returns Popsicle to her cage. She climbs up to the top perch and regards them, her black eyes unblinking.

"As I mentioned, I've had some good talks with the professor recently. He's been reading poems from the local newspaper. Seems Sean is a poet."

"Really? What fun. Did you know?"

"I wondered from time to time, but the professor figured it out. Sean's been seeing a woman who also writes poetry. The professor compared the bar to a kind of *salon*, similar to ones they had in Paris in the nineteenth century. It's surprising how creative some regular customers at Sean's are turning out to be."

"Yourself included, of course. Tell me, what makes people want to pursue art?"

"I don't know about everyone, but for me it has never been a choice. I've always wanted to paint and feel worse about myself when I don't. That's part of the reason I fell into bad ways. Couldn't live with myself."

She nods thoughtfully. "Well, you're painting again, and I can tell it makes all the difference."

"It does. Everyone should express themselves. They don't have to call themselves artists. You, too. You demonstrated great artistry at the pool game the other night. Your assessment of the balls' placement on the board, the angle of your shots, the way you held the cue—you used it to create patterns as an artist uses a paintbrush."

She stares at him, wide-eyed. "I've never considered myself an artist, but I understand your point. Actually, I'm beginning a new project. I'm finishing the family history that my mother started."

Barnaby sits back and flings his hands behind his head. "Good for you. How's it going?"

"Slowly. I've read papers and journals for research, and I'm excited about this. I'm finally fulfilling a promise I made to my mother years ago."

"So wonderful to hear this," Barnaby says. "It means we're both engaged in creative endeavors that we've denied ourselves for years. You know all of this is restorative."

"That's what I'm discovering. You know, I got a letter from Lisa recently. She explained everything and apologized to me for her behavior."

"Good. She's taking steps to improve her life, it seems, like the rest of us."

"Right. It all seems so simple once you find the right direction."

"It's like painting. You have to reach beyond the vanishing point on the horizon for something important you can't quite see, but know is there."

"Spoken like a true artist," Julia grins.

⁂

Two hours later, they lounge at the table with the remains of their dinner.

"I didn't know I liked artichoke hearts on pizza," he says.

"I didn't know I liked olives."

Barnaby understands then that sitting right there in his kitchen with Julia is a moment to cherish. *The present moment.*

Maybe if the present is right, the future will take care of itself. He glances at the clock, surprised at the late hour.

"Would you like dessert?" he asks, wanting to extend her visit, his mind working furiously to recall the contents of his freezer.

"I couldn't eat another bite," she says, "but I'd love to see your studio and new paintings."

He rises and gestures toward the stairs. She peeks into the rooms without being intrusive. As he guides her through the house, he considers it has indeed been an enchanted evening.

"The house has good bones," Julia says. "Just like the doll-house I dearly loved as a child," she continues. "I found it in my father's attic recently and have it now in my condo. Seems strange, but this house reminds me of it. It's a real home, with heart."

"Thank you," he says, warming to her. "It's where I grew up. My parents left it to me. I've let it decline a bit, but I'm fixing it up now. They worked hard to afford it, and I owe them."

When they reach the studio, he flips the switch, and the room blazes with light. His most recent canvas sits on the easel. She crosses the room to examine it.

"I don't know much about painting, but I love those layers of pigment. The whole thing glows. I like the way the sun shines through the windows, bringing out the warmth in the planks of wood. I don't know how to describe it, but it gives me an appreciation for the work those men are doing, stacking the lumber."

"A perfect reaction!" Barnaby says. He looks at her with new appreciation and the sense that he might always enjoy learning new things about her. He lifts the painting from the easel and sets another in its place.

"I like this one even more," she says. "It's O'Malley's, isn't it? And that's Sean, and Charley. Lovely, full of atmosphere. How did you manage to get the brass to shine? It jumps right off the canvas."

"Yellow ochre, a touch of viridian, cadmium red, and a little black for the base color. Titanium white for the highlights."

"Marvelous."

"I'll complete others in this series of oils. Farmers tending a herd of cows. People ice fishing. I may do a watercolor or two as well."

"I'm sure all will be equally good. But I'm curious. No palm trees and sandy beaches? Nothing that represents your dream of going out West?"

"No. I painted beach scenes in Providence. None since then." He pulls one of his old paintings out of the rack. Tanned children build sand castles beside aqua seas, while a girl in a sunhat stares upward to a cloud-pocked sky.

"That's how I remember it all," she says, bending down to examine the painting and fingering the outline of the girl's long braids on her back. "So let me ask again, why aren't you painting scenes of California?"

"Maybe because I don't need to. California is like Bali Ha'i—a place where you dream of going, but can never reach. Something has changed in me as well. This is where I belong, and I don't want to leave."

Surprised by his own words, he senses a distant voice calling. His head swirls as though he's in the grip of a riptide sweeping him away from shore. He grabs onto the easel to steady himself. Anna held special affection for the young girl he captured in the painting. The girl learned to predict weather by observing cloud formations. With uncanny instinct, she was rarely wrong. Barnaby loved Anna for her recognition of people's quiet strengths. He feels her presence in the room and knows at that moment that she wants happiness for him, and for him to live and love again, in strength.

He slumps into the old armchair. The sweeping riptide turns gentle and recedes. When he looks up moments later, he finds Julia's eyes searching his.

"Are you okay?" she asks.

He pulls himself upright. "Never better."

He takes her into his arms and melts into the soft warmth of her body.

Popsicle's voice rings clear from the kitchen.

"Heavens! Lord love a duck!"

# ACKNOWLEDGMENTS

A book needs many players to bring it to completion, and this one is no exception. I'm so grateful to all the people who gave their time and thoughts to *Waterbury Winter* as it evolved from first draft to final manuscript.

Thanks to those who read early drafts: Rebecca d'Harlingue, Carol Masters, Doug Bachmann, Eve Austen, Cathy Hill, Martha Moody, John Moody, Dick Robblee, and James Keul. Special thanks to Dick for his invaluable help with the pool scene and to my son James for his artist's perspective.

Probably every writer needs encouragement, and I've been fortunate to have the support of wonderful cheerleaders during the long writing and publication process. I'd especially like to acknowledge Celia Chandler, Denise O'Neil, my UK family, members of Skyline Book Club, my daughter Jenny Keul.

How could I have polished the book without the amazing editing and coaching given so generously by Ellen Notbohm? She helped me through many dark moments, times when I doubted the story would see the light of day. I valued her presence as though she were a kind friend looking over my shoulder.

All the people at She Writes Press are knowledgeable and responsive, and they were a pleasure to work with for the second time. Thank you for accepting *Waterbury Winter* for the Spring 2022 list, and special thanks to Brooke Warner, Lauren Wise, and Julie Metz.

My publicist Caitlin Hamilton Summie deserves a shout-out, also for the second time.

I'd like to acknowledge Peanut, my family's yellow-naped Amazon parrot as the inspiration for Popsicle. Peanut was with us for years, and his expressions ("Good stuff," "Good parrot," "Hello") were daily utterances and the source of much attention and amusement.

Finally, many thanks to my husband Vince, who offers unfailing encouragement and, importantly, is the cook in our household, providing food for thought as well as meals.

# ABOUT THE AUTHOR

L inda Stewart Henley is the award-winning author of *Estelle: A Novel*. *Waterbury Winter* is her second book. She lives in Anacortes, Washington, with her husband.

*Author photo © Mark Gardner*

# SELECTED TITLES FROM SHE WRITES PRESS

She Writes Press is an independent publishing company founded to serve women writers everywhere. Visit us at www.shewritespress.com.

*Play for Me* by Céline Keating. $16.95, 978-1-63152-972-6. Middle-aged Lily impulsively joins a touring folk-rock band, leaving her job and marriage behind in an attempt to find a second chance at life, passion, and art.

*The Black Velvet Coat* by Jill G. Hall. $16.95, 978-1-63152-009-9. When the current owner of a black velvet coat—a San Francisco artist in search of inspiration—and the original owner, a 1960s heiress who fled her affluent life fifty years earlier, cross paths, their lives are forever changed . . . for the better.

*The Velveteen Daughter* by Laurel Davis Huber. $16.95, 978-1-63152-192-8. The first book to reveal the true story of the woman who wrote *The Velveteen Rabbit* and her daughter, a world-famous child prodigy artist, *The Velveteen Daughter* explores the consequences of early fame and the inability of a mother to save her daughter from herself.

*The Geometry of Love* by Jessica Levine. $16.95, 978-1-938314-62-9. Torn between her need for stability and her desire for independence, an aspiring poet grapples with questions of artistic inspiration, erotic love, and infidelity.

*Beautiful Garbage* by Jill DiDonato. $16.95, 978-1-938314-01-8. Talented but troubled young artist Jodi Plum leaves suburbia for the excitement of the city—and is soon swept up in the sexual politics and downtown art scene of 1980s New York.